My Beautiful England

Michelle Flatley

Cutting

D0268665

A Cutting Edge Press Paperback Original

Published in 2013 by Cutting Edge Press

www.cuttingedgepress.co.uk

Copyright © Michelle Flatley

PB ISBN: 978-1-908122-57-5
E PUB: 978-1-908122-02-5

To all those women who dare to speak out
and all those women who dare not.

I will not cease from mental fight,
Nor shall my sword sleep in my hand
Till we have built Jerusalem
In England's green and pleasant Land.

WILLIAM BLAKE

CHAPTER ONE

Phuket, October 2005

After the big wave, the Blissful Brides Agency was painted white and a shiny new sign hung above the door. Sumalee wandered up Patong Beach with a bag of clothes, just as her sister had instructed her. 'Every Englishman wants a Thai bride,' Mai told her that morning, as they squeezed the mango juice. 'Everyone knows this.' When she spoke she whistled through the gaps of her teeth. It was certain. An elder in the village had foreseen a happy marriage. The man at the agency would take a beautiful picture and then Sumalee could go to England and begin a new life.

Today, like every day for the last year, Sumalee hurried along the dusty road, not looking at the sea. She didn't want to see the ghosts of the dead. No one did. Sometimes she saw the ghost children with swollen bellies, searching for their mothers, wailing and screaming on the shore. Liquid eyes, little bodies coated in black dirt, seaweed wound round their limbs like wire. Often the ghost children whispered to her and tugged her hair. She heard them call her name and every night she prayed that Buddha would send the children up to the warm arc of sky, where they would be free of the water and happy again.

As Sumalee walked she watched the shop signs swinging in the wind. It was lunch time and her belly felt empty and hollow, but there had been no time to eat. Down past Superstars Massage Parlour and Starlight Hotel she found the agency. Beside the blue door there was a poster of a proud Englishman and his young Thai bride. A bride wrapped in a garland of orange and purple strawflowers. Sumalee remembered she had worn a garland like this at her first wedding and her mother had threaded pink krachiao tulips in her hair. Underneath the girl she saw the words, 'NO FUSS. QUICK INTRODUCTIONS. WE PROMISE YOU A JOYFUL LIFE.' Sumalee rang the bell and flattened her hair with her hands. She had come from work and was still in her white apron, dreaming of a second chance, dreaming of a different life.

'Mai send me,' she said to the large Englishman who stood in the doorway, his hair stiff with spray. He wrinkled his nose in disgust and looked her up and down. 'My name Sumalee.'

Calvin Smith ushered her in and gestured for her to turn. 'Do you have a dress?'

'Yes. Me bring dress.' Sumalee nodded and waved her bag in the air. 'Nice dress.'

He pointed to a Chinese screen in the corner and checked his watch. 'I need to take a picture first. The next girl is coming in fifteen minutes.'

'OK sir. Thank you so much ...' Sumalee removed the clothes from the bag. She had carefully chosen the yellow cotton dress covered in white birds and flowers. Yellow, because it was Monday. Yellow, because it was a good colour, bright like the sun.

When she emerged from behind the silk screen, Mr Smith was bent over the mahogany desk pouring brandy in a glass. The ice cubes cracked and chinked. 'That's better,' he said, eyeing her carefully. 'Now we can find you a husband. Can I call you Su? It's more English. English people like names they can pronounce. '

She paused for a moment. 'Su?' The Englishman nodded. She whispered the name over and over. She felt a sudden wave of happiness. A new dress. A new name. A new life.

Sat in the peeling leather chair, opposite the Englishman, Su looked down and admired her strappy gold sandals. Diamante stones twinkled in the light as she turned her feet. Mai had borrowed them from someone in a go go club. Dancing girls had many shoes. Not like maids. Mr Smith tapped the glass with a pen.

'There is just one problem.' The tap, tap, tapping continued.

Su's happiness was suddenly eclipsed and her face darkened. 'Problem, Mr Smith?' The tapping stopped.

'Nothing to worry about my dear … It's just you're a bit older than most of our ladies. You're forty-four. Is that right?'

Su nodded. Her lips were stinging where her teeth protruded. She covered her mouth. 'I too old, eh …?'

'No, no … I'm sure we can find you someone, but it might be an older gentleman.'

'It's OK,' she blurted. 'I need husband. I need husband very much.'

Under a poster showing a turquoise sea, a little boat and palm trees, Mr Smith arranged her hair. Coarse, black hair, thick and long like the tail of a horse. He spoke about the tsunami. Business was good. So many girls wanted to leave Thailand. He grinned. 'If anything, I have *too many* girls on my books.' He stopped for a moment. The wave had done him a big favour, but he realised the Thai woman was about to cry. Pictures glided on the computer screen and Su saw the sea looked real. Mr Smith proudly announced he had photo shopped her. At least that's what she thought he said. He used too many big words. She wasn't sure what he meant but she had signed the forms anyway.

'So, you are free to marry again.' Mr Smith gave her a printout. It showed her photo and the details that would appear on the internet.

'Very good, eh?' said the Englishman, waiting for a reaction. Su smiled in agreement. All she knew was that he had made her skin look smooth, made her appear younger. She wished for a rich man in England and she thought about a home of her own, instead of sharing with her sister Mai. She had seen pictures of

England and Big Ben, and a wheel called the London Eye. But now she needed to get back to work.

Back at the hotel, she continued to clean and change the beds for the visiting tourists. But on the spongy bed in the hotel room she looked at the crumpled paper Mr Smith had given her. She scanned the sheet quickly.

NAME: Su
AGE: 44
HEIGHT: 5ft 2ins
STATUS: widow
CHILDREN: none
OCCUPATION: maid /housekeeper
PREFERENCES: looking for a man who is caring and polite.

She slid the paper back into her pocket and went out onto the balcony of room 86. Today was a good day. She thanked Buddha. She was sure that her luck had changed. For the first time in many months she looked down at the sea, towards the orange sun. She remembered. The last time she had been on this balcony was the day the sea disappeared. That was before the big wave.

CHAPTER TWO

Patong Beach, 26 December 2004

In the hotel kitchen there was a big commotion. Pans were clanging and the chef found the day's fruit rolling on the counter amongst broken dishes and sliding cups. He was convinced it was his assistant's fault. The shelves were empty. Yesterday he had caught the boy singing while tasting the rice. It was clear for all to see. The boy had summoned a ghost and now the kitchen was cursed. So the chef clutched the gold amulet around his neck and began to pray.

When Sumalee entered the kitchen the chef was shouting at the boy. 'Leave him,' she was about to say, but then the whole building shook and the chef was suddenly pulling her under the giant wooden table. In the kitchen the trolleys clattered and the crockery crashed and smashed. 'Earthquake,' the boy stammered above the rumble. He joined them under the table and was seized by the throat.

'Don't eat and sing,' cried the chef, squeezing the boy's neck. 'Understand? I don't want no ghosts. Not in my kitchen.' The boy glared. The chef rolled his eyes and bared his teeth like an angry dog. 'Don't speak boy. Listen to your elders!'

'Shush,' said Sumalee, 'I feel shaking again. Listen …'

Soon the hotel manager appeared. He laughed at the three staff huddled under the table and ordered them back to work. The thunder in the ground stopped. Sumalee was sent to the third floor with a list of fifteen rooms to clean. First the manager wanted her to rescue the Christmas tree. The decorations had fallen off and Sumalee was known for her creative talents. No one else in the whole of Patong district ever generated as much praise for a Christmas tree.

Su found the baubles scattered in the hotel foyer. Knelt on the floor she saw some had cracked and the lights had stopped working. Most of the hotel residents had slept through the earthquake and she was glad they had not seen the tree in this terrible state. She thought about Tai, working in the supermarket on the beach front. He had left at 6am in a bad mood. And she knew why. Her sister Mai was pregnant again. But they had not been blessed. No children. After fourteen years of marriage she had not conceived a child. Tai said nothing. Mai's constant announcements of pregnancy were met with silence. Instead Tai spent his time thinking, or fishing, or both. At the supermarket he chatted up the tourists who came to buy Coke, toys and sweets. Mostly female tourists and she caught him winking at blonde English girls. Sumalee was convinced her husband wanted a divorce. She didn't blame him. She had failed as a wife.

The earth was growling faintly under her feet. Sumalee stepped back to admire her creation. 'Nice,' she whispered. 'Nice little tree.' She stopped for a moment. 'Another quake coming,' someone said in English, rushing past so that the tree shook. Sumalee nodded. 'It will pass.' She placed her hands together, as if in prayer and thought about Tai in the supermarket. Sometimes they joked about the earth shaking. Tai would be cursing. The shelves in the supermarket were bent and the food would be sliding above the counter, toppling on his head. They would giggle about this when he returned home. Tai would swear he would fix the shelves himself. The shop was falling apart. Once he had shown her how marbles rolled down the sloping shelves. He had drawn a pencil line where a shelf should be. Shelves should always be straight because order was everything.

Sumalee grabbed a feather duster and pressed the button on the lift. But the lift did not come, so she walked instead. Up and up she climbed, until she was out of breath. So many rooms to clean and today she felt tired. Tired of life. One day, she thought to herself, I will be someone and do something important. This is not it! And in the hotel room she thrashed at the wall lights with the fluffy pink duster and watched the dust swirl like glitter in the air.

On the bedside table the fruit was brown and ripe. Sumalee sat on the bed and tore at a banana skin. The soft banana top split and landed on the marble floor. She scooped the yellow and brown pulp up with her hands. In Paradise Hotel there were no rotten bananas. The manager would insist it was all thrown in the bin. 'No good for guests. No good for guests.' Sumalee and the other maids collected the fruit and every day it was hidden, squashed in their bags. And every day Mai and her children feasted on squidgy peaches with mashed bananas and ice cream from Tai's supermarket.

By the time Sumalee reached room 86 she was bloated with fruit and her stomach ached. She would give the room a quick wipe, she decided, and not mop. The doors onto the balcony were hanging open and she drew the blue curtain to stop the glare from the golden sky. Now she could see the smears on the mirror and her own reflection staring back at her. She observed the wrinkles that had started to appear on her forehead and traced them with her finger. Frowning lines, Mai called them. Sometimes Mai pulled the loose skin on her own face and imitated her sister in a ridiculous pose that made everyone erupt with laughter. Sumalee grimaced at herself. There was no stopping these lines. They were like the worn paths and crevices in the hills of Phuket. Only her eyes had stayed the same. Honest eyes, said Tai. Like a beautiful animal. But he had never named the animal with honest eyes.

In the shiny sink Sumalee saw an enormous lump of black hair. Water blasted from the tap, sounding like a trumpet, sending the clogged hair spinning around the bottom of the basin. She caught the hair in some tissue and began to hum. In the room the doors were still open. She stopped humming. Outside the birds stopped humming too. Su tilted her head and listened. Something unnatural, something she could not define, made her shudder. For a moment it was as if the world stood still. No birds. No sound.

When Sumalee stepped out onto the balcony she could hear frantic chitter chatter down below. People were on the beach pointing. In the distance a group of black figures huddled together. She looked towards the gleaming horizon and what she saw took her breath away. There was no sea. Just sand, spreading for miles and miles until it touched the sky. The blue sea had disappeared. Another maid on the next balcony spoke in English. 'Look! Sea went away.' She shook her head. 'Something wrong … sea went like magic. Far, far, away …'

Sumalee looked down, confused, amazed. More people came to the beach, now in a buzz of excitement with cameras, searching for the disappearing water. Some had buckets and Sumalee saw the bodies of fish flapping and tails curling on the sand. A small boy bent down and plucked a fish from the ground. He kissed its gaping mouth before dropping it head first into an orange plastic bucket. Others cheered. So many fish. It was a gift. Sumalee watched the boy collecting more fish, heading out into the vast expanse of sand. Soon he was merely a red dot on a strip of gold. She tidied the chairs on the balcony and the sound of wind filled her ears. At least she thought it was the wind. But the sun was shining, almost blinding. She blinked. Suddenly, there was water. The sound of angry water racing. The sea came back. It came back frothy and bubbling like hot water. The sea swallowed the sand and the boy. She stood motionless. Surely the water would stop. She drew a line with her eye, where the water would stop and retreat.

Screaming, wailing. People were running. Sumalee placed her hands over her ears. She imagined she was in the shiny sink, the water blasting in her ears, spinning round and round. For a split second she had closed her eyes. She opened them. The sea did not stop. An orange bucket was carried away. Many arms were raised up towards the sky. Waving, slowly sinking in the stinking black liquid. Bodies were tossed and thrown, dragged down. On Beach Road a cyclist was standing up. He pedalled frantically, away from the growing tide of black. Like a film, Sumalee thought. Not real. She clutched her necklace. She saw the wave grab the cyclist like a claw. She called on Buddha to stop the end of the world. Lin, the other maid, climbed over the balcony and the two women sobbed and clung to one another. But the sound of their cries was lost in the noise of roaring water.

It was some time before Sumalee thought about Tai in the supermarket. She gasped. All at once she was running down the stairs, her hair flying behind her, but something smacked her chest. A wave of people pushed up the stairs, screaming for her to move. The water was in the building. Why was she going down? An American man pulled her up by the strap of her apron. 'No. You can't go down. We have to go up to the top. There's too much water.' Sumalee found herself in another room with about twenty people, competing to get a view on the balcony. An old man lay bleeding on the bed. She saw his leg punctured with glass, a gaping wound clotted with sand. A hotel maid poured water over the gash and he yelped like an animal. The woman picked at the glass with her fingers and dropped the splinters into a porcelain cup. The white sheets absorbed the blood like blotting paper and the stain grew and grew, spreading like the petals of a giant flower.

'Tsunami,' people whimpered and moaned. Sumalee crawled on her knees under the legs of crying women. Through the railings she watched the great dirty water crash over the concrete walls. She saw tangled metal, bicycles riding the waves. Chairs and boxes were spinning and slapping against cars and trucks. Christmas decorations and lights sparkled in the black water, twinkling like stars. A man in a red car banged on the side window with his fist. A fist pressed white. His lips moved. His mouth was open. The car slowly tipped, then slid down into the dark.

There was a thud and a crunch as another car pelted across the water and hit the hotel wall. Sumalee heard the glass windows smash. The shards hurtled through the water like missiles. A boy dangled in a bending tree. Water wound round his legs. He began to chant and sing. The current carried a woman towards them. She squealed. A triangle of glass sliced her like a guillotine and she disappeared. The American man told everyone not to watch. He ripped the sheets. Everyone began to join in. They would need bandages, many bandages. Outside a child was screaming. All around there were the cries of people. What should they do? Where should they go? People were dying. Sumalee watched. She watched the boy in the tree disappear. She watched as the water played with the bodies of the dead, flipping them high in the air. It tugged them back and forth, gulped them whole and spat them out again.

Sumalee stayed on the balcony. The sea and time had beaten her. She had no idea when the water had come, how many minutes she had remained motionless, rigid and rooted like a tree. Then she saw the shop sign floating past. EVERYTHING YOU COULD WANT. Sumalee mouthed the words. It was the sign from Tai's shop. She recognised the crimson red background, the curly white script. She prayed for Tai. 'My husband, my husband,' she murmured, but no one listened. The black water carried the sign away.

CHAPTER THREE

Patong Beach, December 2005

The man was older than she expected. She was arguing with Mai when the phone call came. Mr Smith said she should come quickly in her best dress. Who would believe that he had found her a husband after just five weeks! She hoped for a young man with curly blonde hair and imagined him in a suit like James Bond. For many months she had slept alone and had dreamt of this man. Sleep carried her to many places, sometimes to the world of spies and guns, where the women wore beautiful clothes and shoes with heels, but sometimes to a dark underworld. When the black dreams came she talked in her sleep and Mai's children patted her head and said the tsunami had sent Auntie a little crazy.

Always, she saw the rising black water, thick like oil from a truck. She watched the children dragged under, the small boy with the orange bucket filled with fish. Sometimes he waved at her. On Patong Beach in the daylight she saw the same boy. He called her name and waved. So real was this boy that once she ran towards him, chased him, but he was too quick for her. She heard a playful giggle, an echo and then there was nothing. Just the bare cool sand and she saw the trail of her own footprints forming strange shapes, heading off in all directions. She was not alone. Many people in Patong district saw the ghosts of the dead. At night the cries of the children could be heard for miles. When the wind blew the dead whispered in the trees. Both Su and Mai wrapped the trees in cloth and covered them in flowers and garlands. This morning she had placed some toys at the foot of the bending tree.

15

She remembered the boy who had clung from the branches. He had shouted up at the balcony before the water took him away. About ten years old. She left him a toy, a small Buddha and said a prayer.

Behind Mr Smith's voice she could hear the swish, swish of the sea, lapping gently, teasing the shore. Even now the water seeped into the crevices of her brain. It filled her up, made her head swim and swell. Every day the black water pumped through her thoughts.

Bob Haywood was standing in Mr Smith's office, dressed in shorts and a Hawaiian shirt. Su stared ahead, past him, wondering if this really was the man she would marry. Mr Smith was calling her. So, this was the man who would take her away from Thailand. No suit. He was nothing like James Bond. And he had no hair.

Mr Smith nudged her arm and she jolted. Su smiled. Bob Haywood watched his Thai bride carefully. Already he liked this woman. She had a kind face, unlike his previous wife. Together they walked down Bangla Road, Su staring ahead in silence, all the time trying to hide her disappointment.

In the restaurant she sat awkwardly. The Englishman was still looking at her. Old enough to be her father, she thought. She had dropped a bowl of rice this morning. Mai had shouted. 'You always bring bad luck. Always clumsy! Clumsy bitch! Your name bad luck!' Now this was her punishment, to face life with an old man.

'You don't speak *any* English?' he asked in a desperate voice.

'Little bit,' she replied. 'Want to learn.' She lowered her eyes.

'You're afraid,' he said. 'You feel afraid of me.'

Su looked up at him, scared he might call the whole thing off. 'Mr Haywood, I will be good wife.'

He grasped her hand. 'I don't just want a good wife. I want you to be happy. And don't call me Mr Haywood. Call me Bobby.'

'OK,' she said, nodding. 'Bobby.'

'I know about your life in the past. Your husband…'

'He dead in big wave.' Su gestured with her hand. 'Wave destroy Patong. That life gone.' She looked briefly towards the golden sand.

'Yes, yes, I know,' he paused for a moment. 'Don't worry. I will look after you.'

'Thank you.' Su began to cry. 'I want go England. I want go England with you. New life.'

The Englishman smiled and nodded. His words were stretched and long. 'We'll sort it out. Don't worry, we'll sort it out.'

Su had no idea what he meant. His lips moved and the words sounded kind. This was as much as she could hope for. Also the Englishman would give Mai and her children much money. It was for the best. Best for everyone.

Blue eyes, she noticed, blue as the jewels in Mai's mirror box. Mai would think she was mad, going to England with an old man. The Englishman had a peculiar accent that rose up and down like music and he called her 'lass'. She had never heard this accent before. She had only seen pictures of London. Instead she was going to a place in Lancashire in the north. She repeated the word slowly. 'Lan-ca-sh-ear.' Bobby said it was a beautiful place, but Mai was not so sure. When the Englishman spoke Mai frowned suspiciously. 'Don't go,' said Mai. 'I feel worried about this man. He too old. He drink too much. Forget money.'

Su was angry. What did Mai know? She had everything. Fate had brought her a husband, a home and children. And now there was a new baby, always wriggling, screaming at the top of his lungs. The smell of baby was everywhere, mingled with jasmine. It made her feel sick. Sometimes she wanted to take the baby away. Every scream, every baby sound jabbed at her chest and lungs, told her that she had failed. Failed as a woman and a wife. She would *never* be a mother. She punched her stomach hard. It was bloated with banana. It was time to leave. She thought about Bobby. For once Su saw a small offering of happiness and she embraced her pillow, optimistic about what the future would bring. She imagined life in beautiful England. She imagined a house, a garden and cooking for her new husband. She knew she could be a good wife.

CHAPTER FOUR

After the tsunami, the owners of Paradise Hotel changed its name to Hope. In the glossy foyer Bob Haywood fell to his knees and begged Su to marry him. He produced a small black box. The tourists clapped and cheered as the red-faced Englishman pulled out a diamond ring.

'Tiny,' said Mai. She didn't think this ring cost much money. She hacked and sliced a large water melon and the juice squirted in her eye.

Su flashed the ring in the light. 'Mrs Hay-wood. Su Hay-wood.'

It was decided. Bobby wanted a beach wedding. Su did not like this idea. 'Bad luck,' she moaned, waving her hands in the air. 'Spirits. Many spirits. Me no want see boy.' Bobby laughed and patted her back.

'You're bloody crazy woman! I haven't come to Thailand to get married in a boring hotel. Not when there is a beautiful view like this.' He pointed out at the sea and Su covered her face.

'You no understand. That beach bad.'

'The dead can't hurt you.' But Su wasn't listening. She was shaking, picturing the big wave. 'Water, water,' she murmured.

Bobby shook his head and covered his ears. 'Stop!' he shouted. 'Just stop!'

Su turned. She had made the Englishman angry. 'There is nothing to worry about,' he told her, lowering his voice. But it was too late. Su was afraid. Afraid of the Englishman. Afraid of the sea.

Mai heard everything. There was something about the Englishman that she did not like. She watched him carefully during his visits to the house. Always polite, but still he made her feel uneasy. He had no pictures of this Lancashire and had not given her his full address. At the internet café she searched this place, Lancashire. She found a beach in a town called Blackpool and wondered if Su might live near the sea.

'Where will you live?' she asked him.

'At my house,' he replied. He seemed amused by her questions.

'But where, which place?' She paused for a moment. 'In Blackpool ...?' He did not respond. 'You should bring picture,' she told him.

The Englishman stopped eating. '*Should?*' he repeated.

From his tone, Mai knew she had said too much. Everyone was quiet, including Su. The children giggled nervously, sensing the tension. Bobby laughed too. Mai was sure something bad was about to happen. Also, he had lifted the Buddha in the lounge and tipped the statue upside down.

'Not gold,' he had said, staring her in the eye. It was an insult.

'Please, put it down,' Mai said. 'Please.'

That night she felt the luck draining from the golden Buddha, drop by drop.

Later when Bobby left, Su went to bed. Mai stepped outside. She could hear pounding music from the nightclubs and she groaned. The baby was screaming again, baring his pink gums, arms and legs flaying. She watched Bobby stagger down the street and then turn. The Englishman dressed badly. Like a giant in clown clothes. His shorts clashed with his shirts and he wore rubber flip flops. In the house she had noticed his toe nails were yellow. He was bald like a monk. Also he drank a lot of beer and he had black teeth when he laughed.

Where was he going? Not to the hotel. He had gone the wrong way. Slowly she followed him down the road, wondering whether to tell the English fool. But Bobby did not look like a lost man. He stopped outside the go go bar. Then he checked his watch and went inside. Under the flashing red lights Mai saw him beckon to a slim Thai girl. Gold shoes and a strapless top that was far too tight. A dancer, Mai thought, a sleazy dancer with bright red cheeks. Bobby whispered in the girl's ear. He waved his wallet and drew out a note. Soon the pair disappeared behind the velvet curtain that led to rooms. Mai ran. Up the street, past the massage parlours and past the gaping tourists, panting and gasping for breath. Now she was certain. The Englishman was not all he seemed.

CHAPTER FIVE

The Englishman did not know about Thai ways. Pitying looks and silence followed the announcement of the Patong Beach wedding. Nearly everyone had heard about the wedding between the rich Englishman and the hotel maid. Some made excuses. Getting married at the ghost beach would bring bad luck to both the groom and the bride.

On the day of the wedding Su carried a garland of flowers down Beach Road and headed towards the building that was once Everything You Could Want. After the big wave the supermarket owners had left Patong. Three staff had died, their business was in tatters. It was early, just 7am. Su heard the cheep, cheep of the love birds, followed by the faraway bark of a dog. Now a coffee house with chrome seats and gleaming glass windows, the shop was empty, except for the staff polishing tables, preparing for breakfast. Everything in Patong was shiny and new. It seemed that everyone had spent the year cleaning and polishing, wiping away the grime of the past. Su took the garland to the counter. Nan, the waitress, greeted her and wished her luck. Then she hung the chain on the far wall. 'For Tai,' said Su. She breathed in the scent of the woven flowers. She thought of her wedding to Tai. That day she had been so in love.

She remembered the last time she had seen Tai's face. It was the day after the tsunami. It was 27 December. In the tourism office the pictures of palm trees and smiling children had been torn down. Instead photos of the dead were pasted on the walls. Su joined the queue of people searching for those they had lost. Slowly they shuffled down the long aisles, mostly in silence. Occasionally someone would let out a cry. Mai had offered to come but Su refused. 'I want to be on my own,' she argued. A makeshift path had been cleared so that they could access the office. In town people clambered over uprooted trees, the tangled metal from battered cars. Some wore paper masks to rid the stench of death. The putrid smell of diesel, rotten rubbish and stale water filled the air. She remembered feet, dirty feet, torn shoes dragging on the ground. That was the day everyone walked with their eyes cast down.

Su saw the picture of Tai's bruised face next to the number 168. She went to the desk. She would have to identify the body. Last night she had weaved her way past the lines of bodies wrapped in cloth on the beach. Everyone had seen the swollen little corpses of children.

Number 168 had been crushed in the supermarket. Rescuers found the body trapped under a bent car. Immediately Su recognised the yellow tee shirt with a rainbow. Bought from Patong market a year ago, Tai's lucky shirt had not been lucky that day. She signed the form with the shiny ink pen. There were numbers written on Tai's hand. Numbers curling like thick black ribbons. Tai's metal watch was given to her in a knotted plastic bag. The face was clouded with droplets of water, the time stuck at 11.15. She shook the tarnished watch, but the ticking had stopped. This was it. Bodies, possessions contained. Lives tied in plastic bags. Everywhere there were numbers. Numbers, dates, times. She had never thought about it before. Life was full of numbers. People were defined by numbers.

Nan was hugging her tightly now, crying fat tsunami tears. 'Miss you, Sumalee,' she cried, squeezing her white cheeks. 'Have a good life with rich Englishman.' Su thought of Bobby. Today she felt empty. Today she felt numb. Today she felt nothing. In her pocket was the cold, shiny watch. She gripped it tightly. She held it in the air. She saw the watch was ticking, its rusty arms outstretched, moving slowly, occasionally sticking. It was a sign. She ran back home, all the time listening to the whoosh, whoosh of the sea.

Mai was on the step waiting. 'I have something for you,' she said, smiling. Su saw that she was tired. Again the baby had been screaming all night and there were purple lines under her eyes. Her cheeks were puffy and swollen.

'Why you crying?' asked Su, in a serious voice.

'Because everything is changed,' replied her sister, wiping her eyes. 'I no like change.'

'I know,' said Su, patting her on the back. 'I know.'

She followed her inside the little house. On the table was a present wrapped in gold paper, flowers threaded and wound in ribbon.

'Ah! Very pretty,' chirped Su. 'Can I open, or should I wait?'

'Open. It is for just you.'

Su tugged at the ribbon and the knot uncurled itself, spiralling out in all directions.

The gift was heavy and she was sure it was a book. She enjoyed the sound of rustling paper, paper crunching as she pressed and prodded. 'Is it a book?' Mai was laughing now. 'It will help you, in England.' The paper was crisp and shiny like foil. Inside she saw a glossy book cover, a photo of a white house, green hills and blossom trees.

'Thank you,' said Su, hugging her sister tightly. She read the title aloud, 'My Beautiful England.'

CHAPTER SIX

Like three wise men bearing gifts, the religious elders marched in a line towards the house. Bobby peered through the kitchen window, tiny drops of sweat tipping from his eyebrows.

'You little bit nervous,' announced Mai. 'You look very nice. Nice Thai clothes. Nice Thai wedding.'

Bobby frowned and wiped his head with his hand.

'Don't worry,' said Mai, 'Su will look after you.'

The Englishman said nothing and greeted the monks as if she was not there. In the sitting room Su was kneeling on a rush mat peering into a bowl of water. She saw her own reflection, rippling like waves. Mai's children sat on the many cushions scattered around the room, sleepy-eyed, yawning wildly. When Bobby entered, the monks began the blessing, saying prayers and chanting. A candle floated and bobbed in the bowl, a tiny flame waving and flickering. The oldest monk cupped some water in his hand and emptied it on Su's head. Cool water trickled down her eye. She watched the flame bending and curling. Please do not go out, she thought. If the light goes out, I will not go to England. If the light goes out, I will stay.

Bobby placed an envelope of money on the silver tray before him. Mr Smith had told him all about the ceremony. This was his donation for the temple. Also, there was the *sin sod*, money for Su's family. He had already paid the fee to Blissful Brides. But the wedding was proving to be far more expensive than he had imagined. Luckily Mr Smith had given him a discount. 'I like the woman,' Bobby explained to him, 'but your picture was *hardly* real.' Mr Smith had argued at first, but finally gave in. After much wrangling and much brandy they agreed the price would be dropped by five hundred pounds.

Food and drinks were given to the monks, just like Mr Smith said. Su was smiling at him now. She was smiling because the candle was still alight. Bobby wanted to eat, but knew he had to wait. Tradition. Tradition. Tradition. This country was obsessed. Back in his town there were few traditions. He had his own, of course. He went to football every Saturday, the Queen's every Friday. These were the only traditions he knew.

The beach wedding was to start at 09.09. It seemed ridiculous to Bobby, but he went along with it. He was enjoying being a celebrity. After just a few weeks in Thailand everyone knew his name. Everyone liked the Englishman. He told many jokes, gave big tips in the bar and ate like a hungry horse. Wherever he went people crowded round him, especially women. In Thailand there were so many pretty women.

On Patong Beach the seats were arranged in rows, covered in white silk. There was a beautiful canopy and flowers threaded in the rush mats. Su noticed the tide was far out today. She was glad. But Bobby was disappointed, telling his friends he knew they shouldn't have married so early in the day. There had been so much preparation. He had wanted a sea view.

During *Sai Monkhon*, Bobby looked dark-faced as the elder wound white thread around their heads. Su tried not to giggle. In his Thai tunic and garland she thought Bobby looked almost handsome. But suddenly he was smiling. There was a slight breeze. The tide was coming in. This would be good for the wedding photos.

Mr Smith had told Bobby about the white thread ceremony. Soon an elder, with a tight leather face, blessed the couple and tied their wrists together with white string soaked in holy water. Then the old man ripped the thread and it frayed until the strand broke. 'Whoever have longest piece is the most in love,' said Su. Bobby looked down.

'That's me,' he called, so everyone heard. The crowd clapped and cheered and one by one began to tie string bracelets on the couple's wrists. The sun was burning brightly now and in the distance waves were forming little peaks of white. Su was standing under the canopy, Bobby next to her. She squinted a little. Mai had given her a beautiful flower and she held it to her nose. Down the beach she saw a man running. Faster and faster he headed towards them. Su watched his blonde curly hair spiralling in the wind. He advanced waving his arms in the air. Su jolted. She looked towards the water. Children were playing with a large inflatable ball. Everyone froze. Su could hardly breathe. The children fell silent. The tide was coming in.

'Stop!' shouted the man. 'You have to stop.'

Bobby turned. 'Oh God!'

Su's eyes widened. The man halted in front of the wedding party. He breathed heavily and placed his hands on his knees.

'You have to stop!' he gasped.

CHAPTER SEVEN

The wind was rising now, scattering the sand over Su's feet. She knelt down. She sensed trouble. She listened to the voices ringing in the sky. 'The spirits are coming,' she whispered. Bobby did not hear. He was glaring at the blonde man. The breeze blew the man's hair over his eyes. He pulled a strand away, a wavy strand like a young boy's curl.

Bobby began to shout. 'What do you want?' He pointed a finger at the man's face. 'You have NO right to be here. GO!'

The man squinted in the sun, pushed Bobby in the chest. 'What are you doing? Think about what you are doing.' Bobby staggered back, waved his hands in the air and clenched his fist. 'Don't do this. Not now. Get out of here. You're making a fool of yourself.'

Su looked down at the sand and drew circles with her hand. Bobby's voice was weak, drowned out by the sea, the gasps and cries of worried onlookers. Su saw his face was red and hot. 'Su, there's nothing to worry about. Listen to me—'

She wrote her name in the sand. She wrote Bobby's name. The blonde man shoved Bobby forward. 'And look at her. She's young enough to be your daughter.'

Mai was standing next to the elder. The elder's eyes bulged and he muttered under his breath. Su was crying. 'I want go home. Please, I want go home now.' Mai began shouting. She flapped her arms like an angry bird. 'This is very bad. To disturb a wedding is very bad.'

Bobby gripped the man's shoulder and pushed him back. 'You've always caused nothing but trouble, since the day you were born. Now go, before I do something I regret.'

Suddenly the blonde man lunged at him, both hands around his neck. Bobby pushed against his chest with the palms of his hands. All the time the blonde man continued to squeeze his neck until finally the two men fell to the ground. Soon Bobby could only spit sounds rather than words. Su was screaming, her hands pressed against her ears.

Someone pulled the man away. Bobby was choking, coughing. He crawled towards his wife. 'Su,' he begged. 'Please listen.' He clasped her hands. She heard the sea, saw the water looping round a nearby rock. For a moment she could not breathe. She remembered the boy with the orange bucket. She heard a child crying in the distance.

The blonde man remained seated on the ground, dazed, surrounded by wedding guests. Bobby tugged her dress. 'Are you listening, are you listening?' He turned to the blonde man. 'Do you know what you've done, David? Happy, now?'

'Who that man?' wailed Su.

'He's my son.'

Bobby's eyes were pink. Su looked at his face closely. 'It OK,' she heard herself say. 'Everything will be all right.' She wasn't sure she believed her own words. She placed her hand on Bobby's cheek. For the first time she thought he looked weak. The big Englishman suddenly seemed small. He looked at her now, a little lost.

'I promise you. There's nothing to worry about. I really am divorced,' he said, his voice cracking.

'Come on,' she said, pulling him up. 'Let's be happy. This is happy occasion.'

The wedding party followed them back to Hope Hotel, all except Mai, who sat next to the Englishman, David.

'So, he your father,' she said, in a voice that revealed her disapproval of Bobby. She gave him a cloth to wipe the trickle of blood that dripped from his nose. 'He marry to my sister.'

'Ah,' said David. 'Your poor sister!'

They both laughed. 'You no like your father,' said Mai.

The Englishman shook his head. 'I have good reason.'

'Tell me,' begged Mai. But the Englishman walked away.

She hurried back to the hotel and saw Bobby and Su seated at the wedding table, under a sparkling crystal chandelier. Bobby was thanking the guests. Lights danced on the walls. She watched him carefully. Su waved at her. But even then Mai saw something in her sister's eyes that worried her. It was a haunted look that Su had worn since the big wave. It was that look people have when they lose someone close, the same look people have when they have stared death in the face. Su's eyes were empty black eyes. No emotion. Bobby gave Su a rose and kissed her hand. Always acting, thought Mai. This man is a good actor. My sister is a good actor. Then she thought about the white envelope tucked behind the golden Buddha. It was full of money. This was Bobby's gift to the family. There was enough money to change a life.

* * *

After the reception Bobby and Su got in the lift. The hotel manager had donated the bridal suite, a large room with a four-poster bed and a sunken bath. Su was excited. This room was reserved for very important guests. She had cleaned this room many times and she knew there would be coconut soap, fresh flowers and champagne. Sometimes petals were scattered on the carved, wooden bed. When they reached the room Bobby lifted her in the air.

'Mrs Haywood,' he said, pushing the door with his foot. 'I will carry you over the threshold. This is the tradition in England.'

Su smiled. She liked the sound of Mrs Haywood. Bobby eased her onto the bed, pressing his heavy body on her chest.'

'What's this?' He ran his hands over the bed cover. 'Rice?'

'Yes,' said Su. 'Tradition.'

'Too much bloody tradition,' he moaned, undressing her, kissing her neck.

'Rice is for eating, not for decorating beds.'

CHAPTER EIGHT

When Su woke in the bridal suite, Bobby was missing. She jerked herself up from the silk curtained bed. All that thrashing in the bed of rice had tired her out. There were grains of rice stuck in her hair and she shook her head and prised the rice out with her fingers. It was 9am. Usually she woke much earlier. The life of a hotel maid was a difficult one. But now everything had changed. She wondered about Bobby. Where had he gone? She also wondered about the man called David.

For a moment she sat on the bed thinking. She thought about her old life, her new one. Once the marriage was registered they would leave for England. She picked up her bag. It was heavy. Suddenly she remembered the book Mai had given her. The book fell open, the pages flapping like the wings of a bird. She saw Buckingham Palace, a picture of the Queen. Su snapped the book shut. She was not sure how useful this book would be. Yes, she told herself. She would learn about England. She wanted this marriage to work.

An hour later Bobby appeared with a paper bag containing banana pancakes. 'You missed breakfast,' he told her, stroking her head. He placed the offering in her lap. 'You must be hungry, Mrs Haywood.' He was clearly pleased with himself.

'Yes,' said Su, desperate to ask what he had been doing all this time. She bit into the warm pancake and felt warm honey slide down her throat. Bobby was smiling at her, his face slightly burnt.

31

His nose was dry and peeling.

'You need cream on face,' she told him.

'Married one day and you're already nagging,' he replied in a serious voice.

Su fell silent and continued to eat. She wanted to ask about the first Mrs Haywood. Bobby sat on the balcony reading an English newspaper. He was checking football scores. She saw him pondering over the picture of a topless woman. Sometimes he talked to himself. Probably because he lived alone and there was no one to listen. His phone was belting out English music and he answered in a loud voice. 'Nice one!' he shouted. 'I'll be there.' He stood up and grabbed the baseball cap, hanging on a cupboard door. 'I'm going out to see someone,' he announced, casually kissing her on the forehead as though she was a child.

Already the honeymoon was over. Su stayed on the bed for an hour. She was angry, angrier than she had been for a long time. She went to see Mai. Mai would know what to do.

* * *

Soup smells drifted out of the kitchen window of Mai's house. Noodle soup. She was always cooking. Mai was surprised to see her sister. 'Soon you will not want to visit us poor people in our little house,' she joked. But then she saw her sister's tired face.

'What happen?' she said in a soft voice. She saw Su was crying. 'What happen, Su?'

'I don't know,' said Su, trying to stop the tears because her nieces and nephews were now rallying around their auntie, thinking someone had died. Mai pulled her through the door and pushed her onto the bench.

'Sit down. Have soup. Soup will make everything better.'

Su ate the soup slowly. She could still taste the sweet banana and honey pancake. Her lips were dry and caked with salty tears.

After a while Mai made the children leave the room. 'So,' said Mai, 'Let me guess. The Englishman could not do it, in the bedroom.' She chuckled at her own joke. Carefully she collected the dishes from the table and stacked them in the sink. 'All talk and no action, eh?' Mai looked at her sister and waited for a response. 'Su!' she called. 'You are daydreaming again.'

Su shook her head and blushed a little. 'That fine. He gone out. This big mistake. I feel this all a big mistake.'

Mai turned the tap on and looked out of the window. 'It's not a crime, to go out.'

'I think give him money back,' said Su. 'I have bad feeling.'

There was a long pause.

'But you always have bad feeling about everything,' replied Mai, still with her back turned. 'That tsunami has played with your mind, made you always have bad thoughts.'

'This different,' said Su, swirling the soup with her spoon. She tried to catch the last noodle but it slipped into the soup like a clever sea snake.

Mai began to wash the dishes. 'Don't worry. You will get used to things. You have to try. You want to go England, right?'

'Yes.'

'OK. Go England and try. You're married now.'

Su was still trying to fish the escaped noodle out. 'You like Englishman, then. I need to know Mai, what you think.'

Mai dried her hands on her apron. 'Yes,' she nodded. 'I like the Englishman. Now you must go back to the hotel.'

Su was pleased. Knowing this changed everything. She kissed her nieces and nephews one by one. They looked at her wide-eyed and confused. One minute Auntie was crying and the next minute she was smiling and telling jokes. As Su walked up Beach Road, she felt happy, lighter, like a bird set free from a wire cage. After all Bobby had only gone out.

At the little house Mai was counting the paper money. There

were so many bills to pay. She owed a lot of money and since her husband had lost his job, life was difficult. Five children to feed and then there was her sister. No choice. Su had to go to England. Most of the money had gone. In her hand the envelope felt light, but Mai's heart was suddenly heavy. She tucked the envelope away and it remained hidden behind the fat back of the golden Buddha. She said a prayer for forgiveness.

CHAPTER NINE

At Phuket airport the voices on the speakers were shrill like ringing metal. Su was standing in the entrance with a large trolley holding their cases. Every sound caused her head to pound and throb. She could see Bobby through the glass doors talking to an English couple, laughing, smoking a cigar. He appeared now, pushing her towards the long queue.

'Come on. Let's be going, lass.' He took the heavy trolley and attempted to steer it. Su watched helplessly as the wheels twisted and turned the wrong way.

A man in uniform appeared with another trolley and Bobby grumbled as the staff dragged the luggage from one trolley to the other. Su trudged behind.

'What's the matter with you?' Bobby was shaking his head.

'I have headache.'

'You women always have a headache,' he joked, but Su did not laugh.

'Everything will be OK,' he said, slapping her on the back, so that she jerked. 'Let's get checked in and get a cup of tea.'

Su followed him reluctantly, past the holidaymakers with children. A small girl smiled at her. These people were all going home. Where is my home? Su thought to herself. The girl offered her a sweet.

'No, thank you,' said Su in a loud, clear voice. 'Have go now. You eat.' The girl was still watching her. People say that children can sense when people have crazy thoughts. Su did not look at the girl. Instead she looked at the floor, a swirling mass of squares and patterns. Leaving Thailand was more frightening than she had imagined. Suddenly her ears were filled with sounds. There was the sound of whooshing like gushing water. She felt her chest tighten. Her heart was beating faster and faster. Thailand was the only place she knew. Bobby was speaking to her, but she could not hear. She thought of her nieces and nephews. They had cried, run after her as she said goodbye. Who would look after Mai? And she had never been on a plane. People slid past her in a blur.

'Su!' Bobby shouted. She felt him pulling her up. She stared blankly.

'It's all right, everyone. She just fell,' he told the crowd that had gathered around them.

Su saw the faces of many people, a woman with painted lips whispering, an airport worker bent over them.

'Is everything OK?' asked the woman, surveying Su carefully.

'She tripped,' said Bobby. 'She just tripped over.'

The woman with painted lips looked at Su. 'Is that right?'

'Yes,' Su replied. 'I tripped.' Bobby nodded frantically.

They moved towards a bench.

'Never do that again,' Bobby hissed in her ear. 'They won't let you fly. Do you understand? Never!'

Su agreed. She was not sure what had happened. For a moment she had left this place. She had been in a kind of sleep. Sometimes she thought sleep was better than reality.

On the plane she felt sick. She swapped places with Bobby and looked out of the window. She didn't speak. If she didn't speak she knew she could hold the tears in. But she felt them stinging her eyes. Down at the sea, she saw a golden sweep of sand. The sea was below the plane now. She closed her eyes, felt her cheeks, burning hot. She imagined the sea rising beneath them. Higher and higher she saw the waves lashing until they almost touched the tip of a wing. She heard the sound of her own breathing. She prayed that the pilot would pull the plane up. Then the plane shook a little. Ears popping, eyes swelling, cold air was blasting in her face.

'No!' she shouted. 'Let me off. No! I want go back. Go back now!' She grappled with the seat belt and clawed at the buckle.

Bobby forced her back in her seat and stretched his arm across her chest. His wife was an embarrassment. 'Go back to sleep,' he said. 'Go back to sleep. We'll be home soon.'

CHAPTER TEN

Although it was midday the curtains at number 16 Geoffrey Street were still drawn shut. When Su awoke the first thing she saw was a flamboyant wallpaper of pink roses. The light filtered through the curtains and there was an unnatural, unpleasant pink glow that reminded her of the clubs back home. The room was small. As Su stepped out of bed she took in the dark furniture. There was a mahogany wardrobe with an oval mirror in the middle and a large set of drawers crammed with clothes. None of the drawers was fully closed and various garments trailed over onto the floor.

Slowly, she made her way across the sticky pink carpet to the window. Bobby was downstairs. She could hear shuffling, dishes clanging, a kettle whistling. Cars sped past outside. The rumble of a truck sounded so close the room shook. She tugged the curtains open.

'Hello England,' she said, gazing at the rows of houses in the street outside. From the window she thought the squashed houses looked like a giant centipede with millions of glass eyes. Across the road she saw a grey-haired woman coming out of her door. The woman stopped briefly and continued up the street. Su looked at the houses carefully. They were made of stone. The line went on for ever, the houses sloping down the hill. Then she saw the sky. An enormous grey sky hung low, threatening to tip with rain. In England it was as if someone had painted a grey wash over everything. Grey road, grey pavement, grey house, grey sky. Here there was no colour. Not like Thailand. This place was not like the brochures she had seen. Here she felt very cold. Her heart sank.

As Bobby came up the stairs, she heard him shouting, 'Mrs Haywood! Are you awake?' Su ran back to the bed. Bobby burst through the door with a tray in his hand, a drooping flower in a jug.

'Boiled egg, toast and tea,' he called, setting the tray down beside her. He handed her the flower. 'Proper English food,' he said.

'Me, no like,' she replied, shaking her head.

'Of course you do. You're in England now. Eat up.'

Bobby pulled the curtains back. 'I'll show you around in a minute.' Su stared at the runny egg, the volcano of yolk that had erupted and lashed the plate. Despite the fact her belly was empty she did not want to eat. Bobby perched on the bed beside her and held the toast to her mouth. There was no choice. She realised that her new husband was a difficult man. To say 'no' was impossible. He had paid for her. She had signed a contract. This was the law.

First Bobby showed her the small kitchen. Dark. Everything in the house was brown or pink. Through the kitchen was a walled yard, ivy growing in the cracks, a blue washing line, with brittle plastic pegs, some broken, others black with dirt. But at least there was a tree. Just one tree cast shadows over the yard and sent spots of light spinning round the kitchen walls.

'I know it's not much, but this is home,' said Bobby. 'I've lived here twenty years. Born and bred in Burnley.'

'Nice,' said Su, because she could think of no other reply. Also she was thinking about the tree and how neglected the yard and the house looked. She followed him into the large sitting room. Again there was too much furniture and patterned wallpaper and this time a dark carpet. Bent beer cans were strewn around the room and a cardboard pizza box, soaked in oil, had turned a dirty shade of grey. In the window the curled brittle leaves of a wilting plant disintegrated into crispy flakes as she touched them, scattering like ashes on the dusty windowsill

'It just needs a woman's touch,' he assured her. But Su was busy looking at a photo in a wiry gold frame. The man called David was smiling in front of many books. She held the picture up in the light.

'Son,' she said. Bobby took the picture from her.

'I think we should put that away,' he told her in an agitated voice. 'Just because he sells books, he thinks he knows it all.' He opened a drawer and jammed the photo inside. Then the sound of a truck halting outside made her start. The truck filled the window and blocked the daylight, casting an enormous shadow over them. With a sharp screech the heavy truck set off again and roared down the road.

'Come on,' Bobby ordered. 'I'll show you Burnley. Get yourself ready and we'll go for a walk.'

CHAPTER ELEVEN

She wore Bobby's coat because she did not yet have one of her own. It was large and heavy, covered her hands, and the collar smelt stale, emitting a hint of musky aftershave and tobacco. Beneath the coat her white skirt peeped out and her legs were bare and cold.

'We need to buy you some clothes,' said Bobby, frowning. He looked down at his wife's shoes, little leather moccasins with tassels, threaded with red and yellow beads that tapped and swung as she walked. 'You need some proper English clothes,' he said. 'Those shoes won't keep your feet warm.'

The air was cold and damp as they stepped outside and Su felt the breeze whipping her legs. Down the road they walked, Bobby holding her arm. He held her arm because he sensed she was weak. And she was shaking. Soon the road narrowed and they reached a bridge. Bobby stopped and leant over. 'Look,' he called in a high, excited voice. He pointed down. 'Look, in the canal. Swans. Two swans, Su.'

Su pressed her body against the wall of the stone arch. She had not understood this word, 'canal'. She lifted herself up on her toes. Then she saw the sparkling black water. Two swans circled an abandoned shopping trolley. A child's bike jutted out of the water. It was a girl's bike because the handlebars were shiny pink. Under the bridge a ripped leather armchair was gently spinning in the current. She felt her body tighten, felt her throat narrow. A duck plunged its head in the dirty water. She could not breathe. Bobby's voice was loud now. Like an angry roar of wind, she heard her own breathing. The duck's orange beak emerged. She saw the black glassy eyes. Legs like elastic, bending all wrong.

'Su!! Su!' Bobby shouted, and a man from a nearby shop hurried across the road and stared at the Thai woman buried in a man's coat on the pavement.

'Oh my God, I call ambulance,' said the Pakistani man from the fruit shop. 'What happen?'

Bobby shook his head. 'I'm not sure. Don't worry. I live up the road. I'll take her home.' Together the two men held her up, searching for her arms in the large overcoat. When the Pakistani man left, Bobby glared at his wife on the sofa. 'I didn't pay for this,' he complained. 'I didn't pay for a wife that's mental.' He jabbed at his own head with his pointed finger. 'Do you understand?'

On the sagging sofa, Su was pinching and poking her bare legs, inspecting the red and white marks, checking to see if her legs were still numb. A thread of blood trickled down her knee where she had slid down the jagged bridge wall, like an eel. She nodded frantically.

'Sorry,' she managed to say. Bobby disappeared for a moment and returned with a box of plasters. He gave her a tissue and pressed the plaster on hard. 'Sorry,' she repeated.

'What happened, Su?'

'Water,' she replied.

Bobby ignored the response for a while. From the rigid pose of his jaw, she could see he was angry and so she waited quietly. When he stood up, he rose so quickly she jolted and jerked like a frightened child. He watched her carefully, all the time thinking about his dream of having a Thai wife.

'Tell me about the tsunami,' he said, suddenly. 'Tell me. You do know we don't have tsunamis in England?'

She did not answer. But then he folded his arms and she knew this was a signal for a reply. In a panic she blurted, 'I no like water. I no like sea. Water kill everyone. Dangerous. Kill everyone. My husband. Children. Man on bike. Man in car. Coming back. Big wave always coming back.'

Bobby knelt down in front of her, his face close, his cracked hands on her shoulders. 'Listen to me. You are safe here. The canal is safe. There are NO WAVES.' Already he was learning to modify his language so that she could understand. He spoke slowly in a soft voice, just as her father had done when she was a small girl.

'No wave,' Su repeated.

'Yes, Su. No waves.'

CHAPTER TWELVE

That night Su pretended that she loved her husband. But all the time she had closed her eyes and imagined she was with the blonde man from her dreams. Bobby knew. 'Who were you thinking about?' he asked, as his body left her. She gave him a blank look as if she did not understand and kissed his nose.

In the pink bedroom Su made a decision. She would decorate the house and build a new life in England. First she wanted a white bedroom. At Hope Hotel the bedrooms were all painted white and there were lamps with angular shades. She needed a bedroom that belonged to her alone and she began to imagine the room devoid of the first Mrs Haywood. These pink flowers, that covered every inch of the house, glared at her like angry eyes. She wanted everything to be new. Bobby was pleased that his wife was looking happy and agreed to buy the paint from town. 'Anything,' he said, 'anything to stop you nagging.' In the morning he had to go to work at the chocolate factory. He left her a key and some English money. 'Pounds,' he said, 'for shopping.' He grabbed her face and pressed his lips hard on her cheek. 'We're going to get along brilliantly, you and me.'

Sure that he was gone, Su went into the kitchen and began to clean. She pushed a pool of coffee around with her finger, but abandoned the task. It was difficult to know where to start. Everywhere she looked there were tubs stacked high, the remains of old food glued to the surfaces, stiff as grit. She chipped at a black mound with her finger nail, grabbed the money and her bag and decided to go out.

First she stopped at the Pakistani shop, a dark, cramped little place where everything seemed to be too big for the shelves. She could not read the labels on this food and she scanned the packets quickly, looking for anything that resembled noodles.

'Thai food?' she called to the shop worker, but he simply stared and continued chewing on a brittle stick in his mouth.

Su repeated herself, but the man was as vacant as a blank page and shrugged his shoulders. A few moments later he spoke.

'Thai?' he said. 'No Thai. Town. Go to town.'

'Ah,' said Su. 'Me walk to town.'

The man began to laugh loudly, revealing stumpy yellow teeth. 'No. Get the bus. Number, erm … I forget number. Bus stop outside. Daneshouse to town. Daneshouse to town.'

Su nodded wildly and was thinking about going home when the man went outside and beckoned for her to follow.

'BUS,' he said in a loud voice. 'Big bus will take you.' He pointed to a dirty shelter a few yards away. As the words left his lips a bus rattled up the road. 'Ah, bus coming,' he said surprised. 'Bloody amazing. Never a bus when I need one.'

As the doors opened the Pakistani man shouted to the driver. Su mounted the steps and gave the man a five pound note.

'Where are you going?' he barked.

'Town,' bellowed the Pakistani man and he raised his hand and waved at her.

When the doors slid shut Su made her way down the aisle to the back of the bus. Past teenagers with headphones and mobile phones that buzzed and whirred like fat insects. Clambering over a large boy's trainers she saw there was just one seat near the back and she perched herself on the edge next to a woman with burgundy hair that glinted orange in the sun.

Buses in Thailand bumped and jolted like fairground rides and she had heard the tourists complain, their bodies pressed hot and tight. Here in England the bus was cool and she watched the houses glide past, like slides on a screen. She watched intently and listened to the faint beat of music that drifted from the headphones of the woman with burgundy hair. Occasionally a bell sounded and someone got off. Then someone new got on and she studied their clothes, their hair. No Thai people. Many Indian people wore long clothes, she noticed women wearing scarves that covered their heads and sometimes their faces. Some women were covered in black from head to toe, rectangle cut outs for eyes.

One Indian woman smiled at her. Or was she one of those 'Pakis'? Bobby called all Asian people Pakis and something in his tone, something she couldn't explain, made her think this was not a good word. She would never use this word. Also a boy on the bus was shouting the word at the smiling woman and a shadow had spread across her face before she dropped in her seat out of sight. Su felt angry towards this boy and stared him in the eye. The boy said something she didn't understand and the others erupted in laughter. He turned his body to the side and a large white trainer flashed in the aisle. He observed her closely. 'She's Chinese,' he shouted. 'A Chinky.'

Su turned her head away. Mango. Mango. Mango. On the bus she stared ahead. Not seeing the spotty boy who was threading chewing gum in her hair. Not listening to the cries of 'Chinky.' Not hearing the girls who giggled at her shoes, their eyes fixed on the beads and tassels that swung and clicked like the pendulum of a ticking clock.

Mango. Mango. Mango. This was the English word she had to remember. This was the English word for her favourite fruit. Easy you might think. After all it was just a little word. Five letters. Two syllables. Two sounds. As the bus jolted she pictured the letter 'M' in her head. Thinking about it now she could see the four lines that make up the letter. Like triangles, said her husband.

You just have to remember this is the letter of triangles.

She stared through the smeared glass window and imagined the word again. For a moment she saw an M suspended in a clear blue sky. There it was. She reached up. But then something happened. Separate. Four lines. Four stems as straight as bamboo. She twisted them, turned them, bent them into shape. She attempted to stick them together but the more she tried to mould the letter into shape the more the lines danced and defied her. Soon there were four brittle sticks and as she grasped them they disintegrated, a pile of wood chippings that made no sense.

Mango. Mango. Mango. The word had gone. Now she couldn't see it. Instead she saw images of mangos everywhere. Mangos were dancing in the sky, dipping and diving above her head. Mango missiles fired across the concrete town, the concrete grey sky. She thought about her sister in Thailand. And then she thought about the mango trees back home. In England no one was thinking about mango. Everyone was eating Dixy's chicken. McDonald's. Kentucky. She knew this because Bobby had eaten the Dixy special for three nights.

The teenagers were shouting and Su sensed there would be trouble. The bus driver stopped the bus and told them to get off. Just like when she was a small girl, she sometimes saw things before they happened. Long ago, under the sun in a garden of fiery orange heliconias her grandmother played the thinking game with her. Often they sat on a straw mat breathing in the scent of jasmine. 'Malee,' her grandmother would whisper, 'you have many eyes. Not just these ones on your face, but more in here' and the old woman would tap her head and nod frantically. 'In here you see pictures. Yes?'

Sumalee would smile and make shapes in her grandmother's wrinkled face. Her face was cracked and flaky like the path to school. Always her grandmother called her Malee, meaning flower. One day they played the thinking game. 'Close your eyes,

Malee,' she said. 'Close your eyes and think of a colour.'

Eyes welded shut she thought of the most difficult colour possible. She imagined a large mango and coloured one half yellow and one half purple. She saw the mango suspended in a clear blue sky and smiled, pleased that she would outwit the old woman.

'Tell me when you have drawn the picture in your mind,' her grandmother said in a strange, distant voice.

But the more Sumalee thought about the mango in the sky, the harder the thinking game became. In her mind she bit a chunk out of the side. She gasped out loud.

'It's OK Malee,' said her grandmother, sensing her distress. 'Are you ready?'

'Yes,' Sumalee whimpered, but the mango had disappeared and really she wanted to cry. She wanted to win.

'You ate the mango, Malee,' chuckled her grandmother. 'So, you ate the mango of two colours. You enjoyed the purple and yellow mango, yes?'

Sumalee stood up, amazed. 'Is it magic, Grandmama? Is it magic?'

Her grandmother had a twinkle in her eye that day. 'Now you try, Malee.'

Sumalee didn't argue. She closed her eyes and imagined being in her grandmother's magical world. Soon she was stood on a beach. She saw water, thick, black water that rose and stretched and curled like the tongue of a giant beast.

'I see black water, Grandmama,' she said in a high voice. 'Water is coming.'

'Good, Malee,' she replied. 'Now open your eyes.'

By then Sumalee was tired of the thinking game and her grandmother hugged her tightly and threw her in the air. When she landed on the ground her grandmother spoke in a serious voice. 'Remember Malee. The sea is only your friend if you are a fish.' Sumalee looked up at her. Her grandmother cupped her face with her bony hands. 'You are not a fish. You are a flower. My beautiful, delicate flower.'

The bus driver was shouting, 'For God's sake! This is the last stop. You getting off or what?'

Su jerked in her seat. The bus was empty. The driver was rolling his eyes and pointing at his watch. 'Some of us want to get our lunch. Understand?'

As she stood up Su felt her legs were stiff. She gripped the metal pole and pulled herself up. Once off the bus, she realised she had arrived at a large bus station. The bus driver pushed past her. 'Thank you,' she mumbled after him but he was in a hurry and didn't look back. She had no idea where she was going but worse than this she wished she was small again. She wished she was back in the Thai garden with the heliconias that gaped like bird beaks and the happy faces of wildflowers that baked and bowed in the warm sun. Here she had no idea what the future would bring. And here the sky was grey.

CHAPTER THIRTEEN

Buildings and signs loomed over her and she stood for a while leaning against the sculpture of a metal cow, watching the mothers with screaming children, a man in a grimy van dispensing paper bags of sugary doughnuts. Immediately she recognised the word MARKET. She mounted the steep steps to the market hall and spotted a fruit stall at the far end. Past hanging tutus and spinning red and pink wigs, the market reminded her of home. Only this market was not so busy and the market people were strangely quiet. There was no sell, sell, sell, no one shouting for customers. Like an empty theatre, Su thought to herself. All props and no animation. Where was life? Was this it?

The more she questioned what she saw the closer she came to the fruit stall. A grey-haired man, presumably the stallholder, was sitting on a stool, a newspaper flapping in his hand, but he continued to read and did not move. From here Su could see that the stall consisted mainly of a painted backdrop of fruit and it soon became clear that there wasn't much for sale. She scanned the wooden trays lined with green felt.

'Mam-u-ang?' she said to the man, moving her head from one side of the stall to the other. She couldn't see the fruit she wanted and the English word had escaped her, like sand through her fingers.

'Ay?' replied the man, glancing up at her.

Su paused for a moment. 'Mam-u-ang,' she repeated.

The man grimaced, shook his head and stood up. 'No idea, love. No idea what you're on about.'

Su raised her hands and made a football shape with them. 'Big,' she simply said. 'Big.' She smiled hoping for some reassurance, but none came.

'Big?' the man said, sucking his cheeks. 'I think you need to learn some English, love.' He began to lay some apples in front of her.

'I think she means mango,' said a voice behind.

The stallholder sighed, irritated that another customer had intervened. 'All right … I might have one.' He crouched down and pulled a large mango from under the counter. He seemed annoyed.

'Mam-u-ang,' said Su quietly to the old woman beside her. The woman nodded and pulled a face at the man behind the stall.

'Whatever,' retorted the stallholder, smirking. 'How was I supposed to know? She's probably illegal. England's not bloody England no more.'

But Su noticed he didn't look at her when he spoke and the giant fruit was thrust in front of her so suddenly that it almost dropped to the ground like a grenade.

'Bloody ignorant,' said the old woman. 'Don't worry about him. He's a miserable sod.'

Su stared blankly. 'Thank you,' she said, placing the mango in her straw bag, but no one was really sure who she was thanking. It was more of a natural response, reinforced by her culture, her upbringing. No matter what anyone said to her, she had bought something and she should say thank you. Of course, she remembered this English word now. Mango. Mango. Mango. Never had she known one mango to cause so much trouble. So there was some drama in markets in England after all. But this was not the kind of drama she had expected. And never had she been in the spotlight, not like this. As the stallholder glared after her, she felt her face become hotter and hotter and she raced away, forgetting her shopping list, worried that she didn't know enough English words to survive. Suddenly the only English word she knew was mango. Mango. Mango. Mango. Perhaps she would be condemned to a life of just eating mango. She imagined slicing the fat mango head, the juice bleeding bright in a white dish. And then she imagined it was the head of the laughing market man and she ripped the chewing gum from her hair.

CHAPTER FOURTEEN

It was interesting, she thought, as she walked along the wet path, how at Hope Hotel, they had been told the customer is always right. Once she had glared at a guest and the hotel manager had slapped her arm. 'Sumalee,' he said, 'always be nice to customers, even when they are wrong.' She had heard an American woman calling all Thai women 'tarts'. The hotel manager had also heard the woman. But no one corrected her. Instead they politely took her money and invited her back to Thailand. In England no one seemed to care about customers. She wanted a drink but was too tired and too scared to go to the café, too exhausted to battle with a language she could not understand. And then there was the bus. She needed to get back to the bus station.

In England it was always raining and fat drops pelted her head like bullets from a gun. Beside her was an open shop door and Su stood inside for a moment looking at the world outside, watching the people with huge umbrellas, not really feeling part of it all. The umbrellas were like giant flowers, their petals extended, waving in a world of grey. She stepped inside to let someone pass and soon realised she was in a bookshop. It made sense to stay here for a while and so she wandered up the aisle, plucking books from the shelves and turning crisp pages filled with English words. Some she could read and she extracted them carefully and joined the sounds she could remember. Tai had tried to teach her once, just the alphabet but it was impossible. Now a soup of letters and sounds swirled like hot liquid in her head and she mouthed these sounds until she almost whistled aloud. Then there was someone beside her because she was talking to herself and the man was asking her something, but she didn't hear and he looked at her confused.

Su heard him breathing. 'Are you OK?'

'Yes,' she stammered, pushing the book back on the shelf. 'Mango,' she blurted. She looked at the man now and saw his blonde curly hair falling over his eyes. He seemed familiar and she searched his face, but he was preoccupied. He smiled at her, but only for a moment, for just as he was about to speak a woman called his name and he reluctantly crossed the shop. Su left quickly, glad that it had stopped raining because she didn't have a coat. How ridiculous that she had been to town and not got a coat! There was just one mango and a dreaded trip back on the bus, if she could find it. When she did find the bus she was relieved to see the same bus driver.

'Geoffrey Street?' he said, his eyes widening.

'OK,' Su replied, suddenly aware that this was where she lived. The driver shook his head, slightly amused by the little Thai woman who seemed to have no idea where she was going.

'You need to get off by the language centre,' he told her slowly, as though she was simple. 'UNDERSTAND?'

Su nodded. 'OK.' But really she had no idea and the bus driver knew from her expression.

'All right. Sit down. I'll tell you when to get off.'

'Thank you.'

'Hurry up then, woman,' he bellowed, pointing at a seat. 'There's a queue of people.'

'Sorry, sorry.' Su sat down at the front. The mango was in the bag on her lap and she pressed the skin firmly with her finger. Too ripe. The mango was too ripe. She had so wanted to cook a meal for Bobby, for the two of them. Now she would have to go back to the Pakistani shop. There was no choice. She had to speak English, or not eat. But something else was bothering her. She had a bad feeling. Today had been a bad day. She clutched the little Buddha around her neck hoping for some luck.

'Languagecentre,' shouted the bus driver. Su stood up and nodded at the driver. Soon she saw the bridge and she knew the Pakistani shop was near. Through the door she watched a woman in a shalwar kameez arranging herbs and spices on the shelves. Another woman slapped the hand of a small boy and began to pour coloured sweets into a jar on the counter. 'Too many, too many!' she wailed, but the boy's lips were fixed in a defiant pout and he grabbed at the sweets and stuffed them in his mouth. Su stood in the doorway.

'Chicken … rice,' she called, in a loud voice.

The woman who had been stacking shelves nodded and fetched the chicken from a fridge at the back of the room. 'He naughty,' said the other woman, giggling. Su laughed. A bulging bag of rice with a purple label was placed in a carrier bag. As Su left she was happy, happy that she had been understood. She stopped at the front door of the little house in Geoffrey Street. Painted blue and chipped, it was the only blue door in the road and there were shiny brass numbers. From the path she could see the windows needed cleaning. The windowsill was bare because she had placed the wilting plant in the kitchen. Then she remembered. The photo in the drawer. The blonde man on the beach. The man in the Burnley bookshop. David.

CHAPTER FIFTEEN

Bobby was complaining. 'I don't understand you. You don't understand me. You have to learn English, Su.' Su nodded her head. 'And then you can get a job.' Su was disappointed. All this talk of getting a job. This was not what she had expected, to get a job, to be a maid again. She thought she had left that life behind. But Bobby wanted her to get a job cleaning at the factory.

She said nothing. Standing in the kitchen opposite her husband she did not tell him about David, about the trip to town. Describing her day would be far too difficult. First she couldn't think of the right words but also this morning she had put the photo of David back on the windowsill and now it was gone.

'Yes,' said Bobby. 'Classes are free. Just down the road. You'll be able to make friends.'

Su looked confused, but she liked the idea of 'friends'. In Thailand she had many friends. What would they be thinking now? How would they imagine life in England? She realised that the pictures she had seen of England, they were of a different place. No one in Thailand could imagine that this was England. Not here. She wanted to send Mai a letter, she had written two lines, but then had stopped herself. She had stopped herself because the ink poured from the pen too freely and the letters lapped on the page like angry waves and she knew her letter would be flooded with the truth. She didn't want to tell Mai that England as they knew it was just a dream. She didn't want to tell her sister that the beautiful England they had spoken of didn't exist.

English classes were just a few minutes away and Bobby said they were small, as if this was a good thing. Su repeated the word 'small'. All the time she was thinking that if the classes were small how would she make friends? All of a sudden she felt small. Small as an ant waiting to be crushed.

* * *

The next day Bobby walked her over the bridge and down a steep ramp before kissing her goodbye. He had bought her a coat, a large raincoat in beige with a belt and deep pockets. Su had forgotten the name of the colour already and had struggled to pronounce the word 'beige'. When she spoke it sounded as if she was saying 'age' and Bobby rolled his eyes. Outside the building they stopped. Bobby towered over his wife, looking more like a father with his child than a man with his wife.

'Come in?' said Su, expecting him to follow her.

Bobby shook his head. 'No. I'm going to work. You have a good time.'

'Good time,' muttered Su. She looked at the large red-brick building perched on the edge of the canal. The bricks were peppered with a black sooty substance and there was a sign saying FREE ENGLISH CLASSES. But someone had scrawled the words GO HOME in black pen and there was swearing beneath. Behind the building she saw steps leading to the sparkling black water. As she turned Bobby waved and gestured for her to go in. She waved back and watched him turn at the top of the ramp and disappear up the main road. Should she just go home? She noticed there was a park further down past the language centre. She heard two boys shouting to each other in a strange foreign language. One boy lay on a flat disc that tilted and span round and he spread his arms and legs like a star. The other boy dangled from the knotted chain of a swing that had been wound so tightly, it was impossible to reach. Su was smiling, wondering about the two little boys, wondering about their mother, when someone tapped her on the shoulder. It was a light tap and an Englishwoman with yellow hair was speaking to her in a bright voice.

'Are you here for English classes? Follow me.' That was it. Now she couldn't go home and Su was secretly annoyed. Annoyed because again she was following the instructions of someone else, annoyed because always she let other people tell her what to do. Annoyed with herself. Annoyed with life. She didn't want to feel like this. She wanted to make her own decisions. As she followed the woman with yellow hair she remembered that her husband Tai had once compared her to a beautiful animal. This troubled her. I am an animal, she thought, like a dog on a lead. But I would rather be a wolf. Wild and free.

* * *

There were many language seekers gathered at the centre, women from different countries, women with different languages, different lives. Two women were in the doorway speaking in Urdu, dressed in shalwar kameez tunics and scarves, aqua, pink and gold. They stared at Su, chattering and chirping like exotic little birds.

'Assalam-o-alaikum,' one called. Su smiled and bowed her head.

'You, new student?' one asked, tossing her head back, so that a thick plait swung from side to side. She guided Su towards a curved counter. Soon a man appeared, about twenty-five, a basin haircut resembling a shiny nylon wig hanging in his eyes.

He ticked her name off the long list. 'Room 4,' he said, pointing down the corridor. 'Very good,' he said. 'I'm Chris Chan.

Manager. Just ask me if you need anything.' He flicked the hair from his eyes and began to speak to the blonde woman.

Su found the room at the end of the corridor. Through the glass door she saw some women crowded around a small table. On the wall a large clock with big numbers dominated the room and there was a map of the world beside a white board. Su thought about Thailand. She wasn't sure where it was on the map. Not exactly. Mai had shown her once, but she had forgotten. At school she forgot everything and spent her time watching the hands of the clock, waiting for school to end. Always she wanted to be outside with the trees, the wind, under the sun, or under the moon. She hated being inside. Slowly she entered and made her way to a free seat. Just six women were in the group and they eyed her suspiciously.

'New student, ay, not done no English before?' said one woman in thick glasses, her hair swept back in a large butterfly clip that perched precariously on her head.

'Yes,' Su responded in the confusion. The women looked at each other and waited. The teacher was asking a question, but no one was listening. They were too busy observing the little Thai woman with the crochet hat and frilly skirt. A large Indian woman was yawning, looking at her watch. 'I go to TK Maxx at ten-thirty,' she casually announced.

'But your lesson doesn't finish until twelve o'clock,' the teacher reminded her.

'I go daughter shopping,' she replied unmoved, chasing a rolling pencil. The others watched for the teacher's reaction.

The teacher repeated the corrected phrase loudly. 'I am going shopping with my daughter.' Automatically the woman mirrored the response. Then the teacher looked her in the eye. 'In future you must go shopping on another day. Not during lessons.'

The woman's smile fell. She gripped the pencil tightly. 'OK teacher.'

'I think it would be a good idea if you all start by telling me your names. Tell me about yourself, your family,' the teacher said and gradually they answered her questions, a babble of disorderly sounds and words swirling in the air, few sentences, the repetition of 'nice'.

Su told everyone her name but in the classroom the youngest girl was crying; the women crowding round her, speaking in Urdu.

Kalsoom looked up. 'She crying ... mum in ... bombings. Home ... Pakistan.'

The girl continued to sob. Eventually the others sat down. Someone talked about planes, mountains, Damadola, a place she had never heard of. The teacher stared helplessly. Su nodded and looked blankly. 'Ahh,' was all she could say. Then she remembered there were some tissues in her bag and the packet rustled as she pulled out a white square. She held the tissue out to the girl and watched her unfold the soft sheet and press it to her tiny wet face. In the silence Su was thinking. There was nothing to be said. Language was not enough.

CHAPTER SIXTEEN

The crying girl was called Samina. She was eighteen and lived with her husband Ehsan and nine other relatives. Most nights he worked as a taxi driver patrolling the streets in a battered gold Toyota, trying to steal customers from Star Cabs. In Burnley, Samina spent her time learning to cook and sew with her mother-in-law, a large lady with loose jowls and many children. Many children, who all spoke different varieties of English. And so Samina sat and listened to the strange babbling sounds of Urdu, Punjabi and English that filled the sitting room. Always there was noise. Chitter, chatter, chitter, chatter. She could say her name, address and a few words about the weather. But that was all.

'It very cold,' she said to an Englishwoman once in the street and the woman nodded and smiled an accepting smile. But sometimes others glared and whispered and then she felt as though the quest for English was impossible, pointless. She needed English to stay. She needed a certificate. Everyone in the family repeated 'how long until certificate?' and she repeated the word 'exam' over and over, not really knowing what it meant. She feared it was something very big and life changing and she was frightened. Often at night she didn't sleep and 'exam' was a large beast that clawed at her belly and her brain and dragged her back to Pakistan.

Ehsan listened as she said English words. She repeated them in the mirror, slowly, because the teacher said she spoke too fast.

She watched her pink lips form an O, observed the fullness of her mouth. For a moment he was amused and Ehsan brushed her hair while she dragged and rolled the English words over her tongue. But bored with the game he told her, 'No more English. Speak Urdu.' Ehsan suddenly looked depressed. He said the taxi business was bad. There was a recession. 'Just one fare tonight,' he said in Urdu. Then in English he blurted, 'Shit.'

Samina nodded, knowing what would follow. Her husband was twenty-four, tall and others said good looking. She was thankful for this. Her sisters had not been so lucky. She lay still as he groped at her clothes and frantically undressed her. As usual she transported herself to another place. She pictured herself asleep on the veranda at the house in Pakistan, the sun gently caressing her face, the hot breath of the breeze on her cheek, the sound of leaves rustling. While he crushed her between the starched sheets, she stared up at the ceiling thinking of others like her, their protests unvoiced. Sometimes she wished she had been a man. For the rest of the night there was silence.

* * *

As she gazed out of the window, Samina chopped the chilli just as her mother-in-law instructed. The biryani was bubbling on the stove, depositing spots of water and juice on the white tiles. She wiped her face. 'Shit.' She forgot the chilli and her eye suddenly burnt red like fire. On her own in the kitchen she repeated the word again, then again and again. Now she smiled. Ehsan did this all the time. She felt better, strangely happy that she could be angry. This was anger. She felt real anger rising in her chest. She had never known what it felt to be outwardly angry. All the time her mother-in-law was in the front room relaxing, watching a sentimental film, a romance with beautiful dancers in red and gold, humming along. She pressed the wet kitchen towel on her eye.

'My name is Samina. I come from Pakistan. I live in Burnley.'

Yes. This was English. She liked the sound of the words. She liked the class. At home she cooked and cleaned, cooked and cleaned. Sometimes she visited family members. But life in the UK was very different. The house was small. There was no space. The cooking pot rocked on the stove now, large and ugly, singed brown by the flickering gas flame that licked the base, the glass top lifting and clanging as it fell. The room filled with steam. Warm water drooled down the glass window like a caged animal's spit. The hissing pot was too big for the kitchen. Samina was too big for this house.

And she remembered her house in Pakistan. She closed her eyes for a moment. There were mango trees in the garden, vegetables. They had ten bedrooms, three bathrooms. In Pakistan they sat on the veranda talking about the future, about being married, about life in England. It was the golden egg, to go to England. But this was it. A terraced two-bedroomed house with a cracked concrete yard crammed with dandelions. This was the prize. She lived in Paradise Street. Back home the others were jealous, imagining a grand Victorian house, a perfect English life. They did not see the dirty streets with rows of bins and skinny terraced houses with plastic windows fronted by cars. Not trees.

Then there was a husband whom she never saw, who returned at all hours, who did not speak to her in any language. He communicated to her only with his hands and his body, sometimes there were sounds. When he grabbed her late at night, pressing her to the floor, his hand on her mouth, he breathed a long shush and no one heard.

In the English class Samina learnt how to say 'I like.' She uttered the phrase slowly and it chimed around the room. There were pictures on a large screen that moved and words glided across at the touch of a button. 'I like apples. I like biryani.'

'Do you like England?' the teacher asked. Samina didn't

respond. 'Yes,' the others called together, 'I like England.' But Samina couldn't say the words. She wanted to go back, back to the mountains, back to her brothers and sisters, back to another life. Life in England was strange, odd. Ehsan complained about England. He said the girls in Burnley were 'filth'. They were always drunk, vomiting in his taxi. They had vodka, but she didn't know this word. They wore short skirts. 'Tarts,' he told his brother. Samina understood the word vaguely. She heard it on television once and her mother-in-law quickly changed channels. England was unknown to her. She wanted to go to London. She had seen pictures of Big Ben, Parliament. She knew where the prime minister lived. The house had a shiny black door. He lived at number ten but she couldn't remember the name of the street.

Her life was in this tiny house, in these four closed walls. The language centre gave her freedom, but Ehsan didn't know. She didn't show him what she had learnt. When he spoke to his brother she listened carefully and she understood more and more. In her bag was a battered dictionary. She took the little book out in the bathroom and sat on the toilet seat reading the words carefully, occasionally whispering them in front of the mirror, checking her pronunciation, ensuring that her tongue was between her teeth when she produced a 'th' sound, just as the teacher had shown her.

'That girl is always in the bathroom wasting time,' complained her mother-in-law. 'Why are you always in the bathroom?' And Samina ignored her, hid the book in the folds of her clothes and returned it to the wardrobe where it lay wrapped in a black and gold scarf decorated with sequins, hand sewn by her mother in Pakistan.

CHAPTER SEVENTEEN

Su pulled on the yellow dress and smoothed the folds with her hands. There was a party at the centre for new students and she felt excited. 'Ahh... My favourite dress,' said Bobby, observing his wife closely. 'You look like a little canary.' Su frowned and attempted to mimic him, but the 'C' sound was lost and she could only mouth the word 'gan-er-ee'. Bobby was worried. The dress had grown and as he held his wife's waist he gathered the fabric in his hands. 'You are not eating enough, love,' he said, shaking his head. 'This is bad.'

Su shrugged her shoulders and wriggled away. 'No like English food.'

'Too skinny,' said Bobby, pressing his hands together.

'OK.' Su looked down at her feet. 'Today cook Thai food. Party.'

Bobby nodded. He had seen the large tub in the kitchen containing Thai soup. For a week Su had repeated Tom Kha Gai, over and over. The words stuck in his head and prodded him like sharp needles. Walking to work he found himself chanting this phrase. Tom Kha Gai. Tom Kha Gai. Like the beating of a drum, he thought to himself. Tom Kha Gai. Eventually he found the recipe for Tom Kha Gai on the internet. He hoped the Thai coconut and chicken soup would be worth the effort. But he had trawled round three supermarkets to find the ingredients. 'This is fucking ridiculous,' he found himself saying. 'Fucking ridiculous.'

This was life now, an endless cycle of him trying to understand Su and Su trying to understand him. When he had arrived home with the bag of food Su had hugged him tightly and he felt guilty because he knew his tone was often abrupt, that he lacked patience. Su deserved better. But he had never heard of galangal, or bought lemon grass, or fresh limes. They were for foreigners, the sort of thing you got in restaurants up town. For the past two years he had survived on a diet of Dixy's chicken, pies, black pudding from Bury market and plenty of beer. All this time he had only to think about himself. Now the house was full of mango. This was a fruit that he had no idea how to tackle, no more than he knew how to tackle a rugby ball. He was more a football man. That was his game. Burnley and burgers went together. Not Burnley and mango.

Somehow Su had changed the landscape of his Burnley life. In the beginning he hardly noticed, but friends who came to the house commented on a vase of flowers, a colourful cushion, a bright scarf arranged on the back of the sofa. Others saw the golden Buddha on the fireplace and rubbed its fat belly wishing for money. And the house was clean.

The tub of Thai soup sat on a gleaming worktop and he saw how happy Su was that morning, cooking her own food, smelling the limes, the lemon grass. In her eyes he saw the thrill of tasting her own country, the thrill of visiting her own past again.

Outside the language centre a shiny banner waved on the railings and balloons flapped, some popped, others shrunk in the sun. Su was early and saw there was just one student in the classroom. She hovered by the door like a bird, but then Samina looked up and called out in Urdu.

'Nice day,' said Su, sitting opposite her. 'Bring chicken soup. Thai.'

'Nice,' said Samina, clutching a plastic tub that had turned orange.

'What you bring?'

'Biryani,' the girl replied.

'Ahh. Good,' said Su, not knowing what this meant. She walked across the room and saw yellow and orange rice through the plastic lid, a jumble of chicken and peas.

'Chicken!' Samina cried. 'Chicken.'

The two women laughed. 'Both chicken,' said Su and she noticed that Samina's eyes were large and wide. 'You OK?' she asked the girl. Samina smiled.

'I like dress.' Samina tugged her dress gently. Su sat down beside her and reached inside her pocket. She held up a photo of Mai, her five nephews and nieces.

'Family. Thailand. Sister.' She began to name the children one by one. In another picture was a bony woman surrounded by exotic trees and plants. 'Mom,' said Su. 'Died in big wave.' Samina looked confused and her eyebrows were raised. 'Tsunami,' said Su quietly. 'Take my husband, take my mom.' She raised her hands and imitated the movement of waves.

Samina gasped. 'I know tsunami.' She bit her lip hard, realising that she wasn't the only student whose life had been shaped by death and the past. 'Family bombed,' said Samina after a while. She looked up at the ceiling and raised her hands. 'Village bombed. Boom. Boom. Boom.' She clapped her hands together with a fierce slap.

Su shook her head. 'Life very hard,' she said and the two women shared the silence and breathed in the smell of warm food.

* * *

In the small kitchen the sink was smeared and Su noticed there was no window, just an ugly extractor fan that whirred and hummed. Carefully she placed the Thai soup in the microwave and waited. Samina was standing next to a Polish woman dressed in English clothes. Jeans that were skin tight, a jumper with stripes and shoes so high the woman's body swayed.

'You like class?' asked the Polish woman.

'Me like,' said Su, still observing the woman's shoes, a spiky heel with a band of gold. Also, she was thinking about clothes. She would like some jeans. All free women wore jeans.

But then when she looked at the woman's face, she found herself staring. The woman wore makeup, lipstick, thick foundation and mascara, like the air hostess at the airport. She fixed her gaze on her face and tried to guess her age. About thirty, she decided. The woman felt her looking and turned away. The microwave pinged. Two minutes were up. But the door was stuck and Su could not open it.

'Like this,' said the Polish woman, releasing the door. She was bent over, her face close and it was then that Su saw a bright purple line under the woman's eye.

'Look nice,' said the woman, pointing at the soup.

'Chicken soup,' said Su, vacantly, because she had seen a mark like this one before, on her sister's face. Many times.

'What happen?' she heard herself say aloud. These words were not planned and she covered her mouth, shocked that she had found the English words, shocked that she had spoken her thoughts aloud.

The woman touched her eye.

'It OK,' she said. 'My husband hit. Left now.'

For a moment no one spoke. Samina placed the biryani in the microwave and listened. She had understood this exchange and gave the Polish woman a sympathetic look.

'Call police?' said Su, after a while.

'Daughter, me, left.'

'Ahh ...' Su said, patting the woman's arm.

'Really bad,' said Samina, because this was a phrase that her mother-in-law Suriya used whenever things went wrong.

'Really bad,' repeated Su and she suddenly felt lucky.

'How old daughter?'

'Six.'

'What your name?'

The Polish woman spoke quietly. 'Lenka.'

'Me Su and this Sammy.'

'No!' said Samina, rolling her eyes. 'SAM -INA!' She said her name slowly.

'Sammy from Pakistan,' said Su, but Samina did not correct her. That moment something changed. She decided she liked Sammy. Sammy sounded important. Different. There were too many Saminas in the world.

CHAPTER EIGHTEEN

Sammy sat in the window of the house in Paradise Street waiting for the parcel to arrive. Her mother-in-law was at sewing classes and the men at the mosque because it was Friday, but she was instructed to stay home. The man who came was young and smiled a broad smile. He held out a digital box and the girl was bemused as he pointed at it.

'Do you speak English?'

'I speak little bit,' Sammy replied meekly. 'I go language college.'

The man nodded. 'How long have you been here, in England?' The girl looked blank for a moment, surveyed his spiky hair, a gold ball earring. She noticed his teeth were large and white, as white and square as the napkins she had folded that day.

'Three week,' she said loudly, happy that she understood him, but suddenly embarrassed she lowered her eyes and her voice. He pushed the pen in her shaky hand. 'Here. Name. Here.' She signed her name in large curly letters.

'You speak good English,' he reassured her and he looked at her now, the pretty face, small nose and wide eyes.

Sammy shook her head. 'I no don't know much.'

The man laughed. 'Well, I think you are doing brilliant.'

'Brilliant,' repeated Sammy confused.

'It means very good.'

She giggled, covered her mouth with her hand. 'Thank you,'

she muttered, 'you very kind.'

The courier lingered a little longer than normal.

'What's in your parcel? Something nice?'

'I no don't know,' responded Sammy.

'I don't know,' the man corrected her.

'My mother-in-law say some junk.'

The courier laughed loudly, his teeth flashing bright. 'It's nice to meet you. What's your name?' He tried to read the signature on the box, narrowed his eyes and tilted the screen in the light.

'My name Sammy,' she said, looking at him carefully. Her mother-in-law had warned her about white men and she suddenly realised her hair was uncovered. She folded her arms tight around her body.

'My name is Rob,' he told her. 'See you again, Sammy.'

'Yeah,' said Sammy, because she had heard this expression used by her cousins.

Then he was gone and Sammy sat on the windowsill dreaming of Pakistan and the parcel delivered by the man called Rob sat on the kitchen table waiting to be unwrapped.

She switched on daytime television. There was a programme on dresses. She liked these English clothes. Upstairs she found Ehsan's leather jacket. She put it on top of her shalwar kameez and the black leather was cold and soft. In the mirror she saw herself. 'Cool,' she said, in the same tone as the television presenter. Then she heard a key in the door. Her mother-in-law was back. Quickly, she threw the leather jacket on the carpet and made the bed. Her mother-in-law found her in front of the ironing board, a pile of perfect napkins, crisp and white.

'Where is my parcel?' she called, and the girl told her it was on the table.

Sammy followed her obediently.

'Clothes from Pakistan,' declared her mother-in-law, pleased. 'This is my new business.'

Sammy nodded and watched as the items were held in the air one by one. Silk and shimmering organza, the fabric waved and flapped like the wings of many butterflies. Carefully the embroidered scarves and tunics were neatly folded in the box.

'You like, Samina?'

'Yes.' Sammy smiled. Sometimes her mother-in-law was kind, her voice was soft as wool. 'Good girl,' she chuckled. She patted her head and then suddenly her voice was high again. 'I sell them in the community centre,' said the woman grinning. 'I make lots of money.' But Sammy was daydreaming and the woman saw her.

'Wake up, you lazy girl!' The woman slapped her arm hard. 'Listen, when Auntie is speaking to you.'

Sammy jolted. 'Sorry, sorry,' she said, 'very sorry.'

When her mother-in-law left the room, Ehsan came. He heard his mother complaining. She was always complaining about something. Ehsan clenched his teeth and shook his head. That night he told his wife they were moving house. His mother was driving him round the bend, all round every bend in Burnley and Manchester. The pair of them laughed and held their hands to their lips. 'She is always moaning,' said Ehsan in English. 'Bloody women!'

Sammy said nothing, afraid he might change his mind. In the morning she woke with new hope. 'Where will we live?' she asked her husband, but he shrugged his shoulders as if she was speaking a foreign language and then continued to pull the fluff from his socks. He went to work and Sammy realised nothing had changed.

CHAPTER NINETEEN

The Thai soup had been a success and when Su returned home the tub was light and empty. She wiped a line of sauce with her finger and placed it on her tongue. If she closed her eyes, just for a moment, she was back in the little kitchen with Mai, the sound of birds cheeping, children laughing. And waves. Now her eyes were open she stared into the bare tub and smiled. She smiled because she was thinking of the language class. For the first time she had eaten biryani, pakora and samosas. For the first time she had shared food, laughter, her poor English. Her belly was warm and full. In her bag was a plate of Sammy's samosas, wrapped in foil. She put the plate in the fridge and looked round. She thought of the woman, Lenka. And then she sat on the stool and began to write a letter to Mai.

Dear Mai,
Life in England good my sister. Bobby good man. I have 2 friend call Lenka an Sammy.

Today go party. Eat nice food. Learn much English. Indian food nice.

England always rain an sky black. Not like in Thailand. People is nice.

Misses you an kids. I likes my house. Sum bad things. Bad mango in England. No my England.

I wish me sunshine. Sister. Su. xxx

She put the letter in her bag. There were no envelopes and she had no idea where to buy these. The teacher would help. She pondered over the words 'Life in England good.' Was life good? Life wasn't bad. She wondered how this letter would sound. Life in England was OK, she thought to herself. Not good. Not bad. She prayed a little. She so wanted life to be good.

She was still praying when she heard a cracking sound outside. Through the window she saw a man's face, peering over the yard wall, a pair of metal shears in his hand. With one arm he held the tree branch up high. He began to cut, deep into the wood, so deep the shears jammed and the tree shook. Within seconds she was outside in her bare feet, screaming in Thai. What was he doing? Cutting down a tree. Cutting down her tree.

'Stop,' she shrieked. 'Stop!'

The man jolted. 'The branch is hanging over my washing line. Calm down, love. It's only a tree.' He shook his head, bemused, and began to cut a thinner branch. The man was about the same age as her, perhaps a little older, his face wrinkled and pink, and there were large tattoos on his arm. Big inky green tattoos of dragons and fire.

'No,' wailed Su. 'Bad luck. Bad luck!'

'Nothing you can do,' he shouted back, revealing a broken tooth. He began to laugh and snapped the branch off clean. It landed at Su's feet. She screamed and jumped back. Never would this happen in Thailand.

'It needed cutting down,' he shouted. 'Fucking crazy woman. I was thinking of getting meself a Thai bride, but if that's what you're all like, I won't bother.'

He disappeared, leaving the severed branch on the ground. 'No cut!' Su screamed, waving her arms. She stared helplessly, warm tears rolling down her nose. She stroked the tree trunk with the palm of her hand. In Thailand they say trees hold the spirits of the dead. This tree was old. Very old. Sometimes Su heard the ghosts in the tree, whispering through the leaves. She removed the amulet from round her neck and hung it on the lowest branch.

English people had no respect. No manners. She could hear the man swearing in the house next door. His mouth needed washing with soap, her mother would say. She left the broken branch where it had fallen and collapsed in a chair. Then she laid her head on the kitchen table and closed her eyes.

When Bobby came home Su was sitting under the ticking clock, her hair spread on the table like a fan. She lifted her head and spoke in Thai. Bobby saw her face wet and stained with tears. 'Bad man,' she told him, pulling him out into the yard. 'Bad man.'

'It's just one stick,' said Bobby. 'Just one.' He waved the branch in the air. Su stamped her foot but before she could speak Bobby had hurled the branch into the yard next door and she watched it spinning in the sky.

Bobby called to her from inside. 'What's for dinner, Su?' He had found the samosas in the fridge. From the yard she saw him bite the corner off one, crumbs stuck to his mouth, flakes falling to the floor. What was in them? Were they meat? Were they that halal food? The samosas were good. She heard her name three times. But she didn't answer.

CHAPTER TWENTY

Sammy arrived at the language centre early. Her mother-in-law did not stay today because she had clothes to sell. 'You stand on your own feet for once,' she said. 'Go in on your own. I am too busy to hold your hand. ' As the woman left, Sammy watched her disappear down the street, a shifting black shape amongst the shoppers and students. She halted at the door just for a second and leant against the wall. She removed her scarf and felt the wind in her hair. There was a poster on the building opposite showing a red shiny car and Sammy imagined what it must be like to drive. Everywhere there were Englishwomen driving cars. She would ask Ehsan for driving lessons.

There was a shop on the main street selling drinks and sweets and she crossed the road tentatively, worried her mother-in-law might return. In the shop she walked down the aisles aimlessly. She felt in her pocket for some change. She pulled out sixty pence in coins that rattled and jingled as she walked. She bought a can of Coke.

'Nice day,' said the man behind the counter and the coins were placed in lines in front of him. He suddenly spoke in Urdu. Sammy was disappointed. She wanted to speak in English. 'You live in Paradise Street,' he said. 'I know your husband Ehsan.'

Sammy stared. He would tell Ehsan. There would be trouble. Whenever freedom was in sight there was always trouble. Someone was always watching over her.

In the class the women were kind to Sammy. They spoke about events in Pakistan, about the village raids. One said children had been caught in the bombings. They had collapsed in the road and walked many miles. They clambered over dead bodies to escape. Those who fled had no water, no food. Only the burning sun to guide them. Sammy was crying again. She cried for her aunties, her sisters who were ten and six, her younger brothers and her grandmother. Her mother-in-law Suriya had phoned the family. They told her the news. They told her about her grandmother. The old woman was a hero. She had waited for the bombings to pass. She said she would not move, even if a bomb was planted under her skirt.

When the teacher arrived the women were silent. Sammy wiped her eyes with her sleeve. She looked at the teacher's clothes. She was wearing a skirt with embroidered flowers that wound round the hem and a long white shirt with a belt. The teacher saw her looking. 'I like clothes –es,' said the girl stammering. The teacher smiled.

'What did you do yesterday?' she asked.

'I stay home, parcel,' said Sammy, pausing to think of the words.

The teacher corrected her. She had to remember past tense. The teacher raised her hand in the air and gestured behind. 'Yes,' said Sammy, 'Today I went to the shop. I bought some coke.' She held up the can and the others smiled and cheered. Sammy was thinking about the past tense. She knew the present tense. Always people spoke about the past. She tried not to think about the past. Now the teacher was talking about the future. Sammy imagined the future. But the future was as blank as the paper in front of her and instead she twisted her hair and curled the paper with her pen. Past. Present. Future. And then she wrote her name at the top of the page. In capital letters she wrote SAMMY.

CHAPTER TWENTY-ONE

Lenka Kaminski was standing before the mirror, pulling her eyelid down, checking the shiny purple and black bruise that throbbed and stung. Gently she dabbed on the face powder with a sponge, but her eyelashes were coated pink and in desperation she wiped it off again. Anna was at school and today there was some good news. The people at the women's refuge had found them a house. A small house near the language centre. And hopefully Kamil would not find her this time. Too many times she had given in and called him. Forgiven him, even. Not this time. She was learning English and would get a good job. She would be like Englishwomen. Independent and free.

She lay on the bed and closed her eyes. But today, as always, she saw Kamil's fist coming towards her. Knuckles cracked and dry from working on a building site. Hands tinged grey from mixing cement. Solid as rock. A black boot. A steel toe-cap stamping on her head. A shadow looming over her when she slept. These were the thoughts that plagued her mind. Once she had smiled at a delivery man. Kamil had punched her as she poured water in Anna's paddling pool. Blood splattered in the clear water, swirling pink. A tooth flicked out. Luckily Anna had never witnessed this. She shuddered, felt the gap in her mouth where the tooth had sprung and forced herself awake. On the table were the keys to a new life and she dangled them in the air, scraped the razor edge of the biggest key on her hand. A paper label was threaded through the key with dirty string. She read the address. Number 28

Geoffrey Street. Two bedrooms and a small garden. Enough space for a new paddling pool.

As usual the taxi arrived to take her to the language centre. The keys were cold in her pocket and she gripped them hard. She would go to this Geoffrey Street and see this house after the class. Her stomach churned and she felt sick. It was a mix of excitement and fear.

Today she was late and the students stopped and stared when she arrived. Suddenly everyone was talking at once. What had happened to Lenka? Why was her face purple and black? Su held her hand to her mouth. 'It's OK,' said Lenka. 'It's OK.' That morning when the teacher tried to teach the class the future tense, no one was listening. 'What do you want to do in the future?' she asked the sea of blank faces. No one knew.

At breaktime most of the women lined the corridors, fought over the one flushing toilet. Su and Sammy stayed in the class, delved in their bags and brought out raisins and grapes. Lenka did her homework. 'Past tense,' she said. 'Very hard.' She pushed the paper across the table, defeated. Su told her to copy her work. But Lenka took out her keys and began to jangle them in the air.

'You OK?' said Su.

Lenka nodded and paused for a moment. 'I have new house.' She waved the keys in front of Su's nose.

Su read the label and smiled. 'Near mine house. Near mine.'

Lenka placed the keys in her pocket. 'I go today. After class. Number 28. You show me. Yes?'

'Mine 16,' said Su. Lenka turned to Sammy who was reading a battered dictionary. 'You come too? See house.' But Sammy shook her head and clasped her lips together tightly. 'Not allowed.'

'Ahh,' said Su. She remembered the woman who always stood at the top of the ramp waiting for Sammy. She was a large woman with loose black clothes that covered her whole body from head to toe. She had only ever seen her eyes, heard her voice. Sometimes she spoke English and snapped her fingers. Click, click, click. She was always in a hurry.

'I know,' said Su, her voice excited and high. 'We go house now?' Lenka and Sammy laughed. 'No,' they both said in chorus. 'English class.'

'Tell teacher appointment,' said Su. 'And come back.'

Lenka smacked her arm, playfully. They looked at the clock. One hour. When the teacher came in, Su stood up. 'Sorry. Have go now – appointment. And Sammy. And Lenka.'

The teacher laughed. 'Tests, everyone at doctors,' said Su, surprised by her own story. Before the teacher had time to think the three women were outside on the step, looking up the black ramp. The streets were empty and they rushed through the car park like small girls. Sammy hesitated. 'Mother-in-law see me.' She pretended to squeeze her throat. Lenka stopped and removed her coat. 'Get on. Quick.' Sammy dragged on the English coat and Su buttoned the hood tight and pulled the frayed cord. 'Disguise,' she said giving her sunglasses from her pocket. Su laughed at her friends. 'Funny,' she roared, her body folding over. 'This way.'

Past Su's house the three women skipped arm in arm. Lenka mouthed the number twenty-eight, twenty-eight. As she walked Su told herself that she would not step on the cracks in the pavement. She pointed at number 16 and the others called 'nice house'. Su was proud of the little house. She had cleared the beer cans from the garden, cleaned the windows until they gleamed. And there was a doormat made from straw with the word WELCOME.

Outside number 28 was a ripped velvet armchair, offcuts of carpet, a burst rubbish bag with potato peelings strewn across the path. The women stopped at the gate. 'Lenka house,' said Su. Lenka opened the gate and turned the key in the door. There was the strong smell of paint and plastic. Fresh white walls and a new green cord carpet in the living room. 'Nice,' said Su. Together they wandered around the empty rooms. Lenka felt happy. 'Anna's room,' she called to the others. The smallest bedroom had a fitted wardrobe, a view of the yard and Lenka pictured her daughter playing here, a pink bed and a crate of toys. They arrived back in the living room and Su sat on the floor. She still had some grapes left, a bottle of water. She picked the grapes off the stem and handed them to Lenka and Sammy. In the cloth bag was a pack of playing cards. Su took out the pack. 'Play game.' The others shook their heads. 'I know. Tell you fortune.'

'No!' said Sammy. 'Not in my culture. No magic telling.'

'Tell mine,' said Lenka, bending forwards. 'I like fortunes.' Sammy's face darkened. She folded her arms and checked her watch. 'Quickly.'

Su's grandmother had taught her to read cards, not because she thought she had a gift, but because the English tourists would pay for such things. But soon she discovered that Su had a knowing eye, could see things that other people could not. The cards were shuffled first by Su and then by Lenka and spread on the carpet like a rainbow. Sammy thought about a song she had heard on television. Somewhere over the rainbow and she wondered what lay at the end of the rainbow for her.

CHAPTER TWENTY-TWO

In Patong district people kicked road dust with their toes in the long queues to see Chuenchai, the local Maw Du. Sumalee's grandmother could read a palm, a face, a picture on a card. She was a 'seeing doctor' and could cure troubles of the mind, stop a question before it curled and clawed its way through the brain. The old woman knew that Sumalee had the same gift. Magic blood had passed down through generations. Strangely she had been unable to read Sumalee's future. Always when she stared into her eyes there was black, as if Sumalee had stopped her somehow, refused to let her in.

Kneeling on the carpet at 28 Geoffrey Street Su began to whisper in Thai. Lenka and Sammy stared at one another and giggled. Su scowled. 'Ready!' she announced. 'Pick card.' Lenka tugged the corner of a card with her finger and thumb, but the card escaped her grasp and floated to the ground face down. She was about to retrieve the card when Su gasped.

In Lenka's face Su saw something. It was a fleeting image, so swift, that she found herself speaking quickly. 'Man. Fire,' she blurted. Lenka pulled her hand away. Suddenly she felt cold. She heard the word 'man'. Sammy looked afraid. The card had not been turned. 'Want to go,' she said. 'Now, please.'

'What?' said Lenka. 'Tell me.'

'Dark man,' said Su, her fingers gripping the card. 'See dark man.'

'My husband,' said Lenka, frowning.

'Very bad man,' said Su, but she did not repeat the other things she had seen.

'Yes,' said Lenka. 'Always hit, kick.'

Sammy held her arm. 'Time.' Sammy was pointing repeatedly at her watch.

'Party,' said Su.

Lenka searched her face carefully.

'Party?'

'Yes. Me think big, very big party.'

Lenka smiled. But Su stood up and dropped the cards back in the velvet pouch. This was the first time she had seen something not written in the cards. Seeing was not a gift. It was her curse.

* * *

They walked back to the language centre in silence. 'When you moving house?' said Su, eventually. Lenka shrugged her shoulders. At the bottom of the ramp Sammy tore off the coat and waited. Her mother-in-law came down the ramp, her fat body rippling and wobbling as she moved. 'Hurry up, girl!' she shouted, all the time looking at the Polish woman with scarlet red lips. Lenka glared back.

'I no like that woman,' Lenka said to Su in a loud voice.

'Me no like,' agreed Su, watching the woman push Sammy up the ramp.

They saw Suriya, snapping her fingers, her eyes blinking as fast as she talked. 'I don't like those women,' said Suriya. 'Make friends with your own kind.' Sammy nodded, felt her face drain pale. When Lenka got in the taxi, Su stepped back and waved at the shiny silver car. But then she saw an orange and red flame and it licked the corner of her eye, made her eyes sting hot. She jerked her head as she walked and tried to shake the thought away.

There was something about this woman Lenka. She felt it. Danger. And it was so close it followed her all the way home. At one point she looked back, but there was only her own shadow faltering and waving on the concrete path. But even this was enough to make her run. There was nothing worse in life than being afraid. But her grandmother always said there was nothing worse in life than being unafraid.

CHAPTER TWENTY-THREE

The blonde man David was sitting on the wall of 16 Geoffrey Street, a book in his hand. Su saw him from the bottom of the road and wondered why he had come. As she approached he stood up, ran his hands through his hair and thought for a moment. Su waited for him to speak.

'Come in,' she said, automatically. 'Tea?'

He followed her through the door. 'Bobby, chocolate factory,' she said, looking at the book cover.

'You were in the bookshop,' he said quietly. 'I thought it was you, but I wasn't sure. There aren't many Thai people in Burnley.'

He sat on the sofa and gripped his knees. His shirt was covered in a grid of squares in blue and black and Su found herself tracing the lines with her eye.

'So ... Do you like Burnley?'

'Me like,' said Su, smiling.

'Do you like books?'

'Yes. Tea?'

'No ... Thank you,' he stammered. He looked around the room, focused on a picture of a crying boy, a picture he had always hated. It occupied an alcove with a cabinet full of decanters and glasses.

Su reached for a book that lay open on the leather armchair. There was a picture of a country cottage, sweeping hills and a view of the sea. 'This my book,' she announced proudly. David took the book in his hands and observed the cover. *My Beautiful England.*

'Sister, Thailand,' said Su, nodding. 'Show me England. Buck-in-ham Pal-is.' David bit his bottom lip and looked serious. He placed the book on the table.

'Has my father talked to you about my mother?'

Su tilted her head, unable to understand everything he said. She heard the word 'mother' and repeated it.

'My mother and father are divorced.'

Su nodded. 'Divorce. Yes. Me understand. Everyone divorce in England.'

The man didn't look at her. He didn't see her smile because his eyes were fixed on the carved cuckoo clock. 'My mother lives in Burnley. Not far from here.'

Su started. 'OK.' The woman who liked brown and pink lived in Burnley! She tried to remain expressionless, but it was difficult to stay calm. She didn't want to see this woman. What if she had already seen her, passed her in the street, sat next to her on a bus? She was Mrs Haywood. There was no room for two Mrs Haywoods. David saw her body slump with the weight of his words. Her lips were pursed tight and she stared ahead.

'And there is a baby,' he said, quickly. 'You do know my father has a baby?'

Su stood up. She covered her face with her hands, folded her arms. How could Mrs Haywood have a baby? Bobby was sixty. This was not possible. David stood up, walked towards the door. 'I thought you should know.' His voice had dropped to almost a murmur, as if he had sensed what was about to happen. 'A baby girl. Sorry … I just thought you would want to know …'

Her mind was raging like an angry sea. Thoughts tossed like driftwood crashing on rocks. Driftwood splitting apart into thousands of splinters. Black water carried her further and further away from Bobby, from everything she knew. Dirty water raced through the tunnels of her brain, sweeping any thoughts of a nice life away. All this talk of a baby. She took a deep breath. 'Get out!' shouted Su. 'Mine house. Telling me bad story and you get out.' Her head was about to explode. She didn't understand. If Bobby had a baby and a wife in Burnley, why was she here? She pounded her head on the wall and pulled her hair from her eyes. Why did Bobby want a Thai bride? Maybe there were more wives. With every thought the waves grew higher and filled her up with grief. Her body was full and heavy. She collapsed on the sofa and imagined sinking in black water. She heard the door click closed. Then she saw herself like the children on Patong Beach, wrapped in seaweed, unable to break free, hair tangled, body smeared in thick oil. She tried to wash and rub the blackness away, but it gripped her and she stayed dirty and unclean.

CHAPTER TWENTY-FOUR

At the language centre the teacher told them there would be an exam. Sammy now understood. It was a big test. She worried that she would not pass. Her mother-in-law complained. She asked many questions. When would the certificate come? She shouted at the teacher because the exam certificate would not arrive for many months. The teacher could not give her a date. The old woman became angry. 'Ridiculous,' she protested. Sammy blushed, embarrassed by the tantrum. The teacher smiled at her. 'I am sorry,' said Sammy later. 'My family is worried.' But during the lesson that day Sammy dreamt about her certificate. The certificate meant freedom to stay.

There was much gossip in the class about the Polish woman Lenka. Everyone knew that she had left her husband. At night Sammy lay in bed wondering what it would be like to live alone, to watch television, without a husband and a mother-in-law watching over you. I want to be alone, she thought. I want to make my own decisions. And she took out her English books and began to read, glad that Ehsan was working tonight.

* * *

In the morning Suriya had gone to the community centre to a sewing class. 'You must wait in,' she told Sammy. 'Another parcel … I have my class.' Sammy nodded and waited for her to leave.

The house was empty and she looked out of the window at a woman walking a dog. A group of English boys kicked a can down the street and it rattled on the kerb. They were swearing at each other and one saw her peeking behind the curtains. He stopped and waved across the street and she hid, slightly afraid, listening to the can bouncing down the road. She watched daytime television as she vacuumed, but turned it off worried she might miss the parcel.

The doorbell sounded a loud ding dong which echoed in the narrow hall. She opened the door, bored and tired. And then she saw Rob.

'Ah ... Sammy, it is you again.' He smiled broadly and winked.

She giggled slightly. The parcel was on the floor.

'I have a big parcel today and another in the car.'

'How are you?' she asked.

'I am very well,' he smiled, 'very well, now I have seen you.'

She lowered her head and the courier saw she was embarrassed.

'I am sorry, sorry if I've upset you.' He touched her arm briefly.

Sammy did not speak and looked at him now carefully. 'I no upset.'

'Good, because I don't want to upset you,' he said slowly. 'I will get the sack.'

'The sack?' The girl was confused.

'I will lose my job.' The girl continued to stare. 'NO JOB!' he repeated.

'Yes,' said Sammy. 'I understand. I not an idiot.' She used this phrase because she had heard it many times. When she was shopping with Suriya, her mother-in-law always said, 'I understand English perfect. I am not idiot.'

Rob laughed. 'You need to sign here.' As she signed the screen he returned to the car and brought a second parcel and placed it on the hall floor at her feet.

'Where do you live?' said Sammy blankly.

The courier stopped, surprised at the directness of her question. 'Two miles away,' he said. 'Not far.'

'Can you teach me English? I need certificate.'

'I don't know,' he replied. 'No one's ever asked me before.'

'Me come your house?'

The courier hesitated for a moment. Could he help someone learn English? Once he thought of being a teacher, but he had no qualifications. Flattered, he wrote his address and phone number. 'I don't work on Wednesdays,' he told her 'but I don't want you getting into trouble.' He began to wonder if he had done the wrong thing. But surely there was nothing wrong with helping someone. That's what his mother would say.

'No trouble, thank you,' smiled Sammy. 'I will come Wednesday.'

As he left, Sammy thought about her English class on Wednesday. English classes were three times a week. Monday. Tuesday. Wednesday. She could walk to Rob's house instead. She would ask the teacher for directions to this Beaumont Road in the lesson on Monday. She was learning directions. Turn right. Turn left. Go up. Go down.

CHAPTER TWENTY-FIVE

Bobby arrived home with five boxes of chocolates for his wife. Free because he had been the worker of the week. The other men in the factory enjoyed this Friday ritual of praising the best worker. They joked that he was an Oompa Loompa with his orange tan, that he was the Wonka of the week. Some said 'wanker of the week', because they were sick of hearing about Bobby's adventures and his Thai bride. 'How many Thai women have you had this week, Bob? Did you smuggle a couple in your suitcase?' Bobby turned away and blushed a little. 'Those days are over,' he replied. 'I'll be getting my pension soon, if all this chocolate doesn't bloody kill me first.'

Someone sniggered and shouted, 'She'll be up for it tonight, then. A few choccies and you'll get some.'

'Fuck off, children,' Bobby retorted.

'Yeah, Bobby. It won't be the chocolate that kills you. It'll be all that Thai sex.'

Bobby shook his head. 'I'm off boys. Going home to me nice Thai wife – Jealous are we?'

The others started hollering a rhythmic Ooooooooooooooooo that echoed in the factory hall and raised the attention of a foreman, who promptly told Bobby to piss off home.

When Bobby arrived home, the house was quiet and there was no smell of cooking. Down into the small kitchen he dragged his bulging bags. He dropped the chocolates on the counter. Black Magic and White Magic chocolates were piled high in boxes tied with ribbons. Boxes with silhouettes of a cloaked magician waving a wand. And another box of Turkish Delight he had chosen because it was Su's favourite. Each box was worth at least a tenner. 'Su,' he called. 'I've got something for you. I've got you a present, love.' But before he could speak, Su appeared in the doorway, a broom in her hand, her hair wide and wild.

'Where have you been, love?'

Crack. The broom landed on his bare head and he staggered back and clutched his ear. 'What the fuck—'

Before he could continue the broom swayed in the air, but he grabbed it this time. Su was shouting words in Thai. He heard the word 'baby'. She pulled the broom away. 'Baby. Baby. Baby!'

Bobby's face turned white.

'You no tell me baby!'

'Oh shit,' he blurted. 'David the bastard's been here.'

'Bastard, bastard, bastard!' screeched Su, realising that she had learnt a new swear word. 'Bastard, bastard, bastard!' She threw herself at him and began to punch his face and chest. Repeatedly she hit him until Bobby gripped her wrists and pulled her down onto the kitchen chair. 'OK,OK. Calm down. Let me explain.'

He released his grip. Su was crying now, unable to hear what he was saying. 'I go back Thailand,' she wailed. 'I no stay. I no stay …'

'Yes. I have a baby, but it's a mistake.'

'No baby?' muttered Su.

'There is a baby, Su. Yes. Yes. Yes. But I don't want the baby.'

Su stood up and grabbed the chocolate boxes. She ripped the lids open and began to throw the chocolates one by one across the room.

'Oh God!' said Bobby. 'Don't you understand, woman. I don't want the baby!'

A chocolate nugget pelted him on the nose and he ducked down low. 'I don't want the fucking baby!'

'Yes!' screamed Su. 'And me no want your fucking chocolate.'

CHAPTER TWENTY-SIX

Rain spat on her face as she weaved through the streets towards Beaumont Road. It was Wednesday. Sammy knew the teacher would be waiting and retrieved the mobile phone from amongst scrunched up tissues and receipts. Ehsan had given her the phone, but had warned her that Suriya must not know. Found in his car, down the back of a seat, he had wiped the numbers. It was surprising what you could find in a taxi. Umbrellas, coats, hats and even a walking stick, but the worst thing he had found was a dirty baby nappy. One day Ehsan swore someone would leave a kid in his car. Some screaming English kid. And sometimes he dreamt his car was full of fat babies, dressed only in nappies. That would be a funny story to tell. The phone was pink and he had bought a new sim card from the market. Sammy stopped on the street corner and dialled the language centre. She took a deep breath. 'Please tell the teacher me no coming today ... for I am ill ... very ill.' The receptionist agreed to pass the message on. Sammy was relieved and tugged her scarf high over her head.

Ehsan's leather jacket was in a carrier bag and she pulled it on quickly. No one would recognise her now. Soon she heard the laughter of school children. It was 8.45 and mothers were standing in front of the school gates gossiping and they stared at her as she walked past. She continued up the street stopping every now and then to check the little map printed in class. Then she saw it. Beaumont Road was across the street, a row of semi-detached houses with drives and long gardens.

She found number 33. Like the prime minister's house it had a black glossy door. There were brown plastic framed windows that looked like wood. She worried for a moment. Rob lived in a wealthy street and there were pretty trees on the pavement. There was a smart bicycle on the drive and a garage painted white. She stopped at the garden gate, debating whether to knock. A neighbour saw her, an old man with glasses. 'Are you looking for someone?'

'Yes,' she replied. 'Rob expect me.'

The man raised his eyebrows as the girl mounted the drive and he noticed her sandals, the red painted toes. So, he thought to himself, Rob has got himself a girlfriend. Sammy knocked on the door but she saw the curtains were drawn.

It was 9am. Disappointed she turned, but suddenly Rob was at the door, wrapped only in a towel and his hair dripping wet.

Sammy stepped back and covered her eyes. 'Very sorry, so sorry,' she muttered.

'Don't be daft,' said Rob. 'Come in.'

'No, no better not.' Sammy looked at a garden pot. He took her arm.

'Don't be shy, Sammy. Come in.' Slowly, she followed him through the narrow hall and he led her to a large sitting room with a black sofa and huge television.

'I wasn't expecting you so early.'

She sat on the sofa in silence, with her feet close together. Then she wondered what to say and was surprised when the words flowed naturally. 'Nice house. You have a nice house.'

Rob was twenty-four and had inherited the house when his mother died. The house was scattered with old lady's ornaments, a ceramic dog with bright glass eyes, a porcelain jug, things he could not bear to throw away. He made some tea and appeared dressed in jeans and a tee shirt with a colourful guitar splashed across the front.

'Take off your coat.' She did as he asked and they both sat looking at the television.

'Do you have a garden?'

'Yes,' he said, pulling back the curtains and sliding the doors open. 'Take a look.'

'Like my garden in Pakistan,' she told him in a voice that was now excited and high. 'I like grow vegetables and trees.'

'So what do you want to do?' he asked her. 'Do your family know you are here?'

'No,' she said. 'Kill me.'

Rob sat beside her and listened. This was the first time a woman had ever talked to him so openly. She hated her marriage. Her mother-in-law would not help her. 'What can I do? I need speak English. That is the only way I can be free.'

'Why don't you speak to your teacher?' he suddenly said.

'Do you want me to go?' she said, tears in her eyes. 'I understand now.'

He grabbed her hand. 'I do not want you to go. I like you. You know I like you.'

Sammy looked at the speckled carpet, grey and black. 'Look at me Sammy.'

She turned and hesitated. 'I am afraid.'

He held her hand. 'I will help you.'

* * *

At the language centre Su noticed the clock had stopped. Across the table Lenka saw her concerned expression. 'Where Sammy?' mouthed Su. Lenka checked her watch. 'Me don't know,' she said, shrugging her shoulders and pulling a worried face.

Bright worksheets with pictures of famous buildings were scattered on the table. Su recognised Big Ben, the large clock that loomed over London, and there was a red bus. There were no red buses in the north. She thought about the buses in Burnley. A large black bus travelled near her house, as black as the northern sky. A picture of a witch was on the side of another bus she had seen. And the only clock in Burnley that she could think of was above the town hall. She guessed that the town hall was a grand place with important men, because the building had a dome like a palace.

Citizenship was about understanding life in the UK, the teacher said. Everyone needed to know about life in England.

'English is important for my future,' said one student aloud. 'Need English at doctor.' The woman pointed to her bulging stomach. 'Midwife. Me no understand. Chatter, chatter, chatter, so quick.'

'Yes,' agreed Lenka. 'People in Burnley is always talking so fast. Too fast. On phone, me no understand anything, but life here is easier. Jobs and education is good.'

Su listened to the babble of sounds. She hardly spoke today. She hadn't spoken to Bobby. First there was a baby and then Bobby had gone to the pub. Always he was in the pub. Always he returned smelling of drink and sweat. So much sweat that the bed sheets were damp and cold. And the pillows were stained yellow where he had dribbled in his sleep. Every morning she changed the white covers and boiled them with bleach. One night he was so drunk he sat eating the chocolates under the kitchen table. Deliberately, she had left them there, covered in hair and dust. 'I am not a maid,' she told herself, but really her hands were itching to remove the chipped Turkish Delight that stuck to the floor like pink glue.

'I want learn English, stay in England,' said another woman. 'Help daughter, homework.'

'Yes,' said a woman with thick rimmed glasses and heavy earrings that pulled and stretched her lobes. 'Kids, these days. Always speaking English, not Urdu.' She shook her head and tapped a pencil on the table. 'Forgetting own language, whispering together secrets, thinking we no understand. I know my boy talking about these Burnley girls. English girls with their tight skirts and shorts. Very bad. See everything. And heels. Big heels!'

Lenka began to laugh. 'Oh my God. You cannot say this. Just when girl wear short skirt this does not make her bad person.'

The Pakistani woman frowned. 'No. In our religion. Cover up.'

'But in England, womans has choices,' said Lenka.

'Not in Pakistan,' the woman replied.

'Better to be free,' said Lenka. 'Englishwomans is independent.'

'No one who is married is free,' said another woman and the group laughed.

'I want be free,' said a Bangladeshi girl, dressed in black. 'No mobile phone. Not allowed. Not allowed go out. Husband so, so strict. Husband no let me wear English clotheses.'

'But you should choose,' said Lenka. 'You are in England now.'

'No, no. My husband hit,' said the girl, her voice ringing round the room. She looked at Lenka's face, the lips outlined inky red.

'Men is cruel,' said Lenka. 'Many bad men hit women.'

'Some nice,' said the oldest woman in the group. 'In Pakistan we believe marriage is made in heaven and celebrated on earth. My husband nice. Su, your husband nice, eh?'

But Su wasn't listening. She looked down at her worksheet and thought about the man called David. Perhaps he was trying to help her. If only he had stopped the wedding that day on the beach.

'You are free, Su?' said Lenka in a quiet voice, disturbing her thoughts.

Still, Su didn't answer. She thought about freedom. What did it mean? She had a mobile phone. There was no mother-in-law to watch over her. She could go shopping for mango. Who was really free, anyway?

CHAPTER TWENTY-SEVEN

Saturday was a bad day to move house. Su flapped her arms when Lenka told her the news. 'Other day. Not Saturday,' whispered Su, her eyes gaping wide. 'You so, what the word, super-stit-ious,' said Lenka, in a serious voice. Su was thinking there had already been too much bad luck. Also she had sent a text to Sammy, but she had not replied. She suspected the big fat woman Suriya had taken the mobile phone away and that Sammy was in trouble.

Marriage was not easy, she decided. When she had married Tai, the Maw Du had assured them theirs was a blessed union, one that was heavenly and pure. But the Maw Du had not foreseen what would happen. At first the marriage was good and she and Tai made plans. Plans that included beautiful children with sparkling eyes and soft cheeks to kiss. Plans and dreams for a house near the beach, with a view of the orange sun, banana trees and boats. After three years there was no child. People talked and asked when. It was like pouring oil in clear water. Most days the oil dispersed and there were happy times. Beneath their watery smiles was the grim reality that she would never be a mother, that Tai would never be a father. Sometimes Tai played with her nieces and nephews and she saw the disappointment stamped on his face. The same disappointment when they were in bed together, knowing that physically their marriage was imperfect, lacking in some way. Each of them blamed the other, but this was unspoken and instead life went on, without children, without hope, eventually without sex.

In England Su learnt that marriage meant cooking and cleaning, shining shoes, collecting the empty beer cans that were strewn around the house. Her life was spent always trying to please Bobby. This was not difficult because she realised that he was a simple man. Every week the routine was the same. Chippy on Friday. Watching football at Turf Moor on Saturday. After football there was curry for tea followed by much beer and chocolate. And Su worked out that the more beer he drank the easier life became. When he was sober he pulled her upstairs, called her 'my sexy Su'. On Saturdays she ensured the crate of beer was full and then Bobby slept and snored on the sofa downstairs and she could study her English books in peace. But in the morning she suffered. Bobby's head was heavy and sore from drinking too much and often he swore and shouted, broke things. She counted the glasses. Ten, nine, eight, seven, six, five and now four remained on a glass shelf. She would have to buy some more.

As she got ready for the language centre she thought about these things. She wondered whether England had changed her. Could a country change someone? Was she Sumalee from Phuket, or was she Su from Burnley? Walking down the ramp, she heard someone call her name. Sammy ran behind her. 'Su! Wait for me.' Su stopped and turned. 'Sammy. Sammy. Where you go, Wednesday?'

Sammy hesitated. Her voice was quiet today. 'Me no come every Wednesday.'

'Ah,' said Su. 'Your mother-in-law.'

Lifting the scarf from her head, Sammy nodded, but she felt guilty. She wanted to tell Su about the Englishman. But not yet.

Su said nothing more about the subject. 'Lenka move house at weekend. You come and help.'

'Not sure,' said Sammy. 'I want to help.'

'I know,' said Su, smiling. 'You a good girl.'

'No,' said Sammy, suddenly tearful.

But Su did not see. Lenka was calling the two women from the doorway. 'I wait for you. Stop gossiping.' She chuckled and threw her head back. 'Us three like Charlie's Angels.'

Sammy looked confused. 'Eh?'

'Oh, Sammy ... Film with three beautiful ladies with guns ... American film ... You not seen?' Lenka pressed her hands together and pointed her finger like a gun. 'Us against the world.'

'Crazy woman,' said Su, as Lenka jumped through the air.

'Have to be crazy to live in bloody Burnley,' said Lenka, bright and cheerful. She pointed her finger at Sammy's head. 'And you must come on Saturday to my house. Little party with my daughter. Or I shoot you.' She laughed and Sammy pushed her away.

'I will try,' she said. 'But what do I tell Suriya.'

'She look like a bat in black dress,' said Lenka.

'Bat?'

'Night creature with wings,' said Lenka, flapping her arms. 'In trees.' She giggled loudly.

'Stop,' said Sammy, a smile halfway across her face. 'You very bad.'

'Yes,' said Su. 'Tell the bat you must go language centre.'

'But closed.' As usual Sammy was frowning.

'Always look so sad,' said Lenka, touching Sammy's cheek. 'Be happy. Bat sucking your blood.' Lenka began to dance around and dive like a bat. 'I will get you my Sammy.'

Su had a plan and she scratched her head. 'We meet you on ramp and then she believe you. Say open.'

Sammy thought for a second. 'And where you go on Wednesday?' cried Lenka, suddenly remembering. 'Naughty girl missing class.'

Before Sammy could speak the manager was in the corridor. 'You are all VERY late.' The three women ran and burst through the class door to find the room full of maps. Some were pinned on the crumbling cork board, with bright pinheads in yellow, red and green. Others were spread on the large table, thick creases like white veins cutting through America and Russia.

There were maps of the world, maps of the UK. Together they found cities, places they could not pronounce. Su found Thailand and prodded the green land with her finger. 'Tsunami,' she announced to everyone, thinking how small Thailand seemed next to the vast sea. 'So much water,' she cried. The others looked up from their maps and gave her sympathetic looks and sounds. 'Where Pakistan?' said Su, quickly. 'Show me.'

Sammy scanned the huge sheet. She found India, Pakistan and Bangladesh. 'Ah but where UK and England?' said Su aloud, so that everyone heard. Lenka pointed at the map. 'Here. And here Poland. My beautiful Poland.' She seemed tearful for a moment. 'Poland such a beautiful place. But no jobs. No money. Life better for me in England. Life better for everyone.'

'But England look so small,' said Sammy. She gasped and raised her eyebrows. 'In this world England is tiny.'

CHAPTER TWENTY-EIGHT

Nobody cared about Burnley. Every week someone left Geoffrey Street and another house was empty. From the bus stop Bobby observed the abandoned houses covered in stiff metal sheets that clanged and rattled in the wind. Sometimes Bobby wished he could move away from this area. There had been too many changes. Burnley was not the same place. There were few English people now. It was divided up. Divided into many different worlds, inhabited by many different people. As the Asians moved in, more and more English people moved away. And now the BNP was in Burnley too. Everyone talked about it at the Queen's, about Pakis and immigration. Someone was spouting about Enoch Powell, like they were a historian, or something. But there was no mortgage and the factory was close by. And anyway he never had any problems with the Asians. 'I like most Pakis,' he told Su. 'Your friend is a Paki?' Su did not respond and he narrowed his eyes.

There was rubbish in the street, cans clattering, broken glass bottles. An empty carrier bag fluttered over a grid blocked with sweet wrappers. This bothered him more than the smell of curry or the Asian music blaring from car radios. People dumped furniture outside and never bothered ringing the council. Burnley was sofa city. People were poor. Urban regeneration, he had heard about. But there wasn't much regeneration happening in this area. People had not only abandoned the skinny stone houses. They had abandoned a way of life. People abandoned people.

Even the rats were thin.

On the bus Bobby was complaining. Fares had gone up by ten per cent. This news he had learnt while reading the *Burnley Express*. On Tuesdays he bought the newspaper, from Azrul's newsagent's, but this week was special because his wedding picture was printed on page ten, next to a story about the local hospital. They sat at the front, in silence, Bobby staring straight ahead. A red-haired boy got on the bus and spat on the floor, leaving a frothy ball of white in the walkway. 'Oi, you little shit!' shouted Bobby, but the boy bolted up the stairs. Bobby cursed and muttered. Then he counted the people on the bus, tried to work out how much fare the bus company would collect that day. The bus was packed because it was Saturday. Women, mainly. Few men. But he had promised Su he would take her to the library. She had a list of books. Bobby hadn't been to the library for many years. 'I'm not a reader,' he told Su. 'Books aren't my cup of tea.'

This phrase was confusing but Su grasped that her husband did not like books. Unlike his wife. 'I'll get them on the internet,' he told her. 'It's easier.' But the teacher at the language centre had suggested everyone join the library. They could even borrow music, not just books. 'I need library card,' said Su. Bobby glared impatiently. 'But Su you can't read yet.'

'I read little bit,' she told him, her voice shaking.

'I am buying a new TV today,' Bobby announced on the bus. 'With a huge screen.'

Su rolled her eyes. 'We have nice TV in house.'

Bobby laughed. 'You can join the library and I get a new TV, so me and me mates can watch football.'

Football, football, football. That was all Bobby thought about. The Clarets. He had even bought a bed cover in the same colour. Su wanted a white cover, like the beds in hotels. There were mugs, key rings, wool scarves printed with Burnley Football Club. The man was obsessed.

As the bus weaved through town, Bobby looked at the rows of terraced houses, their stone faces covered in graffiti. These were the houses that would be bulldozed, replaced by squares of green, spindly trees. Maybe they'd build a posh housing estate with red brick houses, integral garages and an ensuite. That's what everyone wants, he thought to himself. Houses thin as paper. Not solid. People these days had three toilets and two bedrooms. Who shitted so much they needed three toilets? Everyone talked about it at the chocolate factory. No one there had an ensuite, or a garage. These terraces had been through wars. They'd still be standing in another hundred years, given the chance. But Burnley wasn't his beloved Burnley any more. Still he clung to it, as though life depended on it, never really having the courage to leave.

Together they walked through the crowded streets, Bobby in his football scarf, his face dimpled and burnt red from his stay in Thailand. Su's step was light and her skirt lifted when she moved, gentle as a floating leaf.

Bobby stopped for a second on a bench outside the baker's. 'Wait here,' he said. 'I'll get some potato pies.'

'Me no like,' said Su, although her stomach was growling with hunger.

Bobby ignored her response and disappeared into the baker's. Sitting on the metal bench, Su stared at the pigeons that scavenged pastry crumbs from the cracks in the paving stones. One bird waited at her feet. She chuckled. 'No food little bird. Away!' As she raised her arm the bird leapt back, watched her with a startled eye. She saw the Burnley people with their heads bowed low, their backs bent and heavy. Times were hard in Burnley. She sat observing life, like a tourist. There was so much to see. A boy was chasing the pigeons, jumping up and down. Stubborn like most children, but so were the birds. Neither was afraid of the other. Neither moved and neither won the game.

There was a miniature fairground ride, a little carousel of cars, and a girl was screaming for a ride. But her mother had no cash and the man with a large pocket in his apron looked guilty as the child was pulled away. She had fifty pence. Not a pound.

The shops were empty. All except Poundland. Everything for a pound. Su imagined the till rattling with golden pound coins, big sacks of money at the end of the day. And the pie shop was busy. Strange that you could buy a book for a pound, but a pie cost more. Sometimes she thought the world was mad. This was one view she and Bobby shared – a sense of things in the world not being right. In this world there were little people and big people. They were the little people, her and Bobby. Like animals. People in Burnley milled around like ants under the shadow of a shoe. Su thought about people living in London, Manchester. She imagined them with their heads held high, men in hats with umbrellas. Tall people. Tall as giraffes. Women in beautiful clothes, with swaying hips, swinging bags and tapping heels. She looked at the shoes of the Burnley shoppers. No heels. For many, their shoes, like their lives, were flat.

Su was lost in thought when Bobby dropped the warm paper bag on her lap. He nudged her gently and told her to eat. Inside the wrapper the pie was pale and flaky. Su picked at the food like a bird. She watched couples walking together. Nobody spoke. The pastry tasted of nothing. Like eating paper.

'This is nice,' said Bobby. 'Coming out together.'

Su nodded and flicked some pastry towards a skinny pigeon. The bird hopped forwards.

'Don't encourage them, Su.' Bobby frowned. He dabbed his mouth with a tissue. 'Burnley is quiet today.' He kicked out towards the pigeon and it flapped its wings in panic.

Su's voice dropped. 'Always quiet. Not like Thailand.' She looked over towards a shop with cloth bags. 'Me like bag,' she said aloud.

'Come on, I'll buy you a bag, love.' Bobby stamped his foot to deter another pigeon. In the shop window there was a large turquoise bag with birds of paradise and pink flowers. The bag was threaded with yellow and pink silk, decorated with sequins and blue buttons. Su looked at the bag carefully. In the shop she swung the bag on the rail. 'This one is beautiful.'

'Mmm. But not good in the rain.' Bobby bought the bag anyway and Su felt the sequins with her fingers. The bag had cost fifty pounds. 'Too much,' said Su. But Bobby shook his head and planted a kiss on her forehead. 'Not too much for you, my love. Now you can carry your library books.'

Su looked closely at the bag and saw the sequins sparkle in the light. In every flower there were two sequins leaning in on each other, linked by a loop of thread, knotted in a lover's kiss.

'My favourite bag!' cried Su, squeezing Bobby's arm. 'Thank you. Thank you. Thank you.' She put her carrier bag inside and placed the new bag over her shoulder. In this country there were so many beautiful things.

Soon they reached the library, a large imposing building on the edge of the shopping centre. It overlooked a square and Su imagined that university would look like this.

'Very old,' she said to Bobby and they both stood in the square and looked up the library steps towards the arched door.

'You want me to wait outside?' Bobby asked. Su held his arm and guided him through the door. 'You help me.' Bobby sighed and checked his watch. 'You know I don't like books.'

'Sit and wait,' said Su, raising her eyebrows. Bobby sat on a seat near the crime books.

'OK. OK. I'll just wait. You just do what you've got to do. Don't mind me.'

Su marched off, wondering why husbands were always so impossible to please. Soon she was at the desk and an old woman with big hair and a pointed nose came to the counter.

'Me join please.'

The woman tilted her head. 'Pardon?'

'Me join i-bry.' Su had forgotten the word, but the woman saw the panic in her face and smiled.

'Do you have some id?'

Su stared blankly.

'I need a letter with your address …'

'Ah,' said Su. 'Me no letter.'

'You need a letter.' The woman waved a letter on the desk. 'Like this with your name and address.'

Su called to Bobby. 'Need letter. Need letter,' she said, her eyes filling with tears.

Bobby reached into his wallet. 'Can she use my card? It's not been used for years, but can she use it.' There was some commotion amongst the staff, who eventually said that Bobby would need to apply again. Bobby shrugged his shoulders and rolled his eyes.

'No books today, Su,' he said. 'Sorry. We can come back next week.'

They were just about to leave but then there was a voice from behind and someone placed a white plastic card on the counter. A white card with a yellow strip. David was standing with a pile of books in his hand. 'Get three books, Su. I'll use my card.'

Bobby thrust the card before him. 'No thanks. We don't want no favours from you.'

'I wasn't asking you,' said David, his voice raised, his eyes hardened. 'Su, do you want to borrow some books, or not?' Su stared. 'I'm getting some books for a friend,' he said.

The woman behind the counter breathed a heavy shush. 'Thank you,' whispered Su, fixing her eyes on David's face and she left the two men at the library counter. The mood was gloomy and dark. No one spoke. Bobby made no effort and David remained rigid and awkward.

Su was beginning to regret the trip to the library. No library card but she went home with two books. One was a history book of Burnley and another book was filled with pictures of gardens and plants in England. At the library she had learnt something. Chuenchai, her grandmother, always told her that life was about learning. Every day learn something new and then you will have a good life. That's what the old woman told her. Today, Su had learnt that life was very complicated. Today, she had learnt that her husband was a stubborn man, who could stand in silence for ten whole minutes.

Chapter Twenty-nine

They arrived by taxi like two holidaymakers. At number 28 Geoffrey Street the light bulbs burnt bright and naked. The walls were bare and a mother and her daughter stood in the centre of the living room with two suitcases. One contained a teddy bear with no name, a school uniform, school shoes, two pairs of jeans and several tee shirts. Anna wore the only cardigan she had, together with pink trainers and some denim-look leggings. She carried a Mickey Mouse rucksack with crayons and a colouring book and a doll that she had grabbed before they left her father. That was all.

The other case contained an English workbook, a wash bag, two pairs of chipped heels, a blue flowery dress, three jumpers, underwear and two pairs of jeans. This was all they owned, but still Lenka was smiling. There were two sofas in the living room and a bed and wardrobe in each of the bedrooms, sourced by the women's refuge centre. And in the kitchen there was a kettle, everything they needed to begin a new life.

'So, Anna. You like?' The child nodded and threw her arms around her mother's neck.

'Let's go find your room. Anna's room.' Anna leapt up the stairs.

'This one,' she cried.

'Ah. No. Other room,' Lenka called.

Anna ran through the open door at the end of the landing, jumped on the single bed and threw her body down flat. She lay on the bed and stared up at the ceiling and so did Lenka.

'Anna and Lenka. Home,' whispered Lenka, pressing her nose against the child's face. They hugged each other tightly. 'New beginning. I see you sleepy.' Anna yawned. 'I want teddy,' she murmured, her fingers tangled in Lenka's hair.

'Let's go downstairs and see garden.' Anna leapt from the bed. 'And I have a present for you.' Anna's eyes widened as her mother led her by the hand into the small kitchen. Anna looked through the glass door. 'Open if you want present.' On the step was a little box. Anna lifted the lid carefully. 'Thank you, Mummy. Thank you!' She ran across the small yard with a new skipping rope in her hands and counted the jumps as the green and yellow rope spun through the air. Warm wooden handles gripped by tiny doll hands. Green and yellow rope speckled with golden thread. Lenka would always remember this moment. She framed it in her mind, the sound of Anna's shoes tapping the ground, hair swishing, a giggle and a yelp. Eyes fixed on her mother's face. Anna was like all children, desperate to get to that magic one hundred. This was happiness

Anna had counted to fifty-six when Lenka's phone began to buzz and vibrate in her pocket. A message from Su. She was on her way with food and she had made a cake. Only in her text she had written 'food ake coming x.' Texting was a language in itself. Lenka decided that neither she nor her friends had mastered it. Sometimes she got messages she didn't understand, but she never questioned this. To receive a message was all that mattered, and somehow, despite their three different backgrounds, and languages, Sammy, Su and she understood each other. This was difficult to explain. To Lenka, it seemed, there was a language amongst women. A silent language that said more than words ever could. There was, she decided, a language that women shared in a look, a sigh, a smile. She wondered if it was the same for men. Sometimes women read a face, like someone reads a book. Su could read faces better than most.

When Su arrived, Anna was breathing heavily and shouting eighty-two. Su and Lenka clapped. Su observed the little girl closely. Her hair was long and blonde, pulled back in a red bobble and she wore dark leggings with a tiny hole in the knee.

'I have present for you, Anna.'

'Ah. That is very kind,' said Lenka. Su gave Anna a shiny pink parcel. Inside the girl tugged out a Princess Barbie. 'Yes!' shrieked Anna. 'Yes!' Lenka began to laugh. 'Say thank you.' The girl hugged Su briefly and began to comb the doll's hair.

'And a present for you, Lenka.'

Lenka hesitated and Su saw she was nervous, tearful. 'You very kind to me. Thank you.' Lenka took the present and began to unwrap it. Inside there was a pen, a diary and a notebook. 'For writing,' added Su. 'You can write your life story.'

'Maybe one day I be famous writer. When I learn English.' Lenka laughed and Su smiled.

'And this pen have your name on. See. L E N K A.' She pointed at the gold lettering. 'Man in Burnley market put name on. Clever, eh? I write down and show him.'

'Thank you,' repeated Lenka and she leant over and hugged Su. 'You, good friend.'

'Put food in kitchen?' said Su.

The two women stood in the kitchen and looked through the window out into the tiny yard. 'You like house?' said Su, after a few minutes.

'Yes,' said Lenka. 'For first time, I feel excited and free.'

Su nodded and squeezed her arm. 'Life is good for you, now.'

Lenka looked at the clock. 'Sammy will be outside language centre at three o'clock. We need go and meet her.'

They walked the length of the street, over the bridge, Anna clutching the Barbie, humming a tune. At the bottom of the ramp Anna ran towards the park. 'Stay in park,' said Lenka, patting her head. 'Mummy coming soon.' Anna sat on the spinning disc and crossed her legs. At the bottom of the ramp Su and Lenka waited. Su felt nervous, sick rising in her chest. She swallowed hard. There was Suriya at the top of the ramp. Sammy hurried down and looked back and waved at her mother-in-law. The woman hovered for a moment and the three women pretended to advance towards the language centre.

'Shit,' said Sammy. 'She watch.'

Su turned. 'It OK. She gone.'

'Gone?'

'Yes. Gone.'

'Oh my God!' cried Lenka, clutching her chest. 'I nearly have heart attack. That woman scare me.'

Sammy shrugged her shoulders. 'This is life for me now. Hiding like I commit big crime.'

'Shit!' cried Lenka. 'I nearly forgot Anna.' She took off her long coat and gave it to Sammy and then she ran through the park gate. Anna was still on the spinning disc talking to the doll. 'We have party now, Anna. Time to go.' Anna was speaking in Polish, making the doll dance on the rim of the wheel. Lenka thought about her mother in Poland. Maybe she would go back one day. But only when she had an amazing story to tell.

In the house, Sammy gave Lenka a card covered in a patchwork of fabric and sequins. 'Very beautiful,' said Lenka. 'You made?' Sammy nodded. Inside was the message 'TO LENKA, GOOD LUK, YOU ARE MY FRIEND ALLWAYS, SAMMY X.'

Su stirred the rice and chicken and spooned it into little dishes. They ate in the living room, the sound of the radio drifting from the kitchen. 'I doesn't like quiet,' said Lenka, listening to a slow love ballad. She pictured Kamil. Whenever it was silent she always thought she heard the click of the door, a footstep outside, a man breathing. With these thoughts her hand shook and the rice sprinkled on the carpet like confetti. Sammy knelt down and plucked the rice from the floor. 'You OK.' Lenka stopped eating.

'I don't want be afraid. Sometimes I scared of everything.' She wiped a tear from her eye. 'Sorry. Sorry.'

Sammy held her arm. 'We all scared, sometimes, Lenka.'

'You scared of the bat lady?' Lenka looked serious.

'Me scared of England,' stammered Sammy, thinking about her words. She paused. 'England scare me. Life different. People is different. Clothes is different. Weather, food, everything is different.'

Su agreed. 'Weather here very bad. Always rain. Always water.'

'Yeah,' said Sammy in a high voice. 'Life in England is difficult for me. I feel bored. My husband always work. Me in house. Suriya is OK. She strict. Everyone too busy in England.'

Lenka gulped a spoon of rice. Anna was skipping in the garden, counting loudly. 'Things will get better for us,' she said, hopefully.

'No for me,' said Sammy. 'You two free. You two can wear English clothes, eat English food. Me no wear English clothes, eat chips.' She stirred the rice with her spoon and made a well in the dish. A wishing well. And then she told Su and Lenka about the man called Rob.

Lenka glared. 'No, Sammy! This is bad idea.'

'Ohhhhh!' cried Su, imagining the angry face of Suriya. 'No go back and see this man.'

Sammy removed her scarf. 'I want to be English. I want to be like Englishwomen and go shopping. Buy clothes. Have an English life. Have English friend.'

'Talk to your husband,' said Su. 'Maybe your husband understand.'

Lenka shook her head. 'No, Su. She can't do this. You have to stop seeing this man, Sammy.'

Sammy began to laugh. 'Rob kind. Have big house and car. He teach me English.'

'On no,' murmured Su. 'You like this Englishman.'

Sammy looked down and made patterns with the rice. 'Su. You are only one who is happy in England. You is very lucky.'

Su smiled for a moment. 'Happy? Lucky?' The others saw her expression change. 'I want be happy but Bobby has baby. Now everything changed.'

Sammy gasped and Lenka placed her bowl on the floor quickly. 'Baby?'

'Yes,' said Su, her eyes fixed on a photo of Lenka and Anna. 'He no tell me before. Me no like secrets.'

'Poor Su,' said Lenka. 'What will you do?'

'Me don't know. He my husband. I tell him no nookie.'

The women laughed. 'Me hide under cover,' said Sammy. 'Always pretending I asleep when husband home.' She closed her eyes and imitated a loud snore.

'Cake and tea,' interrupted Lenka. She grinned at her friends. 'This is cake what Englishwomen have when they is sad. Cake and tea. Cake and tea makes everything better.'

She went to the kitchen and returned carrying a large chocolate cake. 'Big piece,' she said to Sammy. 'I know superlative. I give you the BIGGEST piece.'

'Oh no!' joked Su. 'Sammy cake is BIGGER than mine. COMPARATIVE!'

'See. We are all becoming Englished and laughing at our own jokes,' said Lenka.

Su giggled, crumbs of cake falling on her lap. Today she was wearing a purple scarf and she removed a crumb of cake from the knot. Usually she wore black or purple on a Saturday, because that was the tradition in Thailand. These traditions, she had not left behind. They stayed with her, shaped her life, even in this country. It was then she knew she would never be English. Bobby wanted her to be a British citizen. She needed the certificate. I am Thai, she thought to herself. Like my mother before me. Like my grandmother, Chuenchai. Inside she felt afraid. Saturday was not a good day to move house.

CHAPTER THIRTY

As usual Sammy made her way past the school towards Beaumont Road and just like every Wednesday Frank the old man was next door in the garden, observing the birds and the lives of others. He looked at her Asian clothes, pink and gold. They were beautiful, he thought to himself, and he found himself admiring the sequins and gold thread.

'Good morning, Sammy,' he said cheerfully. Frank walked towards her, weaving his way through a flowery bush with fluffy heads that dispersed and floated through the air. He staggered slightly as he moved. 'Nice day for gardening.'

Sammy waved. 'You are right.'

He looked down at her feet, the perfect polished nails. 'So, how are you twinkle toes?' Sammy pouted and now wore a serious look. She did not understand the remark and Frank hesitated, aware that he had said something wrong, something she did not understand.

'It's all right, dear. I mean you have nice toes,' he explained.

But his explanation came too late for the girl had gone, muttering under her breath in Urdu.

She let herself in with the key Rob had given her. He was in the kitchen standing over the sink. 'I will do that,' she said and she began to wash the dishes, plunging her hands in the soapy water.

Today she was quieter than normal. 'What is this twinkle

toes? What name is he calling me?'

Rob laughed hysterically. 'He's being nice.'

Sammy did not respond. She was flustered and suddenly animated. 'I have just two months. Then it is the exam ...' Rob dried a bowl, unsure what she meant.

'After the exam, how can I come here? There will be no more college.'

'Can you do another course?'

'I am no allowed. I just need one certificate.'

Rob nodded. 'Surely they will want you to learn more English.'

'Perhaps,' she replied.

She used this word often now. She liked the sound of 'perhaps'. Rob used this word a lot. The teacher had also noticed her using this word and smiled and said 'good'.

Sometimes she and Rob went out in his car for a drive. Once he took her to a museum in Manchester and talked to her about history. Today she did not want to go out. Rob was also quiet. She dried her hands on the towel and folded it neatly.

'I do not want you to go home,' he said. 'I want you to stay, to stay with me.'

Sammy understood him. She thought about him at night time. When Ehsan mounted her she closed her eyes and imagined being with the courier. Ehsan had noticed she had become more and more distant. 'You are always tired,' he said. 'These English classes are bad for you. I will be glad when you are finished.' She would nod in agreement, but inside she knew that once the classes were over there would be no more freedom. So she tried to be a good wife, cooking his favourite dishes and telling him he was a good husband, hoping he would not notice that everything had changed.

Rob continued to wait for a reaction. He called her name. She heard him, but the sound was muffled by the buzzing in her head.

She leant her head back and closed her eyes. When she opened them Rob drew closer. He touched her face lightly, stroked her head, her neck, wound her hair in his hands. Then he pulled her close, kissed her slowly. She felt his body close to hers. Through the folds of her clothes he explored her waist, her breasts. He led her upstairs. For the first time she was free. They lay side by side together on the bed holding hands.

'You cannot go back,' he said. 'You must not go back there.'

She pressed her face close to his. 'I am so happy ... so happy, but I must do exam first.'

Rob protested but Sammy whispered, 'Shush. I will get certificate and then everything will be OK.'

He listened to the lilt in her voice and she suddenly became conscious of every word.

'Did I say something bad?'

'No,' he replied. 'You speak better English than me,' and he rolled on top of her and slid his fingers through her hair.

* * *

Suriya was ranting at the receptionist. Staff at the language centre motioned for her to be quiet. They were unable to extract meaning from the confused sounds and language that erupted from her lips. Someone said there was an angry student complaining. Samina was late, very late. Where was she? She had left for her English class as normal, but where was she? Suriya had waited at the top of the ramp for twenty minutes. The teacher had gone. Up the ramp Suriya heaved her heavy body and cursed her daughter-in-law with every breath. English classes were taking too much time and now the girl had gone missing. How could a student vanish in the air, she had asked the manager, and he had stared at her blankly. She was a dramatic woman, threw her arms up in despair and told him she would sue if the girl was not found.

I will have you closed down, she shrieked, for neglect, pointing a fat finger at his face. The manager had stammered and stuttered and tried to ring the teacher, but Suriya had a hot temper and had uttered an angry PAH and left him trembling with the phone in his hand.

* * *

In Beaumont Road Sammy leapt from the bed, naked. 'Oh my God it's late.' Rob was drifting in and out of sleep. 'I have to go.' She kissed his nose and raced down the road. Her sandals were undone and she stooped to fasten them. She rushed to Paradise Street. At the door Suriya glared. 'I so sorry, Suriya. I fell down and English lady take me to hospital.' Sammy was surprised how easily, how quickly the lie had sprung from her lips. She clutched her ribs and bent over low. She had always wanted to be an actress. In the English class she was often chosen for role play. Already she had been a complaining customer, an MP and a patient at hospital. Last week everyone clapped and cheered when she acted the part of a woman desperate to see a doctor. She imagined she was in class now. In English she said, 'I hit my head and I have bad back. Really bad back.'

'You fell?'

'Yes. Before class. Outside the language centre.'

Suriya pressed the girl's head with the palm of her hand. 'Yes. You have a temperature. Samina. Samina. You poor girl! Sit down. I look after you.' Suriya's eyes widened. 'You with child?'

'No. No,' said Sammy, in a panic. For once Sammy felt guilty. Suriya looked disappointed. 'Don't worry,' she said, 'from now on I stay home and look after you.' With these words Sammy lay down on the velvet sofa and slept. She dreamt about Rob. In the dream he was calling her name. She felt herself sweating.

'I think you need to go back hospital,' said her mother-in-law who was bent over her and the girl jolted abruptly. 'No, thank you, you are so kind, I prefer if you look after me instead.'

As Sammy slept Suriya praised her daughter-in-law and told her son Ehsan, 'You are lucky you have such a good wife. She is very brave. When will you bring me some grandchildren?' And she squeezed his cheeks hard, just as she had done when he was a boy. That night he was angry because Samina refused to let him touch her. And he could not find his leather jacket. All she cared about was her damned English classes. She was not such a good wife.

CHAPTER THIRTY-ONE

Intonation was very important. Su learnt this in every lesson. Lenka was good at making her voice rise and fall at all the right moments. But Su listened to her own voice on the recorder and was disappointed. She recognised the flatness in her words, winced because she struggled with pronunciation. English was a battle. Her voice was low and deep, devoid of emotion and expression. At home she practised every day. She listened to Bobby's voice, but this did not help. His accent was strong and he talked quickly. Sometimes he laughed when she spoke. The teacher said 'parth' for 'path'. And 'glarse' for 'glass'. Bobby raised his eyebrows. 'You sound a bit posh, love. Remember this ain't Buckingham Palace.' Always Bobby compared her to the Queen. 'Remember this is Burnley.' Su pulled a face. 'I want speak properly. Not like you.'

Bobby was beginning to think that English classes were a bad idea. Su spent much time at number 28, visiting the battered woman, trying to speak like people on the BBC. He tried to reform her. 'It's not larf, it's laf. I AM LAFFING.' Su tossed her hair back and shrugged her shoulders. 'You no teacher Bobby Haywood!' In the end Bobby gave up. 'I'm not bloody helping you. Sod you. Do it yourself, you silly woman.' Su stormed around the kitchen, slamming plates on the worktop. She wanted more than this. In the kitchen the window was stuck closed, the tap dripped, the skirting board was missing. Bobby had started stripping the wallpaper in the bedroom, but had stopped after one wall. The bedroom drawers jarred and the wardrobe door was hanging loose. These things she saw every day. These things made her grit her teeth. Usually she kept busy and the disappointment about the house faded.

Recently, she had studied Bobby carefully. She watched his face. She watched the way he walked, the way he talked. His fingers were yellow from smoking. The house was full of possessions. But how many were hers? What did she possess? When she thought about this, she counted the things she owned on one hand. A Buddha, an amulet, a cushion, a scarf, a shawl. Everywhere she looked there were ornaments. Someone else's things. A porcelain horse, standing on two legs, was placed on a shelf next to a ceramic clown with beady eyes and a spotty collar. On the fireplace there was a brass shoe. Ugly things. Su took a carrier bag from under the sink and placed the things inside. She cleared every shelf, every picture from the wall of the depressing sitting room. She tore the threadbare curtains from the window, enjoying the light that filled the room. Little tables, a cabinet she pushed into the yard. Extra chairs, she stacked outside. In the sitting room now there was just one sofa and an armchair. And then she took up a paintbrush and whitewashed the whole room. When the paint dropped on the swirling red and black carpet she smiled, satisfied that the carpet would have to be thrown away.

Kneeling down, she began to lift the carpet with a kitchen knife. She pulled it free from beneath the skirting board and saw pine floorboards beneath. She continued to roll the carpet back but the sofa was heavy and she needed Bobby to help. After five hours the walls and ceiling were bright white. But the stone fireplace irritated her. A mix of grey and black, she painted that white too. The room gleamed and when she had finished she sat on the floor with a cup of green tea and picked and peeled the dry spots of paint from her hands and fingers. Looking at her efforts she felt pleased. Light and airy, the room now seemed much bigger. Her depression had lifted. The paintbrush had wiped out all traces of black. It was surprising, she thought, how a room could transform your thoughts. She loved the light. In Thailand the light was white, illuminating colours, flowers and life.

She placed the gold Buddha on the fireplace and wrapped the colourful shawl on the brown sofa back. Red, orange, gold, yellow, turquoise and green, the scarf was bright like English church windows. In the class the teacher had shown them York Minster, a religious building with the most beautiful painted glass. Su wanted to go there and Bobby had promised a trip to York, for her birthday. Bobby said there were once beautiful church windows in Burnley, but the church on the corner had closed down. In the church garden a crooked FOR SALE sign was testimony to the fact that no one believed in God any more. Teenagers had smashed the windows, stolen the crucifix from above the altar. Su gasped. People had abandoned not just the houses in Burnley, but God too.

* * *

Bobby's face began to swell like a pink balloon. 'What the hell? It looks like we've been fucking robbed. Where's the furniture? Su, what have you done?' Su bit her lip. 'Nice?' she said in English. Bobby sighed a loud tut and shook his head, over and over. 'It's a fucking mess, woman. Look at it.' Bobby swung his body round and round. 'Oh fuck. My stone fireplace!' His hands were on his head and he stared in disbelief. He paced up and down. 'The house is empty.' He marched towards the back window. 'My best chair outside!' He rubbed his head and glared at his wife. 'Oh Jesus!'

'I like,' Su mumbled.

Bobby began to shout. 'What were you thinking of? I go out and this is what I come home to. And the paint stinks.' He prodded the fireplace with his finger and inspected the white circle. 'Wet,' said Su. 'I know THAT,' Bobby said sarcastically. He sat on the sofa and looked at Su. 'You're a crap decorator.'

'Crap?'

'Rubbish.'

'Ah.' Su whispered. 'You no like?'

'Get me a beer,' said Bobby. Su jerked upright and hurried into the kitchen. She came back with a bottle of beer. 'Sit down,' he said.

'You angry?'

Bobby looked up at the ceiling. He began to laugh and roar, like a madman. 'I was thinking I needed a change. Not this drastic. But I needed a new change.'

'You want new wife?'

Bobby laughed hysterically. 'A new carpet,' he replied. 'I want a new carpet. Not a new wife. Claret carpet.' He winked.

Su tapped his arm. 'I try and make it look nice. Not like Burnley Football Club.'

'Aye,' said Bobby. 'It looks like a different house, all right.' He gulped down the beer and laughed.

'You no angry?' asked Su.

Bobby rocked on the sofa. 'You're full of surprises. Just tell me next time you plan to wreck the house. And we better buy some new curtains.'

CHAPTER THIRTY-TWO

Ehsan sat in the car and waited. Beep Beep. He punched the horn with his fist and muttered. Always English people were late. Never on time. Soon an elderly man emerged in the doorway, shaking his head. He limped slightly and forced his stick down heavy on the ground. 'I'm coming! Hold your horses,' he grunted. The taxi driver sighed and stepped out of the car for a moment holding the door open.

'That's more like it,' said the man, gulping for air and dropping in the seat. 'To the hospital, please.'

Ehsan eyed him carefully in the mirror. The man was at least eighty and his face was red and puffy.

'Are you OK?'

'Having a bad day with my chest,' he said, reaching for his inhaler. Ehsan watched his chest rise and fall, saw the man lean back exhausted.

'You need an ambulance?'

'No, I'll be all right. I'm always like this.'

'Not good,' said Ehsan, feeling guilty that he had been so impatient. He listened to the sound of heavy breathing.

'No. It's bloody old age.'

Ehsan chuckled and turned the key. The old man looked out of the window.

'Do you mind if I open the window?'

'No,' replied Ehsan, looking at the big houses as they drove down the road. 'Nice street.'

'Yes – I've lived here thirty years. My wife died, so I'm on my own. Are you married?'

'Yeah,' said Ehsan. 'New wife.'

'Lucky you,' called the old man. 'What's her name?'

'Samina,' replied Ehsan, smiling in the mirror.

'Ahh. Nice name. I know an Asian lady called Sammy … very pretty lady with red toes. I'd marry her myself, but she's got a partner.'

'Yeah?' said Ehsan, looking for somewhere to park. 'Do you want me to drop you here?'

The old man struggled out of the car and Ehsan bent to help him up. He shook on the step, a frail figure and reached in his pocket for a ten pound note. He waved it in the air in front of the driver's nose.

'Take it,' he said, coughing and spluttering.

'Too much, mate,' said Ehsan. 'You've given me too much.'

'No problem. Bugger off and look after that wife of yours.'

He turned away and Ehsan stood watching him stagger to the main entrance. A porter took the man's arm and led him in.

Five pounds!

Five pounds was a good tip. Ehsan had a feeling today would be a good day.

* * *

It was Monday morning and Sammy packed her bag for the language centre. She had lost her pen. Rummaging through the kitchen drawers she found a chewed green biro and scribbled in her book to check it worked. The drawer jammed shut as it closed and she saw the time now and was angry because she would be late. She forced the drawer hard but something was stuck at the back. 'Shit,' she cursed and stretched her arm deep into the drawer. She felt a cardboard book and it was bent stuck. She pulled and tugged and out it came, a little black book with gold writing. It was her passport.

She stood still for a moment, thinking about the passport, thinking about freedom. She would need the passport to get her certificate. She put it in the bag, but suddenly remembered she was in the UK, as Ehsan's wife. Frustrated she returned the book to the drawer. The system was so complicated. She did not know how it worked. Ehsan would have to apply for her indefinite leave to remain. She would be forced to stay with him for a long time. She was a woman. She had no rights.

*   *   *

On the way to the centre she saw an Englishwoman driving a sports car with no roof and her blonde hair flew in the wind. She watched her carefully. I want to be like that woman, she thought. Then she saw Su in jeans and a white tee shirt and she waved and advanced towards her. I want to wear normal clothes, she thought, not these heavy robes and veils. I am hot and my clothes are heavy.

'You have too many clothes,' said Su as if she had read her mind.

'You are right. I agree,' said Sammy, 'but I have to wear them.'

'Tell your husband you no want to wear,' said Su, casually, and Sammy's eyes widened. She would speak to Ehsan about the clothes tonight.

There was no air in the class. The students talked about adjectives and places. Beautiful. Boring. Burnley is beautiful, said the chorus of women. England is beautiful. Burnley is boring. Everyone erupted in laughter. Burnley is hot. Burnley is cold. At the far end of the classroom there was a sudden thump. A chair tipped backwards. A loud scream and someone shouted 'Zehnab!'

Zehnab lay on the floor, her eyes closed. There was a big commotion. 'Too hot,' said an elderly woman, slapping Zehnab's face. Zehnab woke up to the crying faces of her classmates. 'Faint,' one woman said. An ambulance was on the way and the teacher made everyone move back. Zehnab sat up, but the ambulance took her away. 'Too many clothes,' said Su. 'Too hot.' Sammy thought about this.

* * *

After the lesson Suriya was in the kitchen. 'What you think about English clothes, Suriya? Today woman faint because Asian clothes too hot.'

'No,' she said. 'It is not possible.' She paused. 'No girls in our family wears English dresses. Now hurry up. There are things to be done.'

Sammy hung the washing on the line as she was instructed, but she ripped the woman's headscarf with her bare hands until the strands hung down, detached and torn.

* * *

Ehsan was outside washing the taxi, a dirty sponge in his hand. Water rolled down the hill along the gutter. 'Another girl been sick,' he said to his wife, disgusted. The odour was strong and he sprayed air freshener on the damp seat. Sammy stood and watched.

'Have you found my jacket?'

'No,' stammered Sammy, remembering she had left it at Rob's house.

'Strange,' he muttered.

'What do you think?' he asked, as he rubbed the car hard with a cotton towel. 'Shiny … Eh …?'

'Nice,' Sammy replied. 'I want talk to you?'

Ehsan looked up. 'Always talking – that's all you women do every day.' He smiled at his own joke, but Sammy looked serious.

'What do you think about English clothes?'

'Clothes from Pakistan are better for women. English clothes are too tight.'

'Oh,' said Sammy. She watched for his reaction but Ehsan ignored her and continued to spray the air freshener shouting, 'My God. That stuff's strong!'

The girl went inside and continued to clean. There was no point in discussing clothes. Ehsan did not listen. He never listened.

CHAPTER THIRTY-THREE

Love made Sammy giddy. In the tiny kitchen in Paradise Street she spent many minutes staring at nothing in particular, thinking about Rob. She didn't hear the conversations around her and caught herself smiling, sometimes singing English songs. She had been listening to the Beatles in the English class and Suriya glared as her voice lifted and she jigged to the sound of 'Twist and Shout'. 'Stop this hullabaloo,' she said, her eyes rolling in her head. 'Anyone is thinking you have much to be happy about.' Sammy stopped, but her mother-in-law smacked her on the back. 'It's a joke! I am joking. Keep singing.' Sammy looked confused. 'I remember learning English,' said Suriya, proudly, 'to become a good citizen. I did Life in UK test. Ask me anything – about womens tied to gates, the sufferers, getting votes for womens. I know all this English stuff. And this word, hullabaloo.' Sammy nodded and cleared the breakfast dishes away. 'And I learnt about Queen Victoria. It's Queen Elizabeth in these days. Queen with crown,' she said, pointing at her head. Sammy said nothing. Suriya always thought she knew everything. It's not WOMENS, its WOMEN, thought Sammy. If only she had the courage to say it. 'My English were perfect,' said Suriya. 'Now I forget.'

Biryani lapped up the sides of the tub in Sammy's hand. 'You need a bag for trip,' said Suriya, fetching Sammy a rucksack. 'Take coat. Blackpool is cold. And put food in bag. Blackpool is nice place. Listen to teacher. Get your certificate, then everything in

England will be good.'

Sammy took the bag upstairs and thought about Blackpool. There was a big tower and the seaside. Inside the bag she placed her English book. One page was loose and the paper had curled at the top. 'I am going to Blackpool,' she told Ehsan. 'Today, I am going to Blackpool. This is future tense.' Ehsan was in bed. He opened his eyes for a moment and snorted, before falling back to sleep again. He was naked and one leg hung over the side of the divan, a sheet tangled in his toes. Always he slept in a diagonal pose, his limbs stretched wide, with Sammy occupying a tiny slice of bed. Sometimes he kicked her, his toe nails scraped her leg and she found herself with her nose pressed against the wall. Once she turned away so quickly she banged her lips and her teeth on the cold wall. When Ehsan had to work the night shift he complained and grumbled, but Sammy put clean sheets on the bed and lay like a star, happy that her husband was gone.

* * *

Together the women at the language centre walked up the ramp onto the main road. The coach driver was standing on the path smoking. He threw the cigarette down and stamped it hard. Su, Sammy and Lenka sat at the back of the coach, Lenka chewing on gum. 'Me travel sick,' she announced. 'No like buses.' Also she was worried about leaving Anna at school. Another mother had offered to collect her and give her tea, but this played on her mind. Blackpool was over thirty miles away. What if there was an emergency?

'Don't worry,' said Su, sensing something was wrong. 'Blackpool nice.'

Lenka smiled and continued to chew on her gum. Su tugged a box of chocolates from her bag.

'Nice bag,' said Sammy. 'Beautiful. Like birds of paradise.' Sammy felt the embroidered birds with her finger. Then she looked out of the window, at the looming grey clouds.

Lenka laughed. 'No paradise in Burnley. Weather is shit.'

'My life is shit,' said Sammy, quickly.

'No!' cried Lenka, gripping her arm. She searched Sammy's tearful face.

Sammy clutched her waist and rocked on the seat. 'I hate my life. I am sick of looking happy. Everything is so bad in England.' As she spoke her lip quivered and her chest heaved.

'No. Sammy! What happen? What happen to make you like this?' Lenka pulled a strand of hair from Sammy's eyes.

'I bad person, Lenka. In England, I am nothing. My husband say I am nothing.'

'Your husband wrong!' cried Su. 'No listen your husband.'

'I have no choice,' sobbed Sammy, raising her voice. 'No choices for people like me. Every day I have to do my duty, think about the family. Always the family. Family. Family. Family.'

For a moment Sammy leant her head on Lenka's shoulder but then she bolted upright and covered her face. 'I so tired of this English life. Sometimes I pray to die.'

'No Sammy! Do not say this. It's a big sin. You must not say these things.' Lenka looked her in the eye. 'You listen. Life is not so bad.'

Sammy continued to cry and Su bit her lip. 'I want to leave,' wailed Sammy. 'Leave my husband and be free.'

'Everything will be OK,' said Lenka, nodding and smiling. 'Everything will be OK. God will help you.'

Sammy shook her head. 'I am bad person, Lenka. No one will help me. I do this.' Slowly Sammy unbuttoned her tunic sleeve and rolled the fabric back. Deep red lines criss-crossed her tiny pale wrists. The skin was jagged and torn and yellow liquid had seeped from one cut forming a line of shiny yellow beads.

'What you do?' shrieked Lenka. 'Oh my God!' She hugged Sammy tightly, felt her body tremble. 'My poor Sammy.'

Su covered her face. 'CUT,' she said loudly. 'CUT. CUT. CUT'

CHAPTER THIRTY-FOUR

Hand in hand the women sat on the bus, listening to the raucous voices of those at the front singing 'Here Comes the Sun'. For the trip, forty or so female students had merged together. No men because they attended separate classes. Sammy said Suriya would have a heart attack if there was a man in the class. Suriya had been careful to check. She didn't want her daughter-in-law in mixed classes. That would be asking for trouble. In private she had told this to the manager. And this morning she had stood in Geoffrey Street, carefully inspecting the coach. Satisfied there were no men, she waved and made her way home. Once a builder had climbed a ladder and appeared at the classroom window. Zehnab the fainting woman had screamed and covered her face. Sammy had giggled and Zehnab told her in Urdu that she was a disgrace to her country.

Su scanned the seats to see if there was anyone else Thai. There was a Japanese woman, two other women speaking in a language that may have been German. The teacher heard, scowled and told everyone to speak in English. 'English ONLY,' she instructed them, wagging her finger. Most of the women were from Pakistan, Bangladesh, India and wore saris or shalwar kameez. None of them saw Sammy crying, or if they did, no one spoke about it.

From the motorway someone saw Blackpool Tower and the women stood and peered through the window. 'Like a pylon,' one woman shouted. 'Horrible.'

Su saw the tower. In Paris there was a tower like this one. Sammy stared ahead, not looking at anyone or anything. Su patted her head. 'Nearly there.' But all the time Sammy was thinking about Blackpool. It was a big place. Bigger than Burnley. Could someone disappear in Blackpool? She thought carefully. A job was not possible because she was not a British citizen. And what did this mean? What did it mean to be British? Eating fish and chips. Wearing jeans. Living in a semi. Visiting the Queen. To her being British was about being free. Choosing a husband. Choosing a house. Choosing clothes. Choosing food.

'Choose a partner to work with,' the teacher shouted down the coach. 'Two people work together.' Su glared. 'Three,' she said meekly. 'OK,' responded the teacher. 'You can work in twos, or threes.'

The coach had stopped on the seafront and the teacher told everyone to go to the beach and eat lunch. Down the steps the women ran. Sammy walked slowly behind Su and Lenka. 'It's OK,' she said, suddenly hopeful. 'I know what I can do.'

'What can you do?' said Lenka, pulling off her shoes and digging her toes in the cool sand. Sammy pulled her dress up and Lenka saw tight skinny jeans. The dress was soon over Sammy's head, revealing a fitted white tee shirt.

'You look like English girl,' said Su, amazed.

Sammy grinned and stuffed the black robe in the rucksack. 'Rob buy me. I have to stay with husband until I am a British citizen. Then I can be like Englishwomen.'

Lenka frowned. 'You have to stop seeing Rob.'

'No,' said Sammy. 'Rob will help me.'

Su said very little and closed her eyes. She watched and listened to the waves whooshing and felt the sun, warm on her nose. But the English breeze was cold and she shuddered. She thought of Mai back home and the children playing on the sand. The voices of Sammy and Lenka echoed in her ear, as if they were far away on some distant shore. She felt like sleeping until Lenka tapped her arm. 'Come on. I buy you ice cream.' Su laughed. 'It too cold for ice cream.'

'Let's pretend it's a beautiful summer day in England,' said Lenka, her voice rising in the air. She tugged Su's sleeve.

'Lenka, you always so happy,' said Sammy, smiling. 'I wish I was always so happy.'

'Hey!' shouted Lenka. 'That was good English sentence. All of us is improving so much.'

'I want to speak as good as the Queen,' said Sammy.

'Queen too posh,' said Su. 'Bobby say why you talking like this posh, posh words and posh voice, like you from London, or something.' Su opened and closed her hands like a moving puppet. The others giggled.

'You want to talk posh, Su?'

'Yeah. Me want to talk like doctor, be like persons who read books. Go university and be educated womans.' Su paused. 'Maybe get job in library. That is a good life. Better than being a maid.'

Lenka thought for a moment. 'Me want to get good job. Interesting job.'

Sammy spoke quietly. 'In my culture women no do jobs. Women stay at home. England better because women can work in jobs.'

The three women fell silent and headed up the steps towards the cabin selling ice creams.

'Three, please,' said Lenka, proudly. 'Please can I have three ice creams?'

'Big, or small?' asked the man, not really looking at the three women.

'Aww. Big, please.' Lenka winked at Sammy.

Lenka paid and the women walked along the beach. 'That is the first time I buy ice cream in the UK,' she said after a while.

She corrected herself. 'I have bought an ice cream for the first time.' She stressed the word 'bought'. 'This English is sooooooooooo difficult,' she said, her lips covered in ice cream. 'Always thinking about the words.'

'My brain hurt with all these words,' said Su. 'I think I forget my own language. No one to talk in Thai.'

'Yes,' said Lenka in a sympathetic voice. 'I speak in Polish with Anna, but she want to speak in English, like friends at school. Don't worry, you cannot forget your first language because it is your own. Part of your heart.' She held her hand to her chest. 'Polish in here.' She patted her chest. 'Polish in here. Always.'

Su watched Sammy's arms swinging as she walked. She glimpsed the red lines on her wrists. She pointed at the marks and clutched her hand. 'Sammy, please no do this again. You have friends. Talk to us. We understand. No one in life always happy. Be thankful to Buddha, your god in the sky.'

But Sammy pulled away. She continued to walk and did not look at her. The sun was in her eyes and she squinted. As the sun caressed her bare face, she was thinking about being with the man Rob. She remembered the last time he kissed her, how his kiss had stayed on her lips for many days, the smell of mint on his breath and coconut shampoo.

CHAPTER THIRTY-FIVE

English people flocked to Blackpool Tower and stood taking pictures of the giant structure. They did this because that was the tradition in England. Su thought the building was a beastly building with no soul. So this was the famous Blackpool Tower – a metal monster that lurked beside the sea, corroded and rusty from the spitting salt water. She stood across the road and looked up towards the top of the tower. She felt dizzy and her neck ached. Lenka took a photo with her mobile phone. 'So tall,' she mumbled, as they dodged the traffic in the road, avoiding a carriage and horse with a patch over its eye.

Inside the building they found themselves in the aquarium. Su was excited. Beautiful fish swam in large glass tanks. Brightly coloured tropical fish like those in Thailand. Turtles with ancient wrinkled faces danced and dived deep into a cave, emerging in the light. She stood spellbound. But then she felt cold. It suddenly occurred to her that this was wrong, all these beautiful creatures together in a glass case, when they should be free, swimming in the ocean. She whispered in Thai. She clutched her amulet. Here was a piece of Thailand, of foreign places, but these creatures did not belong here.

Together the students sat in the ballroom listening to the organ player, watching an elderly couple swing their hips, the woman's gold shoes tapping in rhythm to the music. The music was uplifting and the woman span round so fast that Su felt dizzy.

It was lucky that she had a drink in her bag and she sipped it slowly, wincing as she tasted the warm water.

Sammy was enjoying the music, trying to find the English words to describe dancing. 'In Pakistan I dance.' She corrected herself quickly. 'Past. In Pakistan I danced. I like dancing. Me and my sister always dancing.' The memory floated past her and was carried away like a kite in the wind. Then another thought came. This time she saw the smiling face of her mother telling her to go to England. It was a better life. Through salty tears her mother stroked Sammy's hair and kissed her head. 'I want you have a good life. In England you are safe. Better life for your children.' The day she left Pakistan, her mother had sobbed, given her a beautiful black scarf, woven with love and golden thread. Wrapping it around her daughter's neck she said in a shaky voice 'I will pray for you, pray that you have a happy life.' Sammy wondered about this prayer. It had not been answered. Sometimes she read the Quran and doubted the words. Then she hated herself more than ever. It was then she took the razor blades and began to scrape at her wrists. Now she pressed her wrist hard and felt her veins pulsing like rivers. The woman was flying around the ballroom, her skirt lifting as she moved. Sammy wanted to dance. In Pakistan she had danced in the mountains, in bare feet, her hair knotted and wild. To dance was to be free.

'You like music, Sammy?' Lenka's voice was high like a song.

'Yes,' Sammy nodded. 'Music make me happy.'

'And me,' said Lenka, gripping her knees. 'What music you like?'

'I like all music,' said Sammy, smiling. 'Asian music. Sometime I listen English music on the radio. Sometime when no one in the house I dance to English music and wear English clothes.'

Lenka watched her carefully. 'Shush,' said Sammy, pressing a finger to her lips. 'No tell anyone.'

'I hate it,' said Lenka, 'that you cannot be happy. I wish life was different for you.' Lenka wiped her eye with her hand, smudging the black mascara on her eyelid.

'Please don't worry,' replied Sammy. 'Lenka. Please don't cry. I will get certificate and then everything is changed.'

Lenka listened, but all the time she was thinking these were the words of a teenage girl with a hopeless dream. Sammy would not be a British citizen for a long time. Many years. She tried to appear bright for the sake of her friend. She hid behind a wide smile. Inside her mind was racing. This was England. This was the country of freedom. This was the country where women and men were equal. Yet here was Sammy, a prisoner in her home. The system did not help. If Sammy left her husband, she would have to return to Pakistan. She was here on a spouse's visa. No right to be in the UK. Not on her own.

Everyone spoke about integration. But how could women integrate when they were trapped in their kitchens. The more she thought about it the more exasperated she became. Men had the power. She imagined the men in the Home Office in their shirts and ties, probably white Englishmen, with wives and houses painted white like icing. These men didn't live in terraced houses in Burnley. These men didn't live in streets full of pit bulls and dog shit. These men didn't suffer abuse from people who drank to escape their empty lives. When Lenka thought about these things she felt angry. Being a foreigner in England was so difficult. Being a foreign woman in England was more difficult than anyone could ever know. And how would Sammy survive life in Paradise Street? These thoughts tumbled through her brain like loose rocks falling from a cliff.

Nearly all the women were desperate to see the Tower Circus, except Zehnab, who puffed out sounds like a horse and told them they were like a bunch of silly girls. 'Anyone would think none of you seen animals and tricks in your whole life. How long is this thing on?'

The teacher glared and turned away. Zehnab observed Sammy's clothes. 'Wearing them clothes don't make you English,' she said, sarcastically, a smirk fixed on her lips.

'Yeah, and wearing Pakistani clothes don't make you better than other persons,' retorted Sammy.

Lenka stood between the two women. 'No fight. Be quiet Zehnab.' Zehnab folded her arms and muttered something in Urdu.

'What she say?' said Lenka, clearly irritated. 'Tell me Sammy.'

Sammy pursed her lips together. 'She say she tell my family about my clothes.'

'What?' Lenka pointed a finger in Zehnab's fat cheek and pressed her face close. 'You speak about Sammy and I will smack you. Hit.' Lenka shook her fist and pouted. 'Understand!'

Zehnab nodded violently and stepped back. Her eyes bulged and she spoke quickly. 'OK. Just joking. What matter? No one taking any jokes around here?'

'Big joke when you fell off your chair and we all helping you and Sammy looking after you. Oh my God. There's the sun. Zehnab faint again.' As she spoke Lenka pretended to faint and wiped her brow. 'Aww. Someone help me. The sun is too much.' The other women began to erupt in laughter.

'Sorry, sorry.' Zehnab looked at Sammy now, embarrassed. 'Be friends Sammy.'

Sammy nodded and began chanting in Urdu. 'Stop speaking in Urdu,' said Lenka, out of breath. 'Speak English. We go in circus now.'

'Circus?' said Su. 'You all acting like this is circus. I not want to hear you all fight. Fight, fight, fight.'

'OK. OK. We all stop now.' Lenka continued to glare at Zehnab. The woman annoyed her. How she would love to know Urdu so she could understand what she was saying. How she would love to tell her to fuck off in Urdu. 'Freak,' Lenka, muttered under her breath. Zehnab heard her and narrowed her eyes.

CHAPTER THIRTY-SIX

The argument with Zehnab was quickly forgotten. Outside the tower the women formed an orderly line. Lenka stood at the front and Su noticed how men stopped and looked at her. Yet Lenka was indifferent to the attention. There was something about Lenka that people responded to. Perhaps it was the wide smile, the sparkling blue eyes. In a crowd she shone a little brighter than everyone else. Angelic, Su thought. Blonde, like an angel. Something about her embodied goodness. If someone needed help they would go to Lenka; if someone needed advice, it was Lenka they turned to. Charisma was the English word for it. Lenka had charisma. Su liked this word.

The group chatted and chirped about the circus. The acrobats were Hungarian. 'Fly through air like birds,' said Su, her eyes widening and her arms outstretched. 'Men flying with no wings.'

'I surprised,' replied Lenka, 'I like the circus master, but no animals.'

'Yes,' Sammy said in a loud voice, 'Even animals have rights in this country.' There was an uneasy silence as the others thought for a moment.

'Good day,' declared Su, tapping Sammy's arm. Sammy looked around and stammered. 'Yes. Yes.'

The teacher counted the women and sighed because the line had dispersed and separated into clusters. Su felt the wind bite her face, tasted the salt on her lips. She reached into her bag for the beige coat that Bobby had bought. Suddenly she froze. It was on the beach. She stared blankly. 'Sammy, I go beach,' she muttered in a panic. 'Coat on beach.' Before Sammy could speak Su had dodged the cars and trams and was across the road. Sammy watched her hair flying behind her as she descended the steps.

At the bottom of the steps Su paused. The sea was close. Closer than she expected and the waves curled like claws, gripping the heavy sand and stones. Nearby she could hear whistling and a man with a cap led a donkey past her. He smiled briefly and tugged the animal hard. Fairground music rose and fell in the distance. Quickly she scanned the beach for her coat, but there was no sign. All she could see was a mix of swelling black water and foamy white froth slapping the shore.

She breathed in the cold air and was about to turn away when she heard something else. A faint cry, so faint, she wondered if it was something far off. But then she saw a tiny flash of red being carried in the waves. An arm outstretched. She called out. She felt the freezing water circling her legs, filling her pumps. She heard the scream of a small boy, his face like a torch light in the water. Within seconds she was wading deeper and deeper. The boy's arm reached out and she thrashed through the swirling water all the time calling, 'Chan ca chwy hi kihun.' The salty water filled her mouth. 'I will help you,' she shouted in Thai, swallowing the black sea.

For several minutes she shouted and gulped the water, felt her body lifting higher and higher. The boy had gone. She thought about Tai, about the tsunami children. She let the sea take her. Then she thought about Bobby, but it was too late because everything was dark. This was what dying felt like. Like warmed ice she felt herself melting into the sea.

* * *

Sammy couldn't explain the chill that rolled down her spine, like cold water tipping on jagged rock. She shuddered and found herself crossing the road, heard the teacher shouting for her to come back. Where was Su? First she saw a flash of white, then something bobbing on the waves. In seconds Sammy was in the water. She screamed and shrieked. She swam out and caught Su's hair and smacked her bloated cheeks. The others dashed down the steps and cried. The teacher pulled Su onto the shore and pounded her chest. Water vomited from her lips. A small spurt but it was enough and Su coughed the death water away and bolted upright. No one spoke. Everyone knelt on the sand and covered their faces.

Eventually the teacher wrapped Lenka's coat around Su. 'What happened?' she whispered. 'What were you doing?' Su thought about the boy in the water. She told no one and listened vacantly to the waves whooshing and the approaching sirens. 'Accident,' she said, after a while. She remembered the boy now. It was the same boy that she had seen on Patong Beach, a bucket in his hand, kissing the nose of a flapping fish.

She wondered if she was meant to die that day, whether that had been her destiny. The ghost boy had come for her. She said this to Bobby, but he grimaced and cursed under his breath. 'Don't be ridiculous,' he said. 'The dead can't hurt you.' He made her tomato soup and told her to drink. But all the time he watched her carefully. Su was pale as a dead woman and all this talk of ghosts had scared him.

Chapter Thirty-seven

Poetry carried Sammy far away to many places. It amazed her that one word could evoke a memory, a thought, a feeling. She liked the rhythm of sounds and the teacher told her she was a born writer. Lenka glared because she had chosen to write, but the words escaped her. For Sammy writing was not a conscious choice. The words chose her. Often, when she least expected it, a word and then a line would appear and something she could not define compelled her to write. Sometimes, while she was sleeping, odd words called to her and she would wake up, scribble them down, surprising herself, because the voice that spoke to her was English. Always English.

The day the teacher saw the poem called 'ME', she gasped and beamed a wide smile.

> **I am East and West**
> **Two countries**
> **Two people**
>
> **Like the moon**
> **Two halves**
> **Dark and white**
>
> **Divided like my own country**
> **Sometimes there is war**
> **Sometimes peace.**

A rickety printer chewed and spat out Sammy's words. Typical, thought Sammy. Even the printer tried to sabotage her poem. Once Suriya had found a notebook of her poetry and tore each page out, telling her, 'So you think you are like famous writer? Tcha! This is why no house work ever done and house is like a fat pigsty.' After this Sammy stayed silent and hid her best poems in her husband's wedding shoes.

Soon a copy of 'ME' was pinned on the wall next to a picture of famous landmarks. As the teacher read the words, the other students clapped and cheered. But Lenka was still writing. She was thinking of poems about war. She thought of Kamil. And she wrote a poem about a shoe.

Su was staring at the map of Thailand thinking about Mai. Since the trip to Blackpool she had thought more and more about her own country. 'I want go Thailand,' she said to Bobby that night. 'Next year,' he told her, patting her head. 'Maybe next year.' Su glared at her husband and lowered her eyes. It was times like these when she longed to be independent and have her own money. She went to bed and wrote a letter to Mai.

'I want to visit you,' she wrote, pressing the pen down hard. 'Want to see you and kids and the sun.' She drew a picture of a sun, with long rays that cut and sliced through her words. 'Sometime life too hard,' she continued. She bit the pen between her teeth and heard the plastic case crack. A splinter of plastic fell to the floor. She stopped writing and clenched the paper in her fist. She felt angry with herself. Here she was thinking about the past. What would Mai think? Life in England was not simple. No, she thought. She would make something of her miserable life and finish her English qualification. She would make Mai proud. Maybe she would go to college. Someone had come from the college and talked about courses. In England women did important jobs. She wanted a responsible job and dreamt of working in the town library, helping customers and reading

English books. That night she dreamt she was in a beautiful library with green carpet and velvet seats and a ceiling covered in plaster roses. There were no customers and as she locked the doors something magical happened. The books came alive, the pages flapped and the books danced and waved in the air. Su chased the books down the aisles and the pages fluttered and swooped and teased her. Soon all she could hear was the sound of crisp pages opening and turning, like the wings of paper birds. Paper birds in a paper paradise.

CHAPTER THIRTY-EIGHT

Every morning Bobby smoked in the yard, next to a mouldy urn, crammed with crushed cigarette stubs. Smoke twisted up through the open bathroom window as Su brushed her teeth. Just 7am. Before she reached the kitchen Bobby had gone, slamming the door behind him. She switched on the television and listened to the news, debating whether to have breakfast and then what to have for it. Finally she decided. There was some fresh mango in the fridge and slowly Su poured yogurt on top. She sat with the bowl of mango on her knee, eating with a teaspoon, prodding the chunks, not really feeling fully awake. On breakfast television there were actors talking about movies she had never heard of. All this TV talk was like another world, another language to be discovered and understood.

Usually they watched sport, her and Bobby. Now she had taken to knitting because there was a wool stall on the market. Also, knitting reminded her of Thailand, of lazy days in the garden, making toys and woollen dolls. She saw the knitting on the sofa and checked her efforts. Coloured stripes in red and blue and green. She knitted the scarf for Lenka. Woven with love and tears. They were knitted together, her Lenka and Sammy. Bound by thread. She wrapped the wool around her fingers and tugged the rectangle into shape. Tap, tap, tap went the needles. Click. Click. Click. Knit one. Pearl one. Drop one. Her finger slipped. A shriek and a fierce knocking caused the row to slide off the needle.

Su swore. Who would be banging on the door at this time?

On the path was parked an orange pram with a bent umbrella that slanted over a screaming baby. Beside the pram stood a girl of about twenty, wearing a denim skirt, her swollen ankles brimming over high-heeled shoes. 'Is he in?' she asked, in a low voice, swilling chewing gum around with her tongue. Su looked at the baby. Large cheeks that were fleshy pink and mottled with a raised rash. Tufts of blonde hair stood on end and the chubby fingers clutched a split rubber dummy. 'Well, have you finished looking, or what?' sneered the girl. 'Jesus, where's he dragged you from?' She looked Su up and down. Su stood silent. The girl barged past.

'No,' mumbled Su. 'Go out of my house, please.'

The girl stood in the sitting room and folded her arms. Su hovered in the doorway and observed the baby. 'You look for Bobby?' she called nervously.

'I'll wait,' said the girl, falling back on the sofa. Su heard the sound of a spring snap and clang. 'I need money. Don't mind me. I'll wait.'

Su wheeled the pram in. 'Bobby be a long time,' she said, hoping the girl would leave. But the girl didn't reply and began texting on her phone. Su noticed a ring in her nose, a tattoo on her hand. Some kind of flower and winding leaves that wrapped around her wrist like a chain. 'What you looking at?'

'Nothing,' Su stammered. 'What your name?'

'Chelsea.' The girl grimaced.

Su looked confused. 'Like the place. Like London,' explained the girl, irritated. 'You understand English? Oh for Christ's sake Paris, stop wailing. I've had enough.' Chelsea produced a cigarette and began to smoke.

'Me Su. Me hold baby?'

The girl nodded. 'If you want. Do what you want. I'm not going till Bobby gives me money.'

Su unclipped the buckle across the baby's chest and lifted her in the air. The fat legs dangled like cloth. The baby scrunched her face up and let out a howl.

'Oh, for fuck's sake. Don't hold her like that. Walk around with her, or something.' The girl tutted and checked her watch. Su clutched the baby tightly and began to bounce her on her knee.

'I can't fucking feed her. Not on what the social gives me. Understand?'

Su nodded. So this was Bobby's baby. Chelsea looked around. 'Any cans? It looks like the bailiffs have been in. What the fuck 'appened in 'ere?'

Immediately, Su knew what this meant, but she pretended not to understand. Instead she smiled. 'How much you need?'

The girl looked up and smirked. 'What you got? Anyone would think you don't want me 'ere.' She stood up.

'I got no money,' said Su in a panic. 'No money.'

The girl saw her open bag. 'You sure about that?'

'OK, maybe ten pound,' stuttered Su.

'That'll do for now,' said Chelsea, holding out her hand. Su unfolded the crisp note.

'I tell you what, love. You keep Paris for a while.' Chelsea clawed the note away. 'I'm sick of waiting. It's about time he did a bit of babysitting. Useless shit.'

Su shouted in Thai. The baby shouted too, but the girl with the nose ring and the tattoo staggered down the road and was joined by a man in an army jacket and a dog with a studded collar. The baby gurgled and dribbled on Su's hair. An old woman across the road stopped and stared. 'I'll be back later,' shouted Chelsea. Su shook her head. The baby gripped her hair and pulled and she unclasped the locked little fingers. 'Don't worry, baby.' The baby pinched her cheek. The baby looked like Bobby.

CHAPTER THIRTY-NINE

Blood swirled in the basin and dripped down the white tiles. This time, as the razor sliced her wrist, the blood spurted and Sammy panicked. Ehsan stood outside the bathroom demanding to come in. When there was no response he banged with his fist. 'Samina. Let me in!'

'Just a minute,' she called, tying a flannel around her wrist, watching the red stain spread. Sammy gritted her teeth. The water pumping hard from the tap turned pink. The blade rested on a bar of green soap splattered with droplets of red. Frantically she swilled the soap, wiped the tiles with her hand, hid the blade in her pocket. Blood smeared and smudged on the walls. She felt weak, washed away. Blood and hair spinning faster and faster. Her breathing was rapid and she flushed the toilet to mask the sound. Her wrist was burning hot and red.

'Now, Samina!.' Ehsan's voice sounded urgent. 'What the hell are you doing in there?'

'Toilet,' she shouted in a confused voice, feeling as though she might pass out. She placed her lips over the trumpeting tap and drank some water. In the mirror she saw her eyes sunken and small. Ehsan banged hard. 'You are my wife. Open this door now.' Slowly she nudged the bolt back.

Ehsan rushed towards her. 'What are you doing in here?'

'Nothing.' Sammy lowered her eyes.

Ehsan turned and locked the door. 'Take your clothes off.'

Sammy looked at him. His eyes flared and he stood with one hand on the wall.

She glared. 'You heard me. Take your clothes off, now. It's been three weeks. All the time you hiding in the bathroom, like you avoiding me, or something.'

'No,' said Sammy. 'You are wrong.'

Ehsan pressed her to the wall. 'You are saying I am wrong? Everyone is out.' Slowly he began to lift her robe, sliding his hands up her leg, under her pants. His finger was inside her and she called out, pushed his chest.

'No, Ehsan. No. I tired.'

Ehsan laughed. 'Yeah. Always tired. I don't care if you tired. You are my wife.'

She felt his breath, hot and warm in her ear. He bit her neck, her lip. He gripped her hard. Sammy began to sob. 'No. Get off me. Get off.' She clawed at his chest, his face and Ehsan threw his head back in shock.

'Fuck! What's wrong with you? He punched the wall, but then he stopped. His tee shirt was stained bright red. He looked down, puzzled and then he saw the blood seeping from Sammy's wrist.

'What the fuck have you done? What the fuck have you done?' Ehsan's voice was shrill and high and echoed around the room. He clutched her wrist and saw the gaping cut, blood oozing out. 'What is this?'

'Sorry. Sorry. I sorry.'

Sammy pulled her wrist away, fell to the floor and continued to cry. Ehsan knelt down beside her.

He shook his head and looked down at the wound. 'You did this? I don't understand. How?'

Sammy bowed her head and stared at the floor.

'You better answer me!'

'I don't know. Razor.'

Ehsan held his hand to his mouth. 'Fuck! Is your life so bad?

Am I so bad?' He took her arms and began to shake her. 'You trying to punish me? You trying to punish this family?'

'No. No.'

He disappeared for a moment and returned with a roll of bandage and some small scissors. He sat on the bath and wound the bandage round. Neither of them spoke. When it was knotted tight he led her to the bedroom. 'Lie on the bed,' he said.

Sammy did as he asked. She lay absolutely still, staring at the ceiling.

'You are afraid of me,' her husband shrieked, throwing his hands above his head. 'My God. What do you think I am going to do? What monster do you think I am?'

Sammy lay on the bed and didn't move. She didn't look at her husband. She heard the sound of an angry engine roar down the road. What would happen now?

CHAPTER FORTY

One drunken night with twenty-year-old Chelsea Dobbs had cost Bobby hundreds of pounds and many sleepless nights. She had sworn the baby was his, from the beginning. She had also sworn she wouldn't drink through her pregnancy, or smoke, but had broken every rule in the book. Tied to the pram there was also a Rottweiler dog, called Sid. Chelsea was convinced the dog was gentle. Gentle as a child killer, Bobby thought to himself. He called the creature Sid Vicious, but Chelsea had never heard of the rocker with that name and never got the joke. She was a Burnley girl, had never been as far as Manchester and lived her little life within the Burnley mile. She had notions of going to Chelsea, pretended she had been there to wild parties with the stars. Sometimes she claimed she had been conceived in Chelsea and that's where she'd gained her name. Paris was named after Paris Hilton because Chelsea wanted a kid who'd go far.

From the gate Bobby heard the sound of a baby screaming and was about to turn and run, when Su spotted him through the window. 'Baby!' shouted Su, holding the girl in the air. She ran to the door and thrust the baby in his face. He turned white, looked uncertain.

'Oh God! Where is the mother? Cheeky cow, coming here.'

'Gone,' replied Su, shrugging her shoulders. 'Nasty. Nasty girl. Want money. Money, money, money.'

Bobby sighed a heavy sigh. ' Shit! This is a nightmare.' He

handed the baby back to Su. The smell of sick mingled with milk made him heave. Women coped better with these things.

'When did this happen?'

'Morning time. She come in house. Leave baby.' Su thought for a moment and lowered her voice. 'What you doing with young girl, Bobby?' She wanted to say more, but knew Bobby would react badly.

Bobby paced up and down, covered his face with his hands. 'I was drunk. She was drunk.' Briefly he saw himself waking up to find Chelsea Dobbs leaning over him in a tight PVC basque, her enormous breasts spilling over his face. Lipstick smudged down her chin and was streaked on the pillowcase. He remembered nothing of the night before. He tried to pay her to keep quiet, but before he knew it, the whole of Burnley had labelled him a dirty old man, including David. As he gained one child, he lost another. David grimaced. 'Dad. You're pathetic. Get a grip. What are you doing with your life?' David had stormed out of the house, his face filled with disappointment. There had been many women. David's mother had finally left after finding an earring in her bed. Bobby denied it all. But sometimes the shame of it all sent him cold and in his dreams the women from his past appeared toothless, their hair falling out in large clumps. They were ugly, grotesque creatures. Chelsea straddled him and when he came inside her she laughed like a madwoman. As her mouth opened her tongue grew like a snake, wrapping around his neck and tightening until he could hardly breathe. He shivered and jolted.

'You always drunk!' Su grumbled.

She stormed into the kitchen, taking the baby with her. Finally she sat at the kitchen table. Bobby stood by the window looking a little lost. 'What we do?' wailed Su.

'Let me think,' said Bobby in an irritated voice. 'This is all we need, some bleeding kid.'

The baby gripped Su's hand. 'Ah, baby hold my hand.'

Bobby was not amused. 'Bleeding Paris. What kind of a name is that?'

'Eiffel Tower,' said Su.

Bobby smiled. 'I'll have to go and find the mother. Probably pissed in the pub.'

'Dog and Duck,' said Su.

'Aye.'

'Nice baby.'

'Mmm.'

Bobby barely looked at the child. If he thought about the child his blood boiled. The mother was unfit. And so he detached himself. Sometimes he imagined the baby torn to shreds in the mouth of a giant dog, her body limp as a rag doll. Other times he imagined the baby in an empty council flat, surrounded by drugs and needles and peeling paint. These were the scenarios you read about in the newspapers. Once Chelsea had told him she was going on holiday and he imagined the baby screaming in her cot, home alone. It was easier to pretend she didn't exist, but David didn't agree. Sometimes David gave Chelsea money. Everyone gave Chelsea money. She was a thieving, conniving bitch.

As he was thinking these things the baby was making happy noises, smiling to herself. He looked at the bright blue eyes of the little girl. Like pools of water. In her eyes he saw a reflection of himself. For a moment he felt a pang in his chest. This couldn't happen. Chelsea Dobbs would ruin his life.

CHAPTER FORTY-ONE

Clothes lay crumpled on the floor as Su heaved the empty drawer onto the bed. First she lined it with clean towels and then she laid baby Paris inside. In a Mickey Mouse bag under the pram she found a clean nappy and a bottle of milk. The baby was tired and her eyes blinked and opened again. Su stroked her head and put the bottle to her mouth. The baby sucked a little and then closed her eyes. This was what it felt like to be a mother. Su held the fat little hand and sang a song in Thai.

Bobby watched her from the doorway. Su was a good person and for a fleeting moment he felt an overwhelming urge to hold her, even tell her he loved her. Instead he picked up his coat and left, determined to find Chelsea Dobbs.

In the quiet bedroom Su listened to the gentle breathing of the child. She lay down beside the makeshift cot, heard the baby thrash and move. Her eyelashes were long and damp, her cheeks pink and warm. Perfect. Children were always so perfect. If only life was so perfect. Mothers too. She thought of Chelsea and then her own mother, a feisty little woman, who laughed and cried in equal measure. On the day of the tsunami her mother had gone shopping for mango. She had followed the same route, at the same time, to the same market stall. Before she had left her mother had said the strangest thing. The kind of thing someone might say knowing they might die. Only she couldn't have known this. 'Be happy, Malee. Even when life denies you things, be happy.'

Su had nodded a reassuring smile, but her mother saw beyond this and knew that every day Su craved a child, that this yearning consumed her soul. Every night her mother lit a candle and prayed that Su might be blessed with a child. But always the flame flickered for a moment and then was extinguished by an invisible breath in the air. On that last day she gripped Su's hand and told her that she loved her very much. 'Remember you have people who love you. So many people.' Su kissed her hand. 'You are very wise,' she told her. Her mother had laughed and ruffled her hair. 'Always the joker. Really you are thinking, stop making all this fuss.' That was the last time she saw her. Carried away by the black water, her mother's body was never found. For days Su had waited for the sea to bring her back, but the sea kept her. Su saw a spirit doctor who told her the woman would be transformed, become a beautiful pearl. One day she would be plucked from a foreign sea and return to the land.

Whenever Su thought of her mother she thought of stories, of Thai legends whispered in the dead of night. One day she was late from school and her mother told her that Mae Nak, the ghost girl would find her. Su was never late again. In Bangkok she knew there was a shrine dedicated to the ghost. They say that Nak was married to a man who went to war. While her husband was away she died in childbirth, but her love for her husband was so strong that she retained her human form. When her husband returned the local villagers warned him his wife had died, but he did not believe them. One day Nak dropped a lemon and it rolled under the little Thai house. Quickly she extended her arm and retrieved the lemon, not knowing that her husband had seen her. Realising that she was a ghost her husband fled. Angry Nak began to kill the local villagers and was eventually caught by a brave monk and confined in a jar. The monk threw the jar in the river but it was caught soon after and Nak was freed by two fishermen. It was only after a monk promised Nak that she would be reunited with her husband in another life that she agreed to stop killing.

Like all girls Su feared the ghost Nak. Su imagined loving someone so much that you could never die. She thought of Tai. Their love had been pure, everlasting. She loved him even now, in death. Sometimes she pictured him standing by the bed, surrounded by light. He was such a good man. If only she could say the same about Bobby. She had thought him a simple man, but now she wondered if she knew him at all. Through the open window drifted the smell of fire. She closed the window shut and in the street beyond saw a car, flames rising through the sunroof. Another car burnt out. Ashes scattered. Youths running wild. Bobby had gone to find Chelsea and she felt worried. Burnley was not a safe place.

CHAPTER FORTY-TWO

Thick, red blood oozed from her nostril as he danced and stamped on her hair. She gulped and wailed, then quietly wept, felt the blood filling her mouth. With her broken nails she clawed and scratched at the shoe, then the wooden floor. French polish, or wax, she wasn't sure, but the oily pungent smell mixed with the blood in her nose made her retch. A splinter of wood gouged into her fingernail and she yelped, more aware of the sting in her middle finger than the shoe pounding her head. He rested the glinting kitchen knife against her throat and peeled her clothes like an apple. Then he told her to sit up and close her eyes. From behind he pulled her hair hard. She saw the shadow of the knife swipe over her head in an arc. She was about to cry out when she heard the knife slice through the air. Quickly, Kamil let go of her. She turned. First she saw his shiny shoes. In his hand he waved a clump of her hair. She closed her eyes, afraid there would be more. Nothing. She opened her eyes. He waited until he knew she was looking and then Kamil took the hair and placed it on a plate. He took a match and watched her reaction as the fire whooshed and ate the hair. Lenka covered her breasts. Kamil smiled. 'Everything is mine,' he said. 'Everything.' And then he polished his shoes.

After the dream Lenka woke to find the pillow soaked in blood. Another nose bleed. In the mirror she saw her face smeared red, black blood clogged in one nostril. She smoothed her hair against her head. It had taken a year to grow back. She changed the sheets. For a moment she was sure she could smell shoe polish. She shuddered and went back to bed. Always, she would belong to Kamil. She pressed her arm and with her index finger traced the indentations and welts in her skin. The biggest scar had folded shut, the skin tight as a bud, but she could still feel the outline of the letter K. Like meat he branded her, boiled her in hot water. It was to make her pure, he said. The more she bled, the more Kamil rewarded her with kisses. She tried to run, but always he found her. Whisky was his undoing.

For ten years she had lived like this. Unending cries, broken bones, hiding behind white makeup, her body stiffening, whenever he came near. There had been no one else. He owned her. Even now, he occupied the corridors of her brain. He had held her flesh, her blood, her hair. She was the rotting apple. Damaged at the core. Part of her was dead, something at the centre of her being, something difficult to define in words. She loved Anna, but never would she love another man.

Being in bed alone was when she was most terrified. In bed she never felt safe. The darkness crept over her and every noise was amplified. Tonight she could hear the Bengali boys smashing bottles in the street, the sound of engines racing up and down the ramp. Two, maybe three cars screeched in unison and the boys laughed. The boys were young. They were the same ones who hung around the language centre, sometimes drinking and smoking, selling drugs. Everyone knew there were drugs but no one was brave enough, or cared enough, to tell. Sometimes the police came, but the boys disappeared down the alleyways, the dirty backstreets, with the same skill as the rats that lived there.

She heard a bin tip over nearby and pulled the quilt tight. The scar on her arm now itched because she had been rubbing too hard. She thought of Sammy, her wrists raw and bare. She was a young girl, the same age as her when she met Kamil. Already Sammy was talking of suicide. Lenka had thought of suicide once.

The idea had possessed her after Anna was born. But she had never told anyone.

She remembered Anna, pure and white in her cot, the baby's chest rising and falling in a peaceful rhythm of sleep. She watched her for a while, kissed her hand and spoke to her in a soothing whisper, like mothers do. But Kamil was suddenly in the doorway, calling her, his body swaggering, a bottle in his hand. She recalled a red and black shirt, unbuttoned, the sleeves rolled up to his elbows, a thread hanging loose. He pulled her by the hand to the bedroom. She had said 'no' at first and he slapped her cheek hard. She lay on the bed naked, Kamil next to her, fully dressed in his black boots. He swigged the drink and pinched her breasts. When she protested he plunged the cold bottle inside her.

The next day he kissed his wife on the head and told her she was the most precious woman in the world. Then he kissed the baby girl too and tears flooded his eyes. 'She is perfect, Lenka. I never knew we could create something so perfect.' When Kamil had gone Lenka sat on the bed, clutched her womb and began to cry. Lenka prayed to God, asked him for a sign. What should she do? In the next bedroom she stood over the cot and watched the baby sleeping.

Lenka clutched a pillow to her chest and buried her wet face in the cotton cover. Downstairs there were boxes of painkillers. Many boxes. The birth had been a difficult one and Lenka had torn so badly she needed ten stitches. There were enough painkillers to end it all. She ran downstairs and found the tablets in a drawer amongst disused keys and foreign coins. One by one she flicked them into a bowl. She took the bowl back to the bedroom and knelt before the window. Clutching the crucifix around her neck she begged God for forgiveness. This was against everything she believed in, but there was no choice. Nowhere to run. She heard the sheets rustle in the cot and the baby turned. Lenka breathed hard. The pillow was in her hand. Slowly she brought the pillow down onto the baby's face. The baby didn't murmur. She gulped and pushed down. A shriek and the baby was awake. Lenka felt the little body jolt. She tore the pillow away. Anna's face was pink, contorted, her lips blue. 'Oh my God, Oh my God,' wailed Lenka. 'God forgive me. God forgive me.' She held the baby in the air and slapped her face. The baby screamed and Lenka held her to her chest. 'I'll never leave you,' she said. 'I promise I'll never leave you.'

That night she made her husband a chocolate cake and traditional Polish food. He kissed her hand and smiled. And for a brief moment love flickered in his eyes.

* * *

Someone was knocking on the door. It was a fierce knock and the sound reverberated around the house. Lenka checked the clock beside her bed. Just 2am. She felt her body tighten and listened. Dreams of the past had made her sweat and her nightdress clung to her body. The knocking continued. Maybe it was the wind. She closed her eyes but the knocking was now louder and a man was shouting. Kamil! Anna was calling her and Lenka ran to the girl's room. 'Who is it Mummy? Who is it?' Lenka smiled but her voice trembled. 'Don't worry. Just go back to sleep.' There were many voices now, many raised voices. Lenka looked outside and saw at least twenty people, all pointing up at the window, including Su.

Down she ran and opened the door. Bobby was standing in front of her, flustered, his eyes blinking rapidly. 'Next door is on fire. You better come out, just in case. Jesus, I've been knocking for ten minutes.'

'Sorry, sorry.' Quickly she ran and dragged Anna from her bed. They took their coats and stood with the other neighbours across the road, watching flames roar through the front window of number 26.

'What happened?' said Lenka. 'What happened?'

George, the owner of the house, sat slumped on the kerb. 'He was making chips,' someone said. The fire brigade arrived and wrapped the old man in a blanket. Lenka cuddled him, but saw there was no light in his eyes.

'He's lost the plot,' said Bobby. 'I think he needs help. Poor old sod.'

George observed the crowd of people around him. The smell of fire was strong and Su and Lenka coughed.

'Making chips at 2am,' said Bobby. 'Who makes chips at bloody two o'clock in the morning? I think he's got Alzheimer's. Everyone's thought it for ages.'

'What is that?' Lenka asked, stroking Anna's head. The child was crying, begging to go back to bed. And the smell of fire made her throat sore.

Bobby looked serious. 'It's when you forget everything, even people. My mother had it.'

Lenka nodded. She had never heard of a disease that made people forget everything. She was thinking about Kamil. She would love to paint him out of her life, to forget the past. But then she looked at the old man, bent over, clutching his belly, his braces hanging low. George was arguing with the ambulance man. He didn't want to go to hospital. 'He can stay with me,' Su said, sensing the distress in the old man's voice. But the ambulance crew shook their heads. They led him away. The women cried. They never saw him again.

CHAPTER FORTY-THREE

It was some hours before Lenka was able to enter her house. She sat in Su's sitting room drinking green tea, eating sugar-coated biscuits. Anna was asleep in Su's bed and Bobby smoked in the garden. Su sipped the tea slowly and saw Lenka pause and bite her lip. 'You OK, Lenka?'

Lenka raised her eyes. 'Remember when you tell my fortune.'

Su nodded and gulped the tea down. 'I know.'

Lenka smiled briefly and began to cry. 'I was thinking about my life tonight, about bad things ...'

'No cry,' said Su, shifting along the sofa so that their knees touched.

'Now, I feel guilty,' whimpered Lenka. 'Guilty for old man.'

The two women sat in silence for a long time. 'Horrible to be old,' said Lenka, her voice soft and tired. 'In this country no one care when you old. In Poland when you are old everyone look after you.'

Lenka thought about the house she grew up in. It was a tall house, filled with children, old grandmothers and relatives, who slept in every room. Together they told stories round the fire, watched the logs crackle and spit. Sometimes she watched the ashes flying like blackbirds and it was then she thought about being free and having a room of her own. Not sharing with her sisters, her brothers, who snored and left mice under her pillow because they knew this made Lenka angry. All the family said

Lenka was as calm as still water on a summer day. Only the sight of a little mouse could send her crazy, turn her eyes red and wild.

Death also made her angry. When her grandmother was dying she dabbed water on the old woman's lips with a little wooden stick and prayed she would not die. The old woman turned yellow as a sunflower, her belly was swollen and full. Lenka wrote a story about a sunflower that never died. Flowers sometimes died and came back again. She wondered if her grandmother would come back, just like a flower. And then her mother told her sunflowers only bloom once. That was the end of the story. Her grandmother was gone. God didn't listen.

'Always I have bad dreams,' said Lenka, her hands shaking, as she placed the cup on the table. She could smell paint and noticed the walls were gleaming white and clean.

'Me have bad dreams,' said Su, holding Lenka's hand. 'About big wave. Now I no think about these bad things. Look after baby. You must look after your family. Forget the past.'

'I try,' said Lenka. 'Sometimes I am busy and I forget, but at night I think Kamil will kill me.'

Su said nothing. The magnitude of what Lenka was saying suddenly struck her. Lenka was afraid for her life. Eventually, Su spoke. 'In England you are safe.' She uttered each syllable carefully, stressing her words with a hard precision that sounded almost unnatural, inhuman.

'No,' said Lenka, her eyes sparking. 'England is not this dream place. Think about it, Su. I am never safe, or Anna. I pray I am safe. This is all I can do.'

'If you feel not safe,' said Su quietly, 'come here and I help you.'

Lenka forced a smile. 'At Anna's school there is a man, watching children, at the gate.'

Su raised her hand to her mouth. 'Your husband.'

'I don't know. I have letter. The man is big with black hair. I am afraid Kamil will find us. Always I am hiding. Even in England with all these police and governments and rules I am not free.'

Lenka clasped her hands and picked the skin from around her nails. 'Don't worry,' said Su. 'School will look after Anna.'

There was silence. Lenka said nothing. At the window there were no curtains and the street lamp outside flickered and dimmed.

'Light broken,' said Su.

But Lenka stared into the darkness. She saw the silhouettes of people walking past and she shuddered. Always she felt as though she was being watched.

'Need curtains,' said Su. 'Come in kitchen.'

For many hours they talked in the little kitchen. They talked about family, about foreign places. Lenka had no money. She wanted to visit Poland. It was not possible. In her home village, her mother showed everyone photos of her beautiful daughter and granddaughter. The girl would get an English education and this made the family proud. Lenka was a student at an English college. One day her mother was convinced her daughter's name would be on the lips of everyone. She was a poet, a storyteller, just like her mother and her grandmother before her. She had never seen the scars that trickled along her daughter's body like red rivers. For many years she hadn't touched the bent bones in her back, or stroked her daughter's golden hair. Hair made a woman. Lenka felt the tiny space on her head, where the hair had been pulled from the root. She winced. The bare patch was hardly visible, but she knew it was there.

CHAPTER FORTY-FOUR

As the sun rose, Lenka felt comforted by the light and tugged Anna awake. Together they walked up the street in pyjamas, slippers and coats, like refugees in a war. At number 26, wooden boards were nailed to the windows and the creamy white stone was peppered with soot. In the breeze the smell of fire whirled in the air and Lenka's throat felt tight. When she looked at Anna's eyes she saw they were ringed red. Anna let go of her mother's hand to wipe grit from her eye. Lenka felt exhausted. Up the stairs they crawled, Anna pushing her mother from behind. They lay on the double bed, arms linked and within moments the world snapped shut.

Bobby could not sleep. Su paced up and down the bedroom bouncing Paris on her hip and from the spare room he could hear the child screaming. Paris was teething and had bitten through the dummy. So hard that the dummy leaked saliva and it turned his stomach. For a moment he wondered if the child was screaming for her mother. But he doubted it.

At the Dog and Duck no one had seen Chelsea Dobbs. He had stayed at the pub for a while, drunk a few pints of bitter, convinced Chelsea would appear. Eventually, he called at the flat she shared with a skinny man called Gary, but there were no lights. Outside the flat he saw a burst bin liner flooded with maggots, bottles spinning on the balcony. The kitchen window was blocked out by a piece of stained fabric with just a tiny gap beneath. He bent down and peered through the slit of light. It was then he noticed how dirty everything seemed. A dead fly on the windowsill, the remains of a moth, a sweet wrapper on a greasy tile. The flat was filthy. Chelsea Dobbs was filthy. He wondered how he had come to find himself with a fat, dirty, young girl like that. It made his skin crawl. He turned to walk back and felt something soft under his shoe. Dog shit. The flats stunk of urine, dog shit and beer. At the bottom of the stairwell he wiped his shoe on a patch of dry grass. Here, even the grass was smattered with glass and he went home cursing. He rushed home cursing the world, the youth of today. And then he cursed himself. He had been such a fool.

Despite some warm milk the baby would not stop crying. 'We have to call someone,' said Bobby. 'She can't stay here, love.' He touched Su's arm, but she pulled away, a look of disgust on her face.

'No,' she cried. 'Baby stay.'

Bobby pulled his trousers on. 'I am too old for this, Su. Too old for a baby.'

Su glared. 'You old! I not old.'

Bobby reached for his coat. 'Thanks a lot. And you have college today. What about college?'

Su placed her finger in the baby's mouth and the baby bit hard. 'Teeth,' said Su. 'I take Paris college and you go work.'

'No,' said Bobby, wagging his finger. 'I will find her mother. She needs her mother!'

Su snarled and hissed, said something in Thai. She noticed his tone as he spoke about the baby's mother. It was so unfair that Chelsea had been blessed with a child. She was a child herself. Bobby rolled his eyes. 'This is a fucking nightmare.'

'No swear,' said Su, walking away from him.

Bobby rubbed his eyes. They were still stinging from last night's fire. This marriage was not what he expected. The dream of a Thai wife had been extinguished. The more English Su learnt, the more she argued and defied him. Last night she had called him a 'silly man'. English classes were turning the little Thai woman into a fierce beast with a sharp tongue. Every day they argued. Every day she said 'no'. Before he left the house he told her, 'These English classes have changed you.' Su slapped his back. 'You want a woman who do as you say, yes?' Bobby flared red. 'Respect,' he said.

'Respect. Respect, respect,' repeated Su. 'Where my respect? You always drinking. Never home. Dinner in bin. You sleep on sofa, on floor. Sick on my shoe.'

Bobby raised his voice. 'I'm going.'

'Best shoe,' said Su.

'It was an accident!' Bobby boomed.

'No accident. You pissed.'

'Now who's swearing.'

Su laughed. 'Shut up and go out,' she said. 'I have baby to look after. You go getting pissed again.'

Bobby chuckled and kissed her nose.

'Hey!' said Su, swatting him as if he were a fly. 'I have to look after baby.'

She grumbled to herself and checked the time. She went to the language centre smiling. Inside the centre the staff played with the baby. 'Whose baby?' they asked. 'I look after,' replied Su, proudly. When Sammy came she tickled the baby's belly and stroked her feet. 'Cute baby,' she said. 'I like baby.' Su was enjoying the attention, the responsibility.

At the language centre there was a crèche and the manager led Su into a small classroom with two women and a tub of building blocks. The room was light and airy and a toddler stumbled past with a pram and a doll with wiry hair. Su kissed Paris on the head and the baby smiled briefly as the Thai woman sat her on the floor. But as she walked towards the door the baby began to cry and extended her arms. Su was pleased. She rushed back and held her tight. 'Back later,' she told the baby. 'Su back later.'

In the lesson Su felt distracted. The baby was on her mind. She was thinking about baby food. Bananas. Nappies. Milk. These were the things she needed. And potato. She reached for her bag and emptied her purse on the table. There was enough money to go to town on the bus. She remembered seeing an Englishwoman with a pram on the bus. Suddenly she remembered the dummy. Sammy watched Su fumbling in her bag, heard the sound of change clanging on the table. 'Shush,' said Sammy. 'Teacher watch you.'

They watched a video about holidays. Some people went to Blackpool on holiday, but Su did not want to go there again. The teacher told them to write things down. Su began to write, but found herself writing a letter to Mai.

Dear Mai

I so happy. I look after new baby. Going shopping in England is great and I go on big bus all the time.

Some English people is nice and help me. I neeting scarves for peoples I love.

Bobby buy me bag with birds and sparkling. So nice. I hope you is happy and kids.

Me so nervous. Exam in few weeks. Be lucky, sista.

Su xxx

Su covered the letter with her hand. All this talk of holidays made her yearn for Thailand. She remembered feeding her nieces and nephews mashed-up banana, sometimes carrot. Being a mother came naturally to her and she hoped Chelsea would not come back for a long time.

Inside she felt disappointed. Bobby had sent the last letter to

Mai, but her sister had not replied. Su thought about Mai and imagined her cooking, in a frilly apron with apples on the pockets. Her writing was not good. Perhaps this was why Mai had not been in touch. Mai was ashamed of her English. Reading and writing were so important in this life. For Su reading English was becoming easier. Writing was more difficult. Spelling was impossible. And then there were words that sounded different to how they looked. Like 'centre'. In English there were many rules and sometimes no rules. Even the teacher couldn't explain everything. Su liked the challenge that English presented. She borrowed a book by a man called William. He was famous. But the words made no sense. What kind of English was this? It was old English, Bobby said. No one spoke like that any more. Su read the words aloud. Like a song. Sometimes there were rhymes.

It is the east, and Juliet is the sun.
Arise, fair sun, and kill the envious moon.

Occasionally Su said the words out loud. *Romeo and Juliet* was a play about love and Su wondered about their story. She asked Bobby and to her amazement he had heard of this William. 'There's a balcony,' in this play he told his wife. Su listened attentively. 'And a rose.' Su nodded, waited expectantly. He took her hand and kissed it. 'Forbidden love,' said Bobby in a mocking voice. He began to laugh. Su felt disappointed and never mentioned the play again.

CHAPTER FORTY-FIVE

Summer in England was a mix of warm rain and cloudy sunshine. Suriya complained. Every time she took the washing outside the weather conspired against her. This morning the washing had been pegged out three times. 'THREE TIMES!' she shrieked to anyone who would listen, but everyone was busy, talking about a cousin's wedding. There were plans to be made, dresses to be sewn, presents to be bought. No one cared about the washing and eventually Suriya abandoned the washing to the rain and inspected the fabric that had arrived. When the courier came she was polishing her best ornaments in the hall, making the house nice for visitors. The courier looked pale and she immediately decided she didn't like this young man.

'He look inside house like he rob us,' she told her husband. 'I see him watching my best lady ornament, the one that cost fortune.' Her husband shrugged. 'Nah. No one wants your bloody ornament. It's hideous.' Suriya huffed and sauntered into the kitchen. 'Never trust anyone,' she told her husband, as he followed her. 'This is right, yes?'

'Suriya. Don't always be suspicious,' said her husband. 'No one wants your china. Not unless it is hiding gold.' Suriya laughed. 'All right I know you think I am a fool, but I have bad feeling about this young man. He looks dodgy.'

'Who's dodgy?' called Nasir.

'Your mother no like the courier boy,' his father replied in a sarcastic voice.

'Mother no like young English boys?' said Nasir. 'I don't believe it.' He smirked and winked at Sammy, who had just appeared carrying the washing.

'So, Samina. Is the courier boy dodgy? What do you think? You normally get the parcels.'

Sammy stopped and felt her face freeze. She gawped at her brother-in-law, who was now pointing at her, like a bullying boy. Nasir howled with laughter. 'Your face. Your face. You look like you've been hit by truck.'

Sammy forced an exaggerated smile. 'I don't know what you talk about,' she said, her voice dramatic and high. 'I get washing in.'

'Nasir!' said Suriya, in a serious voice. 'Leave the poor girl. She has a lot on her head. Thinking about her exam. Silly boy!' She rubbed Sammy's back and Sammy held her breath. Nasir narrowed his eyes. 'Always the favourite Samina. Samina, Samina, Samina. Like sun shine out of her arse.'

'What?' Suriya was about to erupt like a volcano. She heard the word 'arse' and that was all, but before she could challenge Nasir, he had run out of the door. Sammy fixed her eyes on the clothes in the basket and folded them meticulously.

'No,' said Suriya, lifting the basket. 'You go and read your English books. Study for exam.'

Sammy hesitated and her father-in-law smiled. 'Do as she says,' he told her, 'or we will all pay the price.'

'Always cheeking me,' Suriya said to her husband, pouting. 'You are worse than the young ones.'

'I am joking,' said her husband, grabbing her from behind. 'You are a good woman.'

Sammy left the room and Suriya shook him away. 'Is there any dhal in shop?'

Her husband sighed. 'When will we ever get any time alone, Suriya? This house is like mad house. Always full of people and kids. This is why Samina no speak. Too much busy. Busy all the time.'

He lifted a newspaper and began to read. 'And this council, always cutbacks. Everything shutting. This council is a disgrace. And all this council tax. Every month paying council and they forget to empty the bins. Rats having a field day.'

He stopped and scratched his beard. 'And today no customers, except Englishwoman wanting a bottle of vodka. I ask you. I tell you. I open a curry house and then there will be hundreds of customers. What you think?'

Suriya nodded. 'English peoples not like cooking, so good idea. In this area, just Dixy's chicken and chips.'

Her husband paused and pondered. 'Ehsan and Nasir could help in takeaway. Ehsan no like taxi driving.'

'Ah. But Nasir, no like work,' his wife joked.

'He's seventeen. No boys like work when they is seventeen. That's it,' said Mohammed, his eyes brightening. 'After this wedding when Samina get certificate we open curry house. I ask my brother, my cousin about it.'

Suriya nodded, but really she wasn't sure. Ehsan and Nasir fought more than most brothers. Last week Ehsan had threatened to kill Nasir. Always they fought over money.

In the bedroom Sammy held her trembling hand still. She was thankful she hadn't seen Rob. Nasir had read the panic in her face. Luckily the family dismissed the boy, hardly took him seriously. At Burnley College he had failed his exams and Suriya shouted at him for wasting his chances. Nasir was indifferent. Qualifications were useless in this country now. Ehsan had a degree and he was driving tarts for a living, cleaning sick off a car mat. Suriya argued back but inside she felt he was right. Business was the key to life. Having a business and making your own money. Not making money for someone else.

Sometimes Nasir helped in the shop, but working there

weighed him down, made him feel listless and heavy. At one takeaway they offered him three pounds an hour to work in the night. He scoffed and turned the job down. Not even the minimum wage. Yet others did it, because they had to.

Suriya put the washing away and sat in the front room. She watched television for a moment and looked at her husband. She had been thinking. 'You are right. The curry house. It will be good for us. Bring this family together. But what about money?'

Her husband was smiling, pleased that his wife agreed. 'Do not worry about money, Suriya. I will look after you.'

Suriya smiled at her husband. It was a good marriage. She loved Mohammed very much. 'Do you think Samina and Ehsan are happy?' she asked. 'Like you and me.'

'Of course,' said her husband, confused, one eyebrow raised. 'Why wouldn't they be?'

Suriya banished the doubts from her mind. She imagined grandchildren and fat cheeks to kiss. She felt reassured. Sometimes when she spoke to her husband she felt very lucky.

CHAPTER FORTY-SIX

Rob was waiting for her when she arrived. 'My God,' cried Sammy, clutching his face. 'Suriya, no like you.' Rob did not speak, but instead took Sammy by the hand and led her into the kitchen. On the table she saw a basket, a bottle of lemonade and a rose. Rob lifted the flower and placed it beneath Sammy's nose. 'A rose for a rose,' he said smiling.

Sammy felt a petal brush her face. 'What going on?'

'Surprise,' said Rob, in an excited voice.

'I am worried, Rob,' she said, stroking the flower on her cheek. 'Suriya …'

'Not now, Sammy,' he said, kissing her nose. 'We can talk about it later.'

In the car they listened to music. 'Where we going?' Rob turned up the radio. Sammy saw Towneley Park glide past. She had been there once with Suriya and women from the sewing class. They had fed the ducks and played with the children on the swings. There was an enormous sandpit with a digger, and a rope bridge that swung as the children clung on. A large mansion overlooked the park. It was a beautiful place dominated by creaking wooden floors that shone in the light and she was disappointed when the car sped past. Soon they were on a country road, hills sweeping down beyond. Sammy opened the window and felt the wind blowing her hair.

'I thought someone might see us at Towneley Park,' Rob said after a while. It was as if he had read her mind.

'Yes. You are right.' His hand was resting on the gearstick and she placed her hand over his.

Soon they turned off onto a dirt track. Here the moorland was rugged and raw, the grass bleached yellow and white. A lone sheep straddled across the track, much to Sammy's delight.

'Once I saw a deer on this track,' said Rob, but Sammy wasn't sure what he meant. He stopped the car and she saw they were high up. 'Like the mountains in Pakistan,' she said, gripping Rob's arm. In the distance they could see Burnley town, the crooked little houses, the football ground.

'You see, Burnley is beautiful.'

'Yes,' said Sammy. Near the car was a bench and she sat down, admiring the view. She clutched Ehsan's jacket to her body and shivered a little. Rob opened the boot of the car and took out a jumper and the basket.

'Put this on,' he said, smiling. 'It will keep you warm.' She did as he said and undid her hair. 'I thought it would be nice to have a picnic.'

She carried the basket and they walked towards a fence. Rob climbed over, took the basket from her. 'English countryside is nice,' she said, standing on a rock. 'I no like Burnley town.'

'Come on,' he urged her. 'I want to show you something.'

As they walked, she felt the wind rising, biting cold on her face. And then she saw it. They stood together, holding hands, like any young lovers on a summer walk. Sammy opened her mouth wide.

'Whoah! What is it?' She ran towards the giant metal structure that stood at the top of the hill, pulling Rob's sleeve.

'Hold on!' he shouted. 'Not so fast.' He tugged himself free and pulled a camera from his pocket. 'Stand still. I want a picture.' Sammy shook her head. 'Just stand still,' he begged. She heard the click of the camera, saw the flash of white and threw her head back. She twisted round and round and stretched her arms wide. Here there was no one; just miles of land and sky and earth and space to love.

Rob desperately captured it all. It was like catching a little bird, in motion, but always knowing that at any moment the bird would take flight. He enjoyed the fullness of her smile, the way her front teeth were not totally perfect and sloped to the left. He studied her face, the way her hair swung and moved as she walked. Her nose was perhaps a little wide but he was mesmerised by the ring that pierced it. Always her makeup was immaculate, like a painted doll. He watched her sometimes putting makeup on her eyes and he sat spellbound, as she lined her eyes and lips. For those brief moments she was his alone. Like now.

She stopped and told him to take a picture of them together. He stretched his arm and zoomed in at his effort. Together they looked at the giant structure ahead.

'What is it?' Sammy wrinkled her nose and laughed. 'I never seen anything like this.'

She listened and heard the chime of bells.

'The singing ringing tree,' said Rob. 'It sings in the wind.'

'I hear it,' she shouted above the din. 'I hear it singing to me.'

She began to dance round and round. At the foot of the sculpture she touched the cold metal tubes, pipes that twisted and spiralled upwards. 'It strange, but beautiful.'

Rob nodded and sat at a picnic table. 'Come and get some food.'

In the basket there were crispy samosas and strawberries coated in sugar. Rob broke a corner off a samosa and began to eat. Sammy called out. 'Take picture of me by the ringing tree, Rob.' Rob directed the camera at her, watched her turn her face to the sky. 'Amazing,' she said.

'Amazing,' he responded, watching her lips as she spoke.

'You like this place, then?'

'I love this tree,' said Sammy, clutching the metal trunk. 'Like a special place.'

Rob smiled as she sat down beside him. He kissed her face. The music from the singing ringing tree warmed her and she thought of the wind racing through the pipes, like breath and blood through a body. She observed how the tree curved and entered the ground. This was to be free. To look, feel and touch anything, everything.

Liquid red on her tongue, she felt the strawberries burst on the roof of her mouth. She held her tongue there for a moment. She felt Rob's tongue touch hers, taste her. Together they fell to the ground where the grass was long and damp. He was inside her quickly, his breath hot, licking her breast, pushing her into the earth. Earth, flesh and bone. Under the sky she came and as she cried out she watched a thousand birds collide and scatter.

Somewhere in the distance they heard a car. Soon they were driving away, the empty picnic basket tipped on its side. Sammy looked out of the window. For a long time she didn't speak. Rob stopped the car at the side of the road. 'What's the matter?'

'Nothing,' she replied. She touched his face and he saw her eyes were watery and full.

'I wish things were different,' he said. 'Maybe you could just disappear, with me.' He cupped her face in his hands. 'No one would find you.' She gently pushed his hands away.

'That is not the right way,' she argued.

'Neither is this.'

Behind them they heard the screech of brakes, high pitched shouting. A grey car slowed down and a group of Asian boys began chanting through the open window. Sammy arched her neck to see. The young boy in the back was swearing, gesturing with one finger as the car drove past. Rob swore. She saw the hooked nose, the baseball cap with the letter N. Nasir blinked and looked back. A flicker of recognition registered in his eyes. She slid down in the seat like a snake.

'What is it?' said Rob. 'What is it?'

'Shit. Shit. Shit.'

Sammy sat up. 'My brother-in-law. I think it was my brother-in-law.'

CHAPTER FORTY-SEVEN

Black was a good colour for Saturday and Su put on her new black jacket and admired the creamy buttons shaped like elephant tusks. She threaded the buttons through the elastic loops and looked at her reflection in the mirror. She decided she liked these English clothes. Especially jeans and the boots Bobby had bought her. The boots were a little too big because her feet were size two and the boots were two and a half. But Bobby had a good eye for a bargain. Tiny feet, just like her mother, thought Su. Tiny feet, like a child, said Bobby to the solemn-faced shop assistant, who was glad to get rid of the pushy Burnley man and his Thai bride.

Paris was in the pram chewing her new dummy, her gums purple and raw. On the bus the baby played with Su's hair and watched the passengers come and go. Her face was bright and animated and she clenched her fists in anger as Su strapped her in the pram. Soon they were outside the shops, Su reading a list of **BABY REQUIREMENTS.**

She found a shop full of baby clothes and rummaged through the frilly dresses. Pink ribbons cascaded down the front of one: another had ladybirds dotted on the front and an enormous white skirt that resembled whipped meringue. She held them up in the light and looked back at Paris in the pram. The child was dressed in pink velvet trousers and a jersey top that was tinged grey. At the back of the rail one dress had yellow and green palm trees on the skirt and boats embroidered on the collar. Su held it up and checked it for size. 'Like Thailand,' she said to Paris. The baby hiccupped and squalled. 'Ah. You no like dress?' Su considered the dress for a little longer. 'Well. I like it.' The baby searched her face and stopped crying.

'How old is she?' said a shop assistant with glasses. 'When's her birthday?' Su paused and confusion spread like a shadow across her face. She stared blankly. She knew Paris was eight months, but that was all. When was her birthday?

'Eight months,' she replied. Quickly she looked at the age on the dress in her hand. Carefully she read the label.

'She's big for eight months,' replied the girl, bending down to retrieve a rattle from the floor.

'Thank you,' said Su, nodding her head and making her way to the counter.

Outside the shop, Su paused. She thought for a moment. Every mother knew the birthday of their child. She wondered when Paris was born and suddenly imagined Bobby and Chelsea together. The thought made her shudder and she wiped the image clean from her head.

On the way back through town she saw the door of the bookshop wedged open and David sticking a poster in the window. He didn't recognise her at first. She called to him through the doorway and tipped the pram up the step. David paused. 'Su?' He looked down at the pram and frowned. 'What are you doing with the baby?'

Su understood his words and recognised the disapproval in his voice. 'Chelsea leave her at my house. Dump her,' she said in an animated voice. She used the word 'dump' because this was the word Bobby used. David patted the baby's head and smiled, but Su noticed he looked worried.

'Where's Chelsea?' he said after a while. 'Where is she?' The poster flapped in his hand as he spoke.

'Me don't know,' said Su, shrugging her shoulders. 'Just disappear.'

David said nothing and placed the poster on the counter. He began to stack books on the shelves. Su read the sign. **ASSISTANT REQUIRED.**

'Me need job,' said Su, watching him bend and arrange the books on the shelves.

'I don't think that's a good idea?'

'Why?'

David stopped and stood up. He was surprised at how quickly Su had learnt English. Su also surprised herself. She had been learning questions and responses at the language centre and suddenly she realised the importance of questions.

'Because …' David stopped and tried to think of an answer. 'Because you are at English classes.'

'How many days you need?' said Su, her face taut and serious.

He smiled and laughed. 'I think you are very busy, Su.'

Su's lip trembled. 'OK. I want to work with books, but I understand you no like me.' She took the pram and turned to face the door.

'No, Su. Wait.' David called her back. 'Maybe you could help one day a week.'

Su rushed past the pram and hugged him tightly. 'Thank you. I work hard.' Su looked around the shop. It was small and cramped, a mixture of old and new books. This was her dream.

'Don't thank me too much,' said David, removing her arms from his neck. 'I can't pay you much.' He wondered about her English. 'We will see how you get on.'

'OK,' said Su. 'Which day? I so excited.'

'When Paris goes home.'

Su heard the words and swung round. Home. That was the word she dreaded hearing. Home. Home meant so many different things. Where was her home? Where was Paris' home? Not with Chelsea. Not with her. Bobby had told her about the dirty flat, the stained curtain at the window, the crawling maggots. That couldn't be home. David saw the panic in her face. 'What's the matter Su?'

'I don't know,' she lied.

'You do know Chelsea will come back for her. She can't stay with you. Not for ever.'

'Yes,' Su stammered.

David looked at the shopping bag tied on the pram handle. 'What have you bought?'

She didn't want to tell him, but already he was in the bag, pulling the little dress out.

'Sweet,' he said. He looked at her for a moment and then at the child. 'It's hard,' he said.

'Yes,' replied Su, tears in her eyes. The little girl was oblivious.

'You can't choose your parents.'

Su agreed. She knew from the tone of his voice what was meant.

'Anyway,' he said in a cheerful voice. 'Why don't you try it on, while the shop's quiet?' He led Su and the baby into the back room and when the dress was on, they both admired the little girl.

'You don't have any children, Su?'

'No.' Su fixed her eyes on Paris, as she crawled across the shop floor 'Can't have baby.'

'Sorry.' David looked away.

'It OK,' she said. 'It OK. Now I too old.'

David gave her a mug of tea. 'How are you finding England?'

'I like England, but life is difficult. I need more English and then life better for me. I want work in library, or bookshop.'

David nodded and looked pleased. 'I will show you the books.'

She followed him up and down the aisles as he talked about different 'genres' of books. He pointed at labels and she read them aloud in turn. There were little seats around the shop, tables with newspapers and ancient books. She saw one now, pages flapped open, like the wings of a bird.

The book of dreams was so large, so old that it remained homeless. Unshelved, unloved and usually untouched. But today Su read the golden script and searched for the meanings of pictures in her sleep. Like a great bible the volume was bound in an expensive leather cover that was speckled and crackled and it sat on a side table, next to daily newspapers.

'Can I read?'

'Yes, yes. Take it home, if you like.'

'Very old book,' said Su. David nodded. She smoothed her fingers down the oily ribbon that peeked between the pages. Pages that were stained yellow and brown, thin as tissue.

The name of some ancient magical person adorned the spine and Su was surprised that no one had bought the book of dreams. The title was worn with time and barely visible. Just a few flaky scrolls of curly gold were left raised on the cover. She was also amazed by the drawings inside of mystical creatures and beasts. Slowly she leafed through the dry crisp pages, admiring the curling tail of a dragon, the bulging eyes of a mythical beast.

Before her was a large oak tree, a wide trunk delicately marked with inky lines. She peered into the drawing carefully until she was almost there. She imagined herself at the foot of the tree and for just a moment she closed her eyes. The sound of rushing water filled her ears. She saw a boy, clinging to the branch, water spiralling around his legs. He called to her, but she remained rooted to the spot. Afraid, she snapped the book of dreams shut. But in her thoughts the inky tree remained, seeping red and black, spreading further and further, leaking through the corners of her eyes.

CHAPTER FORTY-EIGHT

In the park children were running. Su watched them chasing one another, battling with brittle sticks, ducking under skinny trees. She sat on the bench, checking her watch because she was too early for class.

There was much excitement when a small boy with spiky hair produced a black and white football from his bag. Soon the children chanted Me. Me. Me. They kicked the ball high in the air, falling over the roundabout to get a touch. Su watched it bounce close to the pram and shooed them away. Again the ball span in the air, but this time there was a huge commotion. The boys ran through the gate, past the spear-top railings. The ball was still spiralling in the air and the boys gasped and called out. Su turned and saw the ball dipping down straight into the canal. Immediately she stood up and ran. The children were at the water's edge watching the ball as it bobbed frantically away. Faster and faster, it rolled towards the bridge. Like statues the boys stood suspended with their hands on their heads. 'No!' Too late. The smallest boy was in the water, diving on the ball, kicking and splashing his way to the bank.

Quickly, Su dashed to the side and stretched out her arm. 'Very bad!' she screamed. 'Very bad. Water kill you!' The boy took her hand and laughed and shivered and shook. Su led him to the bench and wrapped him in a blanket. 'Never do this again!' But the boy seemed unmoved and pushed the blanket away. Soon he was on his feet, dripping wet. Surprisingly the game continued. Again he kicked the ball. This time the ball plummeted down spinning towards Su, sprinkling her with droplets of water like a shower of diamonds. Then it landed on the ground with a splat, an exploding bomb of ripped rubber. Su raced away.

'Boy swim in canal,' Su told the staff at the language centre. She gestured with her hands. 'Small boy.' The staff tutted and looked out of the window. The boys were still there hurling the split ball in the air.

Su told the class. Zehnab saw she was shaken. 'Bad boys,' she said. 'Naughty! And dangerous!' Zehnab marched outside, the other Pakistani women following behind. Through the railings she saw the small boy, his trousers heavy and wet. She shouted in Urdu. 'Salim Hussain. I know your mother.' The small boy ran to the gate but Zehnab held it closed. 'Swimming with the rats! What are you thinking of? That water is black. It's filthy.'

The boy froze and muttered something under his breath. 'That water's full of poison. POISON.' The boy's face fell and he began to shriek and cry.

'Silly boy. Get your wet little arse home, or I'll throw you back in.' The boy pushed past her. 'Sorry Auntie.' Zehnab shook her head. At the top of the ramp the boys waved and shouted. Zehnab turned to the other women. 'Just because we are in England doesn't mean children should run free like rats.' The others agreed. Together they filed back into the centre.

In the classroom Sammy fidgeted in her seat and tapped her pencil on the table. The teacher was prising batteries from a plastic packet and inserted them in a digital voice recorder. There was silence because the teacher said they would do a practice exam. Sammy looked at the papers stacked in front of her. The teacher's voice echoed around the room, but Sammy was thinking about Nasir. He had said nothing about the day on the moors, not even looked at her.

Consumed by worry, she had spent most of her time in the bedroom pretending to study. Only she was too terrified to study. Whenever she heard the thud of footsteps on the stairs she imagined Suriya grabbing her by the hair and parading her through the streets. She was an adulteress. She needed to be punished. She played with the razor blade and held it to her throat.

The teacher read down the list. 'Samina Ahmed!' Sammy was sweating. Her nose was running. The teacher gave her a bottle of water. Strange thoughts swirled in her head, like fragments of dust whipped up in a tornado. She saw herself in a maze, like the girl in a story she had read. That was it, *Alice in Wonderland*. She looked down at the maze from above and glimpsed herself at the centre. Only she was small and now she noticed there were no discernible entrance and no exit. She was lost. Lost in England. Were there others? She couldn't tell. She saw herself dressed in black, covered from head to toe in a hijab. She remembered a small boy in town, gripping her skirt in Poundland, asking if she was a Muslim. 'They all look the same,' someone said and pulled the boy away.

In the maze she wandered aimlessly trying to find the others, trying to find a way out. If there were others no one said. No one spoke about it. She thought about Rob. Behind her veil she was a woman, with hopes and dreams, just like any other. The teacher called her back and led her to the front. The recorder was on and Sammy heard the sound of her own voice, but it sounded far away, and she was not really there. Past tense, she remembered she had to speak about the past. She could not fail.

'My name is Samina Ahmed. I was born in Pakistan. I am eighteen year old. I am married and I live in Burnley. I came here a few month ago. I lived in a big house with ten bedroom and I have big garden … mango tree … many people in my house … too many peoples … living in Burnley … England is difficult life for me … new family … new everything … I no like England … I no happy … I like … I likes …'

Sammy gasped. The teacher waited. Sammy was out of breath. No more words came. Only tears. The recorder clicked off. 'It's OK. You can try again, later,' said the teacher. 'Don't be nervous.' Sammy began to sob and Lenka took her away to the kitchen. They sat on nasty plastic chairs stained with tea and coffee. Sammy bit her nails, listened to the dripping tap, the sound of water slapping the steel sink. When she spoke, it was with a fractured voice, and her face barely moved. She told her friend, 'I can't take any more of this life in England. I can't do this no more.'

CHAPTER FORTY-NINE

Failing the test was more than she could bear. She cried so much she thought she might disappear. She could smell sweat and pressed the damp patch that spread under the arm of her tunic. She had shot past Suriya and slammed the bedroom door shut. Now she knew this was a mistake. Regret wept and seeped through the pores of her skin. She heard Suriya panting as she pulled herself up the creaking stairs. Sammy had learnt that step number five dipped and bowed. Step number five groaned and squeaked. Next she heard shuffling and saw Suriya's shadow through the gap under the door. The woman paused for a moment and cleared her throat. Sammy held her breath and waited. No sound. Suriya stood still and then she turned and walked away. Sammy bit the quilt in her mouth. Her limbs were heavy, dead as cut logs. But nothing happened. Suriya left the house.

The battered English dictionary was on the bed, the corner peeling, the cover wrinkled like the skin of an old apple. She leafed through the pages and began to read words. Any words. Words that were disconnected. She chanted them as if they were a prayer.

Unclean. Underdog. Underling. Underprivileged. Unfaithful. Unfit. Ungodly. Unhappy. Unhinged. Unknown. Unsightly. Unstable.

She was all these 'un' words. She wondered if answers can be found in a book. Some people say they can. Desperately she took her copy of the Quran and began to read aloud. But it was no use.

She was unworthy and even now she watched as her tears and bleeding wrists stained the cover.

Fingers trembling, she called Rob. 'I need see you, now.'

'OK, OK,' repeated the voice. 'What's happened?'

'Fail,' was all Sammy could say. She sobbed uncontrollably.

'Come now,' said Rob. 'Let me pick you up at the language centre.'

Sammy gulped for air and ended the call. But then the world shattered.

* * *

Suriya burst through the bedroom door, her chest heaving, her eyes flaring. 'Who you talking to? Give me that thing. Give me now!'

Sammy clutched the phone tightly, but Suriya lunged at her, twisted her arm back and began to prise the phone from her fingers. Sammy felt Suriya's nails digging in. 'Do as you are told girl, or I will tell the family.'

'No!' screamed Sammy. 'Get off. Ehsan buy me phone.'

'No phone,' shouted Suriya. 'Give it to me now.'

Sammy brought her knees up and watched her mother-in-law pull back. She saw the shock slide over her face and then anger rise. Suriya shrieked. Sammy threw the phone hard against the wall and the phone broke into dozens of small pieces. The woman stopped and glared.

Suddenly her hand was raised and sweeping through the air. Slap! Sammy's cheek burnt hot.

'Why you make this fuss about phone? Look what happen now! Look what you make me do. Causing all this trouble over a phone. Anyone think you hiding something.'

Sammy sat on the bed speechless. Her cheek smarted and her wrist was bleeding again. Suriya saw the blood dripping.

'Oh my God. You are more trouble than I thought.' She held

the girl's wrist in front of her nose. 'Bad girl! Tell no one about this! NO ONE! Stupid, stupid girl. You will ruin the family. Ruin everything. You listen. You tell no one.'

The woman wrapped Sammy's wrist and gave her a cardigan. 'Put on! Cover up. And no more ringing friends. These girls are making you bad. You are not English. Remember who you are. Remember your family. Always remember your place in this world.'

Suriya glanced around the room. She saw the dictionary, the pages loose and worn. 'And this book, I throw away.'

'But ...'

'No,' said Suriya, passing Sammy the Quran, 'this is the only book you need. Now read and study what is important.'

'English classes ...'

Suriya did not let her finish. 'Yes, you have to go to English classes, but then when you get certificate, you speak Urdu. Urdu only. After certificate, no more of this English stuff. It is for your own good. After certificate you be good wife. I know you are a good girl.'

Sammy scratched her arm. The bandage was tight. Suriya saw and clamped her wrists with her fat fingers. 'If you do this again, you will feel as much pain as you bring to this family.'

Sammy nodded. 'Sorry Auntie. So sorry.'

Suriya hugged her and Sammy held her breath. The woman frightened her.

Sammy's mind was racing. Rob was at the language centre waiting. Suriya bent down and retrieved the plastic parts of the phone. The wall was dented where the phone had hit.

'Broke,' she said, pleased. 'You make friend with your own kind. Then you will be happy, Samina.'

Sammy stared, her face rigid and set. 'I try to be happy,' she muttered.

Suriya's face softened a little. 'I have seen this hundreds of time, Samina. You young girls coming to England thinking this is the land of milk and honey. England is not a land of milk and honey. Life is about working hard for your family. Our ways.'

'I need English book,' begged Sammy. 'Please, I need English book.'

Suriya studied the book in her hand. 'OK, but you must pray and be thankful for what you have.'

Sammy looked up. Her voice was robotic, devoid of emotion. 'Thank you, Suriya. You are right. I should be thankful.'

When Suriya left the room Sammy stared out of the window watching the mist that drifted over the rooftops. She stood and watched the people pass by. She played with a puddle of rusty water that had leaked through the rotten window frame. She thought about Suriya's land of milk and honey. Then she took a pen and paper and began to write.

> **England is the land of milk and honey**
> **People say immigrants get all the money**
>
> **England is the land of milk and honey**
> **They say people there is free from worry**
>
> **England is the land of milk and honey**
> **People say you can be free and still eat curry**
>
> **England is the land of milk and honey**
> **But life here is not so sunny.**

The paper was scored deeply and when Sammy checked the rhythm of her poem she noticed a hole where she had marked the full stop with the pen. She held the paper up at the window and saw the light filter through the tiny hole. The pen was her only weapon against this life and so she took more paper and began to write until her hand ached and every word was OUT.

CHAPTER FIFTY

Dazzling and bright the sun shimmered on the water. People were swimming and she saw a little rowing boat near the shore. With a bag full of squashed fruit she sat on the wooden pier, dipping her feet in the slopping water. It was a mystery to her. The water near the pier looked dark, dangerous and black. Like syrup, it coated you in a dirty substance like tar. This fascinated her. Black water here, but the water near the shore glowed like tinted glass, in shades of turquoise and green. Under it there were mounds of creamy smooth pebbles, the kind people stole away and displayed in their homes. The kind of pebbles you touched because they were the purest of things on this earth. In her dream Su lifted the pebble and held it to her face.

She listened to the whoosh and whisper of the trees and heard the snap of a twig crunch under her feet. She was restless. The wind was restless too and the trees surrounding the lake swished and swayed. She turned and in the corner of her eye saw the rowing boat, rocking in the wind.

There it was, a tiny rowing boat at the centre of the round lake, tipping and swinging like a pendulum. Two oars spun like the broken arms of a clock. Water lapped and bashed and tossed the boat from side to side.

Su was in a panic. The boat was empty. She couldn't be sure, but she wondered if someone had fallen in.

Within seconds she dropped the pebble to the ground and ran

through the water. She swam to the boat, took a deep breath and shot down. She remembered her father's words and they echoed in her ears. 'You swim like a magical creature. Sometimes I think you could live on land, or sea.' Green water and worms floated round her head. At first she couldn't see, but then there was a light in the water, almost like a spotlight on a dark stage. Perhaps it was the sun. Now she noticed the disc of yellow light spinning, weed dancing like wild hair. She followed the light. And suddenly she saw the glowing body of a girl, enveloped in weed.

A girl suspended in the water, like a mermaid. Her eyes gaped like the eyes of a fish. The gold buckle of her shoe was trapped in the weed. Su hurtled upwards. She needed more air. Back down again. She ripped at the weed, tore it with her hands, but it was like thick wire. She grasped the shoe and pulled. She pulled and pulled and clawed the girl up by the hair. Up and up, into the little boat. But she wasn't breathing. Chelsea Dobbs wasn't breathing. She lay lifeless, her face waxy and pale, her limbs tangled in slime and weed.

Su was choking, felt water in her mouth. She heaved and sat up in bed. Her leg was cold and numb. Bobby was smacking her back. She coughed some more.

'It's just a dream. For God's sake, what were you dreaming?' Bobby frowned. 'You scare me when you do that.'

'I dream Chelsea dead,' Su muttered half asleep. 'Drown in water.'

Then the baby was crying, but this time Bobby went to her and Su heard him singing a song. She smiled in her sleep.

CHAPTER FIFTY-ONE

Sammy had been in the bath so long her skin was wrinkled and peeling. Like rotten fruit, she thought to herself, tearing a slither of skin that flapped near her thumb nail. Ehsan was in bed waiting for her and the idea of him touching her made her feel cold and angry. For weeks they had hardly spoken. Sometimes she caught him looking at her wrists and he seemed disappointed and far away. Now, whenever she felt the urge to cut herself, she took the pen instead and wrote her thoughts. As the words spilt out, she felt the same sensation of blood dripping from her veins.

At the language centre she had shown her poems to Lenka and Su. Su admired her writing and told her that this was a gift from God. Sammy smiled. She tried to explain. It was impossible to suppress the rage she felt. When Suriya told her to stir the curry, she wanted to throw the food, shout and object. To Sammy, writing was a form of protest. Silent protest. Sadly, she knew silent protest wouldn't change anything. But it allowed her to escape the monotonous routine of her life. When she wrote, she could be someone else, or somewhere else. But not tonight.

Ehsan looked bored. 'You no want be with me,' he said suddenly. 'I know.'

Sammy stared up at him. 'I fail my practice test.'

Ehsan rolled over onto his side. 'You telling me this, now. Why you no tell me before?'

Sammy blinked. 'I disappoint you.'

'Practice, right? It was just a practice.'

'Yes.'

'Then it doesn't matter.'

Ehsan looked at his wife closely. 'I don't know what you want, Samina.'

This was an opportunity to speak. Sammy paused and thought about the right words. 'I want to be free, Ehsan. Free.'

Ehsan looked confused. 'You are free.'

'No.'

'What do you mean? You are as free as me.'

Sammy stammered. 'I mean, I want choices.' Before she could speak again Ehsan sat up.

'You mean you want other men.'

'NO!' she fired back at him. 'It's not about that. I want choose clothes, job, where I live.'

'You mean you want to be like Englishwomen.'

'Yes, but also Pakistani too.'

'In our culture–'

Sammy interrupted him. 'In our culture women do not do these things. I want more. Don't you ever want more?'

Ehsan considered her words carefully. 'We need a new house. Then you will feel better, away from here.'

'I not happy.'

Ehsan glared. 'If any woman say this to me before, I would hit her. I trying to do everything for you. Trying to make you happy. Buying you clothes. Working for money. Saving up.'

'I know.'

'No, Samina. I think you is selfish. Thinking about yourself and not the family. Nasir was right about you. He say you not good for marriage.'

Sammy began to cry and Ehsan held her hand. 'What can I do?' Sammy buried her head in his chest. 'I so sorry. I so sorry. I wished I love you.'

Ehsan replied. 'Samina. You seen love marriage in England. All divorced. Maybe you learn to love me.'

That night Sammy tried to love her husband, but all the time she thought to herself, this is not how it should be. The mattress groaned and creaked beneath her. A metal spring dug in her back. She imagined she was on the moors, surrounded by purple heather and rock. She pictured water rolling off the craggy hills and a clear sky where the outlines of the birds were pointed and black. And then she thought of the mountains in Pakistan and swimming in a giant lake that gleamed like glass.

In the morning Ehsan woke to find his wife had already gone to the language centre. Images of houses filled his head. He had seen a semi for sale. A big house, with a garage and a garden for children to play in, was his dream. But it would take a long time to raise the money. He thought about asking his father. Maybe his father would help. At the end of the bed he sat and saw his clothes rumpled and carelessly strewn on the bedroom floor. He smiled, pleased that he and Sammy had finally shared some love. He retrieved his shirt and under it was Sammy's rucksack. He had seen this bag before and sure enough, just as he thought, he spotted the scruffy English book, peeking through the top. Sammy had forgotten her college bag. He would take it to the language centre, he decided. This would be sure to make his wife happy.

He lifted the bag onto the bed and began to fasten the buckle. It was a struggle because the book was stuck. Slowly he pushed the book down into the bag but then he felt something sharp jab his hand. He tried again, reached back down and pulled out a foil strip of pills. Most of the foil blisters were empty and there was just one tablet left. He read the label. This medication, Ehsan had never heard of and for a moment he was troubled. Perhaps his wife was ill. He took the pills downstairs and found the laptop. He was curious and worried. He typed the word. That was the end.

Sammy remembered the bag and was asking the teacher to go

home. She ran back to Paradise Street, her mind in a whirl. Ehsan was on the computer, the pack of pills in front of him. His eyes were red and she could see he had been crying.

'Ehsan.'

'I trusted you,' he stormed. 'Where did you get these?'

Sammy lowered her eyes. 'Doctor.'

'Since when have you ever been to the doctor on your own? You never go anywhere on your own.'

'Doctor give me.'

Ehsan banged his fist on the glass table. 'You tell me you want kids. All the time you lie! Taking bloody contraceptive pill! How we gonna have kids if you take these?'

Sammy pursed her lips tight. There was nothing to be said. Ehsan kicked the laptop off the table. She flinched. She considered running. Lenka would help her. Maybe Su.

'I've finished with you,' said Ehsan calmly. 'You will have to go back to Pakistan.'

Sammy bellowed, 'No, Ehsan. No. Please. Let me stay.'

His face changed. 'Begging me, now. What did you expect? Go back to your family and explain what a disgraceful liar you are. Shaming me. Shaming the family. Cutting your wrists. Taking pills.' He shook his head. 'I can't believe this has happened. You changed. Why you change?'

Sammy stood still. She tried to find an answer. 'How can I come to England and not change?' she suddenly said. She was breathless now and her voice was no longer confident. If she went back to Pakistan her mother would be ashamed.

'Lots of girls come here and are fine. Burnley life is fine.'

'No,' argued Sammy. She waved her arms, frustrated that her husband could not see the truth. 'They not fine. They just pretend. Close their eyes and pretend everytime. Close their eyes and pretend everytime that everything is OK. They all living a lie.'

Ehsan laughed. 'Samina. You need to know you have ruined this marriage. All this talk, like you are English, or something. You are not English.'

'In England life is different. We should be different.'

'No,' said Ehsan. 'You still my wife. Live our way. What about culture, religion?'

'I just want to wear English clothes.'

'Like those tarts.'

'No. See, you are like everyone else, judging me. You are not Allah. You cannot judge me. You cannot judge peoples by clothes they wear on their backs.'

'No one in our family wears English clothes. No one. Only mens.'

'Why?' Sammy glared. 'Why just mens? I don't want this life.'

'You are going back,' said Ehsan, pointing his finger in her face. 'In Pakistan maybe you learn some respect.'

Sammy stopped. Her voice was low and resigned. 'OK. I go back. Have everything your way. There is no choice for me. See, even now, I have no choice. Be thankful you are not me, Ehsan. Be thankful you are not a woman.'

CHAPTER FIFTY-TWO

In Towneley Park the mist curled and swirled like thick black smoke above their heads and over the hills beyond. Anna was running, behind her a red and yellow kite dipping and rising. The string was tight and dug in her hand leaving a deep groove. But still she would not let go. The wind gripped the kite hard and the fabric flapped and billowed. Pulling and tugging, up, up it went, so high her neck ached. Lenka chased after her and called her name, but Anna ran on blindly. Faster and faster the string unravelled. The girl was smiling brightly. The kite was rising. But then the wind whipped the kite away. Lenka saw the kite spin off over the horizon, disappearing in a plume of grey. Anna stood with her arms upstretched to the sky. Her mouth was open, but she made no sound.

They left the park and headed back into town. 'I will buy you a book,' said Lenka. 'Yes. A new book.' The girl smiled. 'And a burger,' added Lenka. Anna clasped her hand and followed her mother into the little bookshop. The children's books were at the back of the shop and the girl sat on a beanbag and began to look at a picture book about a fat cat. She giggled to herself and Lenka was glad she had forgotten about the kite.

Lenka had not meant to buy a book of poetry, but she found herself, standing there in the aisle, reading the words aloud. First she noticed the name. The book was by a woman called Sylvia. Also Sylvia was her mother's name. But the title was a strange name, or place she wasn't sure of. A-R-I-E-L. She tried to sound out the word. The man in the bookshop turned and smiled. 'Sorry,' she mouthed, aware that he had heard her.

'It's OK, ' he said, walking towards her. 'That's a good choice. Sylvia Plath. You like Sylvia Plath? She's one of my favourites too.'

'I don't know, I think I does, I do,' said Lenka, stumbling over her words. 'First time,' she said quickly. 'Sorry. My English is bad. I am learning.'

'Where are you from?' David guessed she was Eastern European and he surveyed her face closely. Her teeth were small, her eyes looked blue and sleepy. But it was her blonde hair and height that caught his attention. She was at least five feet nine and with her heels she was the same height as him. Lenka knew he was looking and focused on the book as she spoke.

'I'm from Poland.' Her voice was clear and bright.

'Your English is good,' he told her. 'Do you live in Burnley?'

'Yes, me and Anna.'

David looked at her hand. No wedding ring. 'And your husband?'

Lenka was surprised by the directness of this question and hesitated. Finally, she replied, 'No together.' She smiled as she said the words. She saw the badge with his name. 'Your name is David? I am Lenka and this is Anna.'

He shook her hand. She called Anna's name. Anna pouted and frowned.

'What's the matter?' David asked, bending down to look at her book.

'I lose my kite,' the girl told him in a tearful voice.

'Oh no!' he replied. 'How did that happen?'

'This is true,' said Lenka. 'In Towneley Park. The wind took it away.' She patted Anna's head, but the girl was in no mood for affection and sulked down the aisles.

The man called David went to the back of the shop and returned. In his hand was a book on how to make a kite. 'It's damaged,' he said, 'so I cannot sell it, but you can take it.' He flicked through the pages.' If you have some fabric and a stick, a kite is easy to make…'

'No,' protested Lenka. 'Thank you, but no.'

'It's free,' he said, 'but Anna must show me the kite she makes.'

'OK.' Lenka laughed and the man smiled. She bought the book about a cat and the poems by Sylvia Plath. 'Thank you,' she called. 'We will show you the kite.'

'Don't forget,' he said.

On the way out of the shop Lenka repeated his words 'Don't forget.' In McDonalds she read the Sylvia Plath poems. She was thinking about the last line of 'Morning Song'. 'The clear vowels rise like balloons.' She thought about David's voice. Sometimes you meet people who speak in such a way you want to capture their words on paper and write them down. This was how she felt about the man called David. The way he phrased a line made her stop. His words danced in the air, he could influence, persuade someone to buy any book with that voice. Anna was looking at her now. Milkshake was dribbling down her chin and the girl dabbed her mother's face with a napkin. Lenka laughed. This behaviour was ridiculous and unexpected.

Outside the rain showed them no mercy and they huddled beneath a collapsed umbrella with a bent metal spoke. 'We need new umbrella,' said Lenka, pulling Anna's hood over her head. She sighed. The rain trickled down her collar and neck. Her jeans were wet and clung to her legs. 'I hate the rain.' They ran across the town centre and stood under a shop canopy, waiting for the rain to subside. 'Good day?' she said to Anna, dropping a mint in her hand. The girl sucked on the mint and nodded, but it was clear she hadn't forgotten about the kite.

They watched the shoppers speeding along, children skipping in puddles, annoyed mothers struggling to carry bags. A group of rowdy men in black jackets came down the road, chips steaming in cones, boots thrashing in water. Lenka looked up. One man whistled at her. She turned and faced the shop. A hand pressed down on her shoulder.

'Lenka.' She swallowed hard and froze. She knew this voice. She would know this voice anywhere. Anna was shouting, 'Daddy! Daddy!' Kamil picked the child up in his arms and threw her in the air. 'How's my best girl?' Lenka's world stopped. She choked on her words. 'Kamil. Please put her down.'

'OK. OK.'

The rain blew hard like grit thrown in her face. She looked down and saw Kamil's shiny boots. He staggered slightly and waited for her to speak. Her mouth was dry. No words came to her. She wanted to tell him to go away, to tell him he had ruined her life, that she hated him. But in his eyes, she saw it. He knew everything. She was going to ask him about the man outside Anna's school, but she stopped herself. In that moment she knew it wasn't him. Something in his face, his manner, aroused her sympathy. Despite everything she felt pity for him.

He took a receipt from his pocket and wrote his number down. There was no sense of urgency in his voice, no demands. 'If you want, you can ring me.' He spoke quietly. His words were careful and considered. She saw his hands shake and tremble, the outline of the numbers zigzagging across the page. Like a child's first writing. Lenka nodded blankly. 'I have to go,' he said simply, pointing at the group of men. The group cheered and whistled and he gestured for them to stop. 'I changed, Lenka. No drinking. I have a counsellor. Get my life back.' He shouted for the men to stop. His voice dropped. 'You look different, Lenka.'

Lenka nodded. 'I have to go, also.' She turned and walked back into town, afraid he might follow her home. But when she looked towards him, he was behind the men, his back stooped and his head hung low. This was not how she remembered him. Anna was chattering on. Lenka stopped and watched Kamil disappear. The sound of the men's heavy boots trailed away. The large bodies dissolved in the misty grey. Soon they were just dots in the distance. She was no longer afraid.

CHAPTER FIFTY-THREE

Preparations for the family wedding took over and distracted everyone from their troubles. Sammy was grateful for this. She suspected Ehsan had said nothing about the pills. Not yet. Suriya took her to sewing class and they made new dresses with silk and gold thread. The woman was a skilled embroiderer and Sammy watched her create swirling patterns with the needle and thread, so fine that the others gasped and applauded when the garment was finished. Suriya taught her how to sew trailing leaves and the rhythm of the needle and thread soothed her thoughts and made her forget the past. In these brief moments Sammy was happy. Creating something lifted her soul and Suriya saw this.

'I have an idea,' Suriya announced as the family ate. Everyone stopped eating and looked suddenly curious and interested in what the woman had to say. 'It's about Samina.' Sammy almost choked. She swallowed the lump of chicken in her mouth whole. She began to cough frantically and gulped her water. Now she was sure she was going back to Pakistan. She clasped her hands together in prayer under the table. She glanced at Ehsan. He was expressionless. This was the last supper.

'Sammy is a gifted sewer and I think she should teach the sewing class, when she has learnt more.'

Everyone clapped and smiled and Suriya told Sammy to fetch her sewing. 'The most beautiful leaves I have ever seen. Such skill. And after just a few lessons. This makes me proud. Well done, Samina!'

Sammy turned to her husband, but he did not look at her. He continued to chase the fluffy rice with his fork and told Nasir about a footballer he had picked up in his taxi. 'He gave me twenty pound tip. These footballers have too much money to give away. Earning one hundred thousand a week.'

'As long as he give money to you, who cares?' said Nasir, amazed. 'All that for kicking a football.'

'Pick up more footballers,' said Suriya, clearly happy. This was her favourite time, everyone together, sharing food and stories. Her husband began to speak.

'This is good time for us. Wedding next week. Samina will have certificate soon, so she can stay in UK.' Sammy looked down. Her father-in-law did not know that she had failed the practice test. 'When big test, Samina?'

'Next week,' Samina mumbled.

'Don't look so terrified,' Nasir told her. 'Any fool can pass. No one ever fail.'

'Sometimes people fails,' said Ehsan, raising his eyebrow at his brother. 'English is hard. Not everyone is the same.' Sammy smiled at him and he almost smiled back.

'She will be OK,' said Suriya, in an authoritative voice that warned Sammy she better pass.

'I will do my best,' said Sammy, but inside she was feeling like a balloon with too much air. The pressure she felt was enormous and her stomach was bloated. The food in her belly swam round and she felt sick. Mohammed continued to speak. 'OK. Now for biggest news. I have spoken to my cousin and we are buying takeaway in Daneshouse.'

Everyone sat open mouthed. Ehsan stared at his father dumbfounded. 'But when was this decided. Who will be working in the takeaway?'

'Ah,' his father replied, waving his naan bread, 'this is where you and Nasir have big part to play.' Nasir smirked. 'You and Nasir work together, manage everything. I keep shop and see how things go.'

Ehsan thought for a moment. 'You think this will work?'

'Yes,' said his father, grinning wildly. 'People need takeaway in this area and this is good for yours and Samina's future.' Ehsan did not reply and his father searched his face, waiting for a response. 'Ehsan. You not looking happy.'

Sammy frowned at Ehsan. He looked serious now. 'I am happy. Me and Samina are happy.' He looked towards her. 'We are going to find a new house so we can have a family. This takeaway is good for everyone. New beginning.'

Suriya stood up and hugged her son. 'I don't want you to leave, but bring me grandchild and I will forgive you.' Everyone laughed. Sammy pushed her plate away. There was no mention of Pakistan. Instead a new house, a new life. She was both relieved and confused.

After the meal Ehsan went upstairs. Sammy followed him. He sat on the bed watching television. Sammy stood before him. 'Why, Ehsan? I don't understand.'

Ehsan rose from the bed and stroked her hair. He held her face in his hands and saw the makeup streaked down it. He wiped the makeup away with his hands and paused. 'Because I love you,' he said. 'Because I love you.'

They stood facing each other, their fingers knotted together, wondering about the past, wondering about the future. Sammy's thoughts were racing, faster than flood water. Always, she had presumed theirs was a loveless marriage. Love had never been mentioned. She looked at her husband with new eyes. She believed he loved her. This was her chance to make things right.

'Oh, I have been thinking, about clothes. When we move maybe you can wear some English clothes, but you show me first.'

Sammy held him tight. Downstairs they heard the sound of Asian music. 'She is watching film again,' said Ehsan. 'Romantic film.'

'Yes,' said Sammy, biting her lip.

'What do you want to do?'

'Go for a walk.'

Ehsan laughed. 'OK. That costs no money. I'm happy with that.' She nudged him playfully and he kissed her hand. 'Your wrist is better.'

'Yes,' she replied. 'Better. No more.'

Together they walked down the street, Ehsan with his arm around his wife. On the path a white car was parked. 'People always parking on pavements. So annoying,' grumbled Ehsan. Sammy walked round the car into the road. The window was down. She saw the driver watching her. She saw Rob. Ehsan saw him watching too. 'What you looking at, mate?' Ehsan called in a sarcastic voice. Rob glared and Sammy shot him a startled look. Ehsan led her down the street. She looked behind. The car turned round in the road and screeched away. 'Mad man!' shouted Ehsan

On the canal bank they sat and watched the ducks. Machinery from the factories opposite whirred and hummed. Over the bridge they could hear people talking in different languages and outside the factories the Polish workers sat on boxes eating sandwiches in plastic packets. Today the park was empty. Ehsan held Sammy's hand. Sammy stared vacantly into the water. She was angry that Rob had come to her street, angry that he was watching her. Ehsan hurled a stone in the water. Rings of water rippled and spread across the canal. Soon the water settled again and the couple saw their reflections joined together. Sammy was lost in thought. Sammy and Rob were over. But Sammy and Ehsan were just beginning.

CHAPTER FIFTY-FOUR

In the kitchen the chicken soup was bubbling and condensation formed pools on the windowsill. Su stirred the soup and tasted it with a wooden spoon. More salt, she thought, licking her lips. It needed more salt. But the pot was crusty and clogged with damp. Gently she shook and tapped the lid. Still the salt was stuck. She prised the top away and saw the salt had formed one big lump. With her fingers she crumbled the lumpy salt in and watched it dissolve to nothing. She thought of her mother. She left a small amount, just like her mother would. She remembered the Thai saying that when the salt runs out, your luck runs with it.

Bobby was due home soon and Paris was asleep in the pram. Su smiled. Life had settled into a routine that was timed and orderly. Routine pleased her, but for Bobby it was different. Sometimes she saw the boredom in his face, the frustration when the baby was crying to be fed. It was times like this when she became aware of the age gap between them. Bobby was tired and he looked suddenly older. He talked of holidays and spent his days dreaming of trips abroad. None of his plans included a child.

Su turned the soup down low and opened the window. The kitchen walls were mottled with black spots and Bobby had promised to deal with it, weeks ago. She took some bleach and a cloth and rubbed the damp away. But she knew it would return again, in a few days, and the kitchen would look exactly the same. Still, there were no curtains in the sitting room and this annoyed her. Today she would buy some material and make the curtains herself. She would ask Sammy about these sewing lessons. She stood at the window with a ruler and attempted to measure the width and the length. Bobby said there was a tape measure somewhere but she couldn't find it. She wrote the measurements down and out of the corner of her eye saw someone come through the gate. There was a knock at the door and she ran quickly, worried the baby would wake.

'So Susie. I'm back. What d'ya think of me tan?' Chelsea Dobbs was dressed in a yellow vest, her body glowed orange and her hair was bleached white.

Su gasped. She heard the sound of her own breathing. Her voice was breaking. 'Where, where you been?'

'Lanzarote,' she replied. 'Can I come in, or what?'

Su slumped on the sofa. Her voice was weak and slow. 'You come for baby?'

'Yes.' Chelsea saw she was about to cry. 'How is she?'

'OK.' Silence stretched between them. 'Baby out,' said Su, quickly. 'Come back later.'

Chelsea looked confused.

'Baby with Bobby,' Su lied. 'Not here.'

Su stood up and the girl did the same. Chelsea seemed puzzled, as if she sensed something was wrong. 'What time is he back?'

'Six,' Su said, praying that Paris would stay asleep. She walked towards the front door. Chelsea folded her arms and looked round the room.

'All right Suze.'

'My name Su.'

'Whatever.'

Chelsea left, but on the step she hesitated. Quickly the door slammed shut and Su fled to the kitchen. Paris was now awake and Su stuffed the dummy in the child's mouth and cradled her in her arms. She was thinking about life without the baby. She couldn't bear it. Outside there was shouting and she heard banging on the door. Chelsea was knocking with her fist, demanding she open the door. 'I know you're there. Give me my baby!'

Su stayed in the kitchen and fed the baby girl soup. She washed her face with a flannel and imagined she was a mother. 'You want to stay with me, yes.' She sang Thai songs about love and floating boats.

Eventually the shouting stopped. Su played with the baby and built a house with bricks. The little girl giggled as she pushed the house down. Just as the house of bricks collapsed Su heard the sound of a siren. A police car with flashing lights parked outside. Someone was at the door again. She cried with fright and clutched the baby to her chest. She stayed in the little kitchen and wondered what to do. After a few minutes a policeman climbed over the yard wall with a thick stick. He knocked on the window and told her to open the door. The policeman took the baby.

When Bobby arrived home from the chocolate factory Su was sat at the kitchen table, her eyes flooded with tears. And Chelsea Dobbs was waving her arms at the police, her mouth gaping, as if she was a celebrity on stage. 'She wouldn't give me my baby back,' she said in a dramatic voice. Chelsea was busy proving she was a good mother.

Bobby stared and pushed past. 'You,' he bellowed, 'have no idea what you've put us through!' He turned to the policeman who was writing notes. 'She left the baby here and pissed off on holiday.'

Chelsea stammered and stuttered. In the kitchen Bobby placed his hand on Su's shoulder. She pulled away. 'I want my baby. Please, I want my baby.'

'Su, love. She's not your baby.'

Su continued to cry. He rubbed her back. 'I knew this would happen. You got too close.'

Bobby called the policeman over. 'I'm the baby's father,' he said. 'This girl, she's not telling you the truth. Go to her flat. You'll see. It's a shithole. That place isn't fit for a baby.' The policeman gave him a sympathetic look. 'What will happen?' Bobby asked.

'We need to speak to Miss Dobbs,' he replied in a scientific tone.

'It's a misunderstanding,' Bobby argued. 'The girl's been on holiday. Look at the colour of her. You don't get a tan like that in Burnley. She's been missing for two weeks. Ask her neighbours. Ask anyone. We were helping her. My wife's just got a bit close, that's all.'

Chelsea glanced over at him. Bobby marched towards her. He wanted to slap her, but instead he spoke calmly. He imagined what the police were thinking, when they looked at him, when they looked at her. It was the shame, a total disgust for himself, distaste for the whole miserable situation, which stopped him from lashing out. How could he tell Chelsea Dobbs she was a failure, a bad mother? That would be hypocritical. Now he thought of Su. Poor Su, and it was Su that guided his words. 'If you care for that child at all, do the decent thing and let Su say goodbye.'

Chelsea became flustered. She groped for words. 'OK. She can say goodbye.' She looked at the floor, suddenly embarrassed because the police were watching her and the neighbours were in the street.

Bobby continued, his voice broken and stilted. 'Su was trying to help. Paris is happy here. She's bought her clothes, done everything for her.'

'So you're saying she's a better mother than me.' Chelsea's nostrils flared. She was restless and she bit her nails.

'No. I'm saying she wants to help you. We both do, love.'

For the first time he saw Chelsea Dobbs weaken. Chelsea lifted the baby in the air. Paris was screaming, her legs and arms flaying. A look of anguish spread over Chelsea's face. 'She don't know me.' Bobby reassured her. 'Of course she does. You're her mother.'

Chelsea carried Paris to Su and the baby held her arms out. A string of dribble hung from the baby's chin. Su tried not to appear as if everything was hopeless. 'You can say goodbye,' said Chelsea, her voice flat. She seemed uncomfortable, unable to look anyone in the eye. Su cuddled the child and kissed her head. Suddenly Chelsea was crying fat tears. 'I'm sorry, Su.'

'It OK. She your baby. Beautiful baby. Precious baby.'

In the doorway Chelsea stopped. She saw Su clutching her skinny legs. Fragile as a bird. She sensed her grief and felt herself shrink away. Any kindness always unnerved her. All the time the baby continued to scream. 'Will you help me, Su? I'm rubbish at this baby stuff. You can visit me, yeah?'

Su stood up and touched her arm. 'I will help you. Anything. Just ask.' Hearing this made Chelsea emotional. These were things no one had ever said to her before. Even her own mother. She mouthed the words thank you and followed the police out.

The police took Chelsea Dobbs and her baby away. Su muttered to herself in Thai. Her eyelids were wet and heavy. She felt detached. All at once the world she inhabited was strange to her. She forgot English words. Forever a foreigner. She stood in the doorway and looked down the Burnley streets, at the bridge, the graffiti daubed on metal shutters. She surveyed it all as if she was viewing it for the first time. No flood water, but she felt the same as before. There was that same empty pain, as though she had lost everything.

CHAPTER FIFTY-FIVE

To Su language meant power. Nations were built on words. Nations were also brought down by them. She had been reading for what seemed like hours. The light that emanated from the table lamp bathed the book in a magical glow. The pages were almost transparent, moon white. Reading like this gave her a sense of peace she never found in the outside world. She read the story aloud and listened to the sound of her own voice. Sitting alone with just a ticking clock for company she realised how different her English voice was to her Thai voice. Lower, more assured, she decided. She detected a confidence in this voice that was never present in her mother language. When she spoke her pronunciation was as sharp as the blade of a new knife. She cut through the words and sliced the sounds with her tongue and teeth.

She glanced across the room. Bobby had bought her a bookcase and the cardboard boxes were stacked on the floor. Tomorrow there would be no baby, but instead there would be a new bookcase waiting to be filled. And tomorrow she would offer to help in the bookshop. Maybe she would buy some books, learn some new words. These possibilities excited her. Language was the key to a new life.

*   *   *

When she arrived at the bookshop David was surprised to see her. 'Baby gone,' Su muttered. She attempted a smile. 'Chelsea go holiday. Back now.' David hesitated and pointed at the counter. 'You can help me put these away.'

The books smelt of ink and dust. Old books about flowers, cookery and places in Britain were piled on the counter. Su cleaned the books with a cloth and wondered about the owners. Inside the cover of the book of flowers, someone had written the message, 'To Mabel, from your ever loving husband, forever yours.' Su wiped the cover carefully and thought about Mabel's story. Old books fascinated her. Their history was unknown and could only be imagined.

Finding the correct places for the books was more difficult than she anticipated. It was easy to locate the cookery section. Here the covers were brightly covered, the books oversized. Also, she found herself reading everything, testing her reading skills, saying words aloud. David laughed. When an elderly customer came, Su helped her find a book about cats. The woman seemed happy and grateful and wished her luck with her exam. For the first time Su realised she could speak to anyone. She could make herself heard. She could make herself understood. Already she had decided to go to the big college in town. First there would be an interview, but then she could do more qualifications.

She thought about David now. Every week he drove to houses and collected unwanted books. Sometimes he paid small amounts of cash; occasionally he stumbled across rare first editions. He told her that fewer people came to the shop these days. It troubled him that more and more people rid their homes of books. The customers were getting older, he said. Less people seemed to appreciate books, or no one had the money to spend, or both. Some days he made ten pounds from the sale of second-hand books and that was all. Only the students from the local colleges ordered new books. Sometimes he wondered how long the shop would last. Then, what would he do?

Sad little books filled the poetry shelves, their covers worn and torn. Su held one up and inspected it. A label on the front said 50p. She took the book to the counter and told David, 'Me buy, please.'

David waved his hand. 'No, no. Take it. You can take it.' Su left the book on the counter. 'Thank you. I have new bookcase.'

'Ah. Choose three books you like and take them home.'

Su made her way down the shop, but felt her foot sticking to the floor. She paused for a moment. Lifting her shoe, she saw chewing gum hanging down. The grey gum clung to the carpet pile. She sighed and took some mashed-up tissue from her pocket and began to stretch and pull the gum away.

'It's those school kids,' David complained. 'Sometimes they come in here and hang around. No intention of buying anything. Let me help you.'

He emerged from the kitchen at the back with a cloth and some washing-up liquid but the gum was stuck fast. Kneeling down, he heard the doorbell chime. He stood up and stepped over a pile of books. 'Wait. Don't step over a book. In Thailand they say it bad luck,' she called. David shook his head, bemused. Already he was speaking to the customer, directing him to the correct shelf. Su continued to scrub the nasty patch of carpet.

The customer with the baby chatted about the weather and bought a book about the war. The baby sat in a smart navy blue pram with shiny chrome wheels. There was a rattling sound as the baby kicked a line of plastic ducks. Su watched David serve the man and continued to rub the carpet with her cloth. She heard the baby cry. The baby's cry rang in her ears and reverberated in her head. She didn't look. Instead she held her breath and tried to block out thoughts of Paris. The air was stuffy and dry and for a moment she couldn't breathe. She dropped the cloth and ran to the kitchen. The man turned and looked baffled. After he had gone David locked the shop door.

In the tiny kitchen Su bent over the sink. She heard the sound of her own breathing. Her chest was tight. David was standing over her now and passed her some water. She took the glass and gulped the water fast. When she raised her head, David was still there. 'What's the matter?'

Again she couldn't find the words. Her chest heaved and the blood rushed through her head like a torrent. All the time she was thinking the current of her life had brought her here to England. Now she was drowning. Without realising she dropped her head on his chest and stayed there. She felt her body shaking, her eyes stinging wet.

'Su,' David whispered, lifting the hair from her eyes. 'It's OK.'

She felt his fingers pressing on her neck, his body warm next to hers. His shirt was slightly open and she pushed her face into his chest, half expecting him to reject her. But David stood still. His hands rested on her waist and she heard the steady rhythm of his breathing. Gently he lifted her up onto the sink and wrapped his fingers in her hair. He looked at her for a brief moment and parted her lips with his finger. Su unbuttoned her shirt, slowly. She guided his face to her breasts and pulled him close. With his tongue he explored her; his hands were under her skirt, sliding her pants down, his fingers gliding up. She grappled with the buttons on his jeans and yanked them down. Quickly she forced him inside her, thrusting her tongue in and out of his mouth. He gasped for breath and cried out. Gripping his back with her nails, she wrapped her legs around him. He was deep inside her now and for the first time she felt the tide swell inside her, a giant wave, a rush of water that gushed and sent them both spinning.

It was over as quickly as it had begun. David pulled away, a look of horror spreading over his face. 'This can never happen again.'

Su buttoned up her shirt and felt her lips dry and chapped.

She was still panting. David covered his face. 'My God. You are married to my father.'

Su looked at her wedding ring and thought of Bobby. 'Yes,' she replied, suddenly numb. She watched David carefully. 'Bad idea. I no come here again.'

'It shouldn't have happened, Su,' he whispered.

Su's voice was calm, devoid of emotion. 'I know. I know. We both make mistake.'

David rubbed his eyes. 'Just forget about it,' she said casually. 'Mistake.' David glared. 'Just sex,' said Su. 'Just sex.'

David looked shocked, his eyebrows were raised and his eyes bulged. Su shook her head. 'You men make me sick. Looking at me like this. Like everything my fault.'

She retrieved her pants from the tiled floor and eased them up her legs. 'Do not tell Bobby,' she said in perfect English, smoothing her hair flat, but it was more of a command than a request.

David continued to stare at the wall. He didn't move, or look at her. 'I am going,' she told him. He didn't see her smile. She smiled because for the first time in her life she had felt in control. Also, she smiled because this was the best sex she had ever had.

CHAPTER FIFTY-SIX

Behind tinted windows the three men waited and watched. The car had been parked in Beaumont Road for five hours. Together they watched mothers turn out the lights and put their children to bed. They watched the pizza delivery bikes come and go. They watched the teenagers sneaking kisses behind parked cars. And they watched Rob Bannister stagger home from the pub with a bag of chips for company.

They were dressed in black and the smell of sweat and nerves filled the air. At their feet were hammers, a crowbar and a cricket bat. They drank Coke to fill the hours and bickered over strategies and tactics and time. These were the words they used to justify the plan, but really there was none. Soon the last light went out and the whole street was thrown into darkness. The time was 1am.

Opening the patio door had been easier than they expected. They used the crow bar and the mechanism had simply slid open with little noise. But no one expected the man to be asleep downstairs.

Rob woke to the sound of angry voices. He had barely opened one eye before he felt a terrific blow to his head. It was dark and at first he wondered if he was dreaming. His reactions were slow and he threw his arms up in an uncoordinated manner, wondering where he was, what was happening. 'What the—' Another blow, this time to his cheek and he felt the blood oozing. He slumped back in the armchair and looked around, dazed, confused.

He saw the three figures now, looming over him, but his vision was blurred. He heard them shouting for him to stand up. He pushed himself up from the seat and felt his body sway. He tried to speak. Then a kick to his right shin and his legs buckled. He was bent over on all fours. The men were laughing. The tallest man leant over and waved something in front of his face. 'This is my fucking wife.' Rob recognised the photo of Sammy. The man threw the picture on the ground and stamped on it hard. Glass shattered and then a crack on his back sent his spine into spasm. His face hit the carpet. The man tore the photo from the frame. A boot in his head and Rob shouted 'Please, please stop.'

'He's begging now,' said one man, swinging the cricket bat. 'Smack him.'

'Hold him up,' said the man with the photo. The other two men pulled him up from the floor while the biggest man punched his nose. Another smack and his lip split. A fist in his eye and he couldn't see. The cricket bat pounded and slapped against his legs. They dragged him to the kitchen, by the hair, a trail of blood spilling behind. One of the men turned the gas hob on. 'You won't touch her again, you bastard. You understand.'

The flame was blue, rising high. They held his hand in the fire, smelt the flesh burn. He shrieked and screamed. A tea towel was stuffed in his mouth, he kicked and thrashed, almost passed out. Then the other hand, this time for longer, and his body shook and he felt as if he was splitting into a million pieces. Words were spoken in a strange foreign language. Words were rapid, frantic, fired like bullets. The men kicked him again, just for fun. For a few seconds there was just blackness and the pain ceased. But then a sharp jabbing like needles in his arm forced him awake. Alone in the dark his wrist was hot and he saw orange flames riding up his arm. He rolled over, not sure whether he was dead, or alive, not sure whether this was hell.

* * *

Frank Nuttall turned on the light. The cat was crying to come in. The damned cat refused to use the flap, refused to chase the mice. He should have got a dog instead. Downstairs he opened the back door. He saw a man in Rob's garden, running down the path and then towards the drive. He jerked, stepped back into the kitchen and took a deep breath. The screech of brakes outside told him something was very wrong. He dialled 999 and tiptoed to Rob's house.

The back door was open, but no lights. He called out. Nothing. He flicked the kitchen switch. It was then he saw Rob on the ground, his face caved in, his head bleeding, shiny like black rock. The old man grabbed a towel and pressed it against his head. The boy was breathing, but his breathing was all wrong. 'Hold on lad,' he said, clutching his arm. 'Hold on. The ambulance is on its way.' Now he saw the gas cooker was on and quickly switched it off. Rob's eyes blinked. 'It's OK,' said Frank, his voice shaking. He found the kitchen phone and called 999 again. He needed an ambulance now. Blood had formed a pool under the boy's head and Frank saw the burns on his hands. 'God almighty. What have they done to you! What happened here?' He wet a dishcloth and placed it on the boy's hands. Outside the sirens were loud and shrill. Frank gulped. Rob's breathing was now laboured. 'Come on lad,' he shouted. He shook him slightly. 'Don't die on an old man. Don't die on me. It should be me before you.'

CHAPTER FIFTY-SEVEN

Together they went to the woods where the ground was damp and wet, where mushrooms sprouted like spotlights in the dark. Some were velvety and white and grew in fairy circles and Anna was convinced that elves and pixies hid in the bark of the trees. Other mushrooms were black and withered and groped through the ferns, inedible and strange. David plucked a crop of large chestnut-brown caps, sticky and shiny under the trees. 'Penny Buns,' he said, laughing. Lenka listened as he named the mushrooms one by one. He pointed at something called a Shaggy Parasol, an umbrella-shaped mushroom that had a woolly top. Lenka pressed her face close. The mushroom was like a bride at a garden party with a slender stem and frilly skirt.

The strange shapes intrigued Lenka. But in the moss David pointed at a group of brown bell-shaped mushrooms. Like a crowd of old men in tweed silky suits these mushrooms stood, their fat stems bulging like knocked knees. '*Cortinarius brunneus*,' said David. 'They are poisonous.' And they knelt down and watched the wrinkled shapes bent and twisted on the bright carpet of moss.

In the woods Anna chased the water that trickled down the slope. Lenka and David wandered behind, Lenka talking about the language centre, David realising that Su and Lenka were friends. It had never occurred to him that Lenka and Su might know each other and now the reality frightened him. Why was the fabric of his life always stained in some way by his father?

Already he had decided that he would not see Lenka again. As they walked Lenka sensed something was wrong. David was suddenly quiet and looked lost in thought.

'What's the matter? Did I say something wrong?'

'No, no,' he reassured her. He stopped and picked up a fallen pine cone. 'No. It's not you.'

He hadn't intended to tell Lenka about his father, but the words spilt from his lips automatically. 'Your friend Su is married to my father.'

Oh,' Lenka replied. 'Really?' She looked back at him again, wondering why this was a problem.

'I don't get on with my father,' he said after a while. 'We are not very close. So much has happened, in the past.'

Lenka nodded. 'OK. I have past. People in my past. Some things are bad in the past.'

'If you could change anything in the past, what would you change?' he suddenly asked.

'Everything.' Lenka laughed. 'Everything, except Anna. Oh and finding your bookshop.'

'So you like books?'

'Yes. I love books. I read stories all the time. When I was small my mother told me stories about Poland, fairy tales.' For a moment, Lenka was lost in thought. 'Yes. And my grandmother made stories. A different story for every day. She forgot them all but I remember them. I tell them to Anna.'

They continued to walk under the whispering trees, Lenka waiting for him to say more, but he said nothing. She watched the light filter through the leaves of the trees, casting shadows around them. 'This is a beautiful place,' she said in the silence. She felt his hand accidentally touch hers and then his fingers wrap around her own.

On the moorland they inspected the kite. Lenka had sewn and glued it tight, terrified the fabric would rip and tear in the wind. But David took another kite from the car. 'Just in case,' he said, 'just in case, you know what I mean.'

Lenka smiled. 'Mine is better,' she joked. He pushed her gently and smiled. 'Cheeky. I spend hours making this,' she said, tugging the string. Anna was screeching, the wind knocking her sideways. 'It's a good day for flying a kite,' he called.

'I'm afraid the wind will take me away,' shouted Lenka, her hair wrapped around her face.

David held onto her. 'I won't let anyone take you away,' he said, suddenly.

* * *

Outside the house, David stopped. 'You want to come in,' said Lenka, fumbling for her keys. 'No, no,' he said. 'Thanks. I have to go.'

There was an awkward silence. 'OK,' she said. 'Thank you. We had good time.'

David walked towards the gate. This could never work. He pictured Su and Lenka chatting and laughing. He had to walk away. Lenka watched him for a moment. She tried to read his face, his walk, the way he touched his head. The bookseller seemed nervous and shy. He struggled to open the gate and when it was finally open he stood rooted to the spot.

He turned and pushed his hair away from his face. 'Lenka. I changed my mind. I will come in, if that's OK.'

'Yes,' she smiled. 'Of course.'

He followed her into the little house. He left Su behind.

CHAPTER FIFTY-EIGHT

In the cities young boys got guns and blew each other's heads off. In Burnley they blew their own heads off. Sammy listened to the women in the shop, gossiping and sighing about the state of the world. 'There's nothing for them,' said the older woman with broken hair. 'No wonder they're all on drugs. And this area's gone downhill.' She glared at Sammy. 'And we all know why.' The other woman gave her friend a knowing look. 'Pakis,' the woman whispered. Sammy cast her eyes down, paid for the newspaper and left. But inside she felt angry. She hovered on the step and thought about arguing back. The women were still talking, their eyes bored into her back. She heard a loud cackle. There was no point. When she looked up Ehsan was in the car waiting. He waved. She waved back.

She passed him the newspaper and they drove round looking at the for sale signs. Ehsan wanted a semi. 'Terraced houses are too small,' he said. 'All these English houses are like little boxes.' Sammy thought about houses in Pakistan. In Pakistan the houses were big and spacious. And they had land. Not concrete yards. She saw the houses boarded up, the smudged and dirty stone. She wondered who had lived there long ago. Places changed. People too.

Down one road a group of boys swung hammers like women with handbags on a shopping trip. 'Not this area,' Ehsan said. 'I don't want my kids in this area.' A ginger boy in a satin tracksuit grinned wildly as they drove past. He spat in the road, a pellet of chewing gum fired out. 'These boys are always wasting their time.

Always hanging around, causing trouble. And where are their parents.' Sammy agreed. Sometimes the Burnley boys frightened her. Gangs came down the streets at night shouting, hurling abuse. She looked out of the window. It was frightening. One boy looked about six. He kicked a parked car and waved his fist at her. 'Thugs,' Ehsan said. 'Some of these kids make me sick.'

'Maybe life is better in Pakistan,' Sammy said suddenly.

'No,' Ehsan argued. 'Education is better here. I will never go back to Pakistan. My life is in England with my family.'

Soon Ehsan was in a good mood because he had found a semi near the hospital with three bedrooms and a big garden. They got out of the car and peered through the windows. The house was empty and Sammy could see the rooms were big and clean. Round the back they wandered into the garden. There were bushes and shrubs, a clipped lawn and a small wooden shed washed in blue. 'I think this is the one,' Ehsan said, pleased with himself. He kissed Sammy on the cheek and looked at next door's garden. 'This is a good area, yes?'

Sammy nodded. 'This house is really nice.' She held back slightly, afraid he might suddenly change his mind.

'Come on, Samina. This is our dream. And there's a school up the road. And a park. And a shop. You should be happy.'

Sammy squeezed his arm. 'I hope we can be happy.'

'There's nothing to stop us being happy,' he said to her. 'Nothing.'

* * *

In Paradise Street Suriya was in a temper. Nasir had switched off the news to watch the music channel. 'You, give me that remote,' she screamed, 'or I'll give you my piece of mind.'

'Nasir!' his father said in a drowsy voice. 'Put it back on.'

Nasir turned to Ehsan, his eyes bulging. 'So Ehsan, how was the house hunting?'

'Good,' Ehsan nodded.

'Is no one listening?' interrupted Suriya. 'Someone been attacked in Burnley.'

'Listen to Ehsan,' replied Nasir. 'He's found a house.'

Suriya stopped complaining, went to the kitchen and washed the dishes. 'Too many men,' she said to Sammy. 'Sometimes I think this world has too many men.' She chuckled and threw a tea towel over the girl's head.

'And so you like this house?'

'Nice house,' said Sammy, watching a bubble rise and pop.

'This house make Ehsan happy,' said Suriya. 'Good for kids.'

'Yes,' said Sammy.

In the front room the men were still bickering. 'Who been attacked?' said Mohammed. 'Is this English boy in coma? I heard about this. Very bad. Put the news on.'

Nasir played with the remote for a while. The news had finished. 'Missed it. Gone off,' he told his father.

'Burnley going downhill,' his father said. 'Always crime, even in good area. You find house Ehsan, away from trouble. Even kids have guns in these days. Little kids. My God. I shocked by this stuff that happens. Some of these people have no rules. No respect.' He fumbled for his words. 'I watch it on *News at Ten*,' he declared. 'Someone remind me.'

* * *

When Suriya's visitors came Ehsan had gone to work. Sammy's embroidery was held up for everyone to see, but the young children were bored and sleepy. 'Take them to shop, Sammy. Get them some sweets,' Suriya ordered. Sammy pulled her coat on reluctantly. It was windy and she had reading to do. The children followed her down the street, chattering about school, slipping their hands in hers. In the shop Sammy bought some sad little lollies. The sticks were bent and the lollies had melted in the sun. She fiddled in her pocket for the money and began to count it out penny by penny. The money was laid out next to the pile of newspapers and she counted it again. It was then she saw the battered face of a man. She tilted her head. Swollen eyes, broken nose, broken jaw, dented head. The headline read: LOCAL MAN IN COMA AFTER TERROR ATTACK.

'Poor man,' said the woman behind the counter. Sammy picked the paper up and began to read. The children were fighting. The woman was tutting. 'They set fire to him. Left him for dead. '

Sammy began choking. She gulped. Not Rob. Not Rob. Not Rob. She read the name. Rob Bannister. Priti the youngest girl was now crying, grabbing at her arm. 'Shush!' said Sammy. 'Just SHUSH!'

'Are you buying that?' said the woman. 'Erm, yes,' said Sammy, scrambling for more change. 'I want …' Her words hung in the air. Outside the shop she tore the front page away and folded it into a tight square. She placed the tablet of paper in her pocket and threw the rest in the street. She walked home in a daze. Just silence.

In Paradise Street everyone was in a celebratory mood. She smiled and joined in, helped with the food, served drinks, played hide and seek with the children. She gave the performance of her life. At ten she went to bed and pulled the square of paper out. She read the article a hundred times. Over and over.

* * *

The first thing Sammy noticed about Frank was that his face was grey and his skin crumbling. He was dressed in his pyjamas when Sammy called, not pottering in his garden as usual. Slippers that were too big slid away from his feet as he walked. The police want to speak to you, he told her, trying to push a slipper back on. They need any help they can get. He brought a tray of tea and biscuits, but Sammy felt sick. 'I saw them,' he said. 'I saw the bastards leave.'

He looked out of the window. 'Running away. I keep thinking about it. Asians. Running away.' He paced up and down for a while. 'Why would they hurt Rob? Why would anyone hurt Rob? He's never done anyone harm in his life.' He scrubbed at his head with a cracked finger nail. Dandruff floated and lingered in the dry air. 'I expect you'll go and see him. I think only family is allowed.'

'Asians,' Sammy said, horrified. For some reason she had not expected this.

'Yes. Something to do with that white car that was here all Saturday night, I'm sure of it.'

Her mind was racing. She could smell cabbage and then coffee. 'You told police about me.'

'Of course I did. You're his girlfriend. You know him better than anyone else.'

Frank looked confused. 'Something about that night bothers me.' His lip began to tremble. 'My memory's going,' he said. 'Since that night I can't think straight. They tell me it's the shock. I'm not the best company right now.'

Sammy stood up. 'I have to go, Frank. I have to go now. Sorry. You are a good man, but I have to go.'

Frank stared after her, raised his hand to stop her. But he was out of energy. She ran faster than she had ever run in her life. At Paradise Street she burst through the door, out of breath. Ehsan was standing in the front room with Nasir and another man, a bin liner in his hand. 'Why aren't you at college?'

'I sick,' she told him. At that moment she heaved and vomited on the carpet. 'Oh God,' Nasir said, backing away. 'I hate sick.'

Ehsan fetched a bowl. 'I'll clean it, Nasir. You two go.' He nodded towards his brother and the other man. They took the black bag away and Sammy heard the clang and clink of metal as it was lifted. He rubbed her back. Fear gripped her. He placed his hand on her knee. She looked at it carefully. No one else could see, but she knew there was blood on his hands.

Chapter Fifty-nine

Fresh graffiti covered the wall at the side of the language centre and the caretaker was perched on a ladder scrubbing away the words FUCK OFF PAKIS. Sammy watched the grey water rolling down the wall, smearing and smudging the paint. The caretaker frowned. His arms ached and he was sick of cleaning obscene language from every surface of the building. 'Bad boys,' he said, his face scrunched up in disgust. Sammy nodded. 'They no think about me cleaning it up.' He descended the ladder and pointed at the water slopping in the bucket. 'Look. Black. I need hundred buckets of water to clean this mess.' Sammy gave him a sympathetic look and was glad to see Su appear at the bottom of the ramp.

'Where you been?' said Su. 'You always missing class. Me phone you and phone no working. Class all day today. Long day but good to revise.'

Sammy checked the caretaker was out of earshot. 'Suriya,' she whispered. 'Took phone. I need talk to you and Lenka.' She paused for a moment and gritted her teeth. 'I have to tell you some important thing.'

When Lenka came they hurried away to Su's house and sat in the yard. Out the back there were four bikes propped up against the wall.

'Whose bikes?' said Lenka, baffled.

'Bobby bring them for me. EBay.' Su chuckled. 'Always buying on eBay.'

Lenka sat on the largest bike, wobbling from side to side. 'Ah. Me have bike in Poland. I like going cycling. Come on. We go for a ride.'

Sammy looked solemn. 'I need to talk to you. Not playing on bikes.'

Su tried the smallest bike for size. It was an ancient looking thing with a basket on the front and a working bell that tinged. 'Nice bike,' said Su, removing leaves from inside the basket. 'You like, Sammy?' Sammy made a face, but before she had a chance to protest Su and Lenka were in the alley behind. Within minutes Sammy had packed her robes in her rucksack and the three women rode through Burnley.

'Which way?' cried Su, jolting down the kerb.

'Follow me,' shouted Sammy. 'I want show you amazing place.'

She wasn't sure if she could remember the way to the singing ringing tree but somehow they arrived at the top of the hill overlooking Burnley and the sculpture was before them, spectacular and breathtaking, just like she remembered.

'Wow! What's that?' Lenka threw her bike down and ran her hands over the metal pipes.

Su muttered under her breath. She could hear bells chiming, the wind singing and raging over the land. She shivered slightly. 'This place scare me,' she said to Lenka and Sammy. 'Like tree is real. Like tree has a voice.'

Lenka rolled her eyes. 'Su can hear voices.'

Su narrowed her eyes. 'You should no joke about ghost. Ghosts are everywhere.'

'Stop!' said Sammy in a serious voice. 'I need speak to both of you.' They sat at the foot of the tree, the wind howling in their ears. Sammy took a book from her rucksack and gave it to Lenka. The book was covered in fabric and sequins, tied with a silky black ribbon. 'I need you to do this one thing for me.'

Lenka shot her a puzzled look. 'What is this?' She teased the ribbon loose. 'No! This is your poems. Why you giving me this?' Lenka handed the book back.

'I want you to look after for me,' said Sammy, pushing the book away. 'Suriya take my phone and now something bad happen. Look in back.' Tucked inside the back cover Lenka saw a newspaper cutting. Carefully she unfolded the paper. 'I seen this. No! This is your Rob.'

Sammy suddenly became tearful. 'Yes. It is Rob and I know Ehsan did this.'

'No!' said Su. 'Your husband?' She had seen this on the news. Bobby had known the boy's mother. 'You sure, Sammy? You sure your husband would do this?'

'Yes. I am so sure.'

There was a long silence. 'What about police?' Su suggested.

'No,' said Sammy. 'If anyone know about this, they will kill me. I have to go away.'

'No!' Su and Lenka said together.

'First I try and get certificate. Then I go away. After certificate.'

'I don't want you to leave, Sammy,' said Lenka, her face solemn. 'Stay with me.'

Su began to cry. 'Stay. You have friend in England.'

Sammy held their hands. 'You both such good friends to me. You both make me so happy. You both like my family. I never forget you. But this life in England has all gone wrong. Now, if Rob die, it will be my fault. Not just Ehsan. I am guilty as those men.'

'No, no,' repeated Lenka. 'Stop it. Stop it. You are a good person. You are not a bad person. Stop this thinking. Stop thinking like this.'

'Tell the police everything, Sammy. The police will help you. Someone in England will help.'

Sammy shook her head. 'There is no one who can help me. I

am a foreigner. They will say I belong to Pakistan. My family will never forgive me, so I can never be happy.'

'You can. You can,' protested Lenka. 'You have to try.'

'I tired,' Sammy replied. 'Always trying to make people listen.' She stopped for a moment and listened to the pipes of the tree chiming. 'Remember when we came to England. All of us had dreams of perfect England. England not so perfect for any of us. I remember pictures of beautiful house. My mother say go England and live a happy life and be safe. I believed everything. I thinking England is paradise with equal rights for men and womens. I believed in England everyone matter. I believed speaking this language would make me independent and free. I wanted to come here and be free. I wanted choices.'

'You do have choices, Sammy. Listen to me.' Lenka shook her. 'Everyone has a choice.'

'You no understand Lenka. Family. Culture. Religion. These things come first in Pakistan. The way is different.'

'The way is wrong,' Lenka shouted. 'Wrong!'

'No, not wrong for everyone. Just wrong for me. I is changed. I not Pakistani. I not English.'

'Sammy. You are both,' said Su.

'No,' Sammy said smiling. 'I am not Pakistani. I am not English.'

'You are our beautiful Sammy,' said Su, her voice raised.

Sammy laughed. 'Let's talk about something happy now. Tell me something happy. Always we talk about bad things.'

Lenka pulled up a clump of grass and knotted the strands together with her fingers. 'I have something to tell. I meet a lovely man.'

Su's eyes widened. Sammy giggled. 'Who is he?'

'Very special person,' said Lenka, raking the soil with her nails. 'He know you, Su.'

Su appeared confused. 'I don't know any men in Burnley.

Only window cleaner!'

'David,' said Lenka, a little embarrassed. 'You know David.'

Su felt her face drop. She picked her laces undone. 'David Haywood?'

'Yes. He is nice kind man.'

Sammy clapped her hands. 'You see, you are happy and now I feel happy.'

Su forced a smile. 'When you meet him?'

'In the bookshop a few week ago.'

'You are together?'

Lenka shrugged her shoulders and dug the soil from her nails. 'I see him on Saturday.'

Su stayed calm. The more she thought about David, the more she realised he didn't matter. Strangely, she felt happy for Lenka. But listening to Sammy talk about England made her think. Where did she belong? Her stomach was churning. If only life was different for all of them. She stood up and cast her eyes over the sweeping land. Burnley town was at the foot of the hill. Ugly buildings and closed-down shops. Empty houses, empty fridges, people with empty pockets. She gazed at the dots in the distance. Little flecks of colour on the hill. Fractured sky, slicing the sun. She watched it all. She saw the land tilt and plunge down. A sheep lay in a boggy trench, surrounded by flies, its body stiff and matted with dirt, a gaping liquid eye. Despite everything the wheel of life continued to turn on the land, digging, churning, slipping, but always leaving its mark.

CHAPTER SIXTY

Rob was dead. On the news the police were appealing for an Asian woman called Sammy to come forward. Ehsan bolted across the kitchen and turned the radio off. He played with a pool of milk on the table, pushing it round in circles. He didn't look at her.

In her pocket Sammy felt the cold razor blade, resting on the tip of her finger. She pressed hard and held her breath. Ehsan said nothing and left. She watched the dark patch spreading across her pocket and took a tissue. The blood waved across the paper like the branches of a tree. Her blood. Rob's blood.

At the language centre the sign board said **EXAM IN PROGRESS. PLEASE BE QUIET.**

Su was leaning against the door, her lips moving, talking to herself. 'I practise this future tense. I will go. I would like to go.' She shook her head and sighed. 'You OK, Sammy.'

Sammy nodded. 'Rob ...'

'I know,' Su said, pulling her close. 'I heard.'

No one mentioned the word death. No one mentioned the word murder. 'What will you do?'

'Future tense,' said Sammy quietly.

'Yes. But what will you do about everything.'

'I will do my exam,' Sammy said, imitating a smile. All the time she was thinking, there is no future. No future.

When Lenka arrived they looked solemn. 'Don't be nervous,'

she said. 'We will pass. This is future tense I talking in. We will pass.'

Su whispered. 'The man Rob. He …'

Lenka covered her face. 'Oh no! Oh no, Sammy.'

Sammy raised her hand. 'No talk about this now. We have exam.'

In one test Sammy listened to a recording about being a good citizen. She read the question sheet. 'What's a good citizen?' Her mind was blank. She squeezed the pen hard. 'Someone who helps others is a good citizen.' Then she wrote, 'Someone who no kill.'

During the speaking test she stared at the white board. She imagined letters on the board. Big black letters. **I went. I saw. I was.** Then she glanced at the map of the world. In every corner of the room there were maps of the UK. She craned her neck and frowned. She stared at the map beside her. No Burnley. Burnley was not there. She was not there. She laughed. The teacher waited for her to respond. She stood up. 'I no need certificate,' she declared. 'Thank you, but I no need.' The teacher called her back, but Sammy continued out of the classroom into the kitchen and made some tea.

'So,' said Lenka, 'how was your exam?'

'Good,' said Sammy. 'I remember everything.'

Lenka hugged her. 'I feel so sad there is no more classes.'

'Me too.'

Su appeared waving her papers. 'My God. I forget past tense. Always present. Hope I pass.'

'Last class,' said Lenka.

'But party tomorrow,' Su said happily. She glimpsed the plaster on Sammy's finger. 'What happen, Sammy?'

'Ah, me trap in door.'

'Oh.'

They sat in the kitchen in silence. Everyone knew that Sammy had cut her own finger. 'I think we should say a prayer,' said Lenka. 'A prayer for Rob.'

The others fidgeted and waited. Lenka recited the Lord's Prayer and followed it with a prayer of her own. 'Bless Rob, dear God and bless our friend Sammy who is having difficult time.'

Stale air filled the little kitchen. Lenka was thinking about funerals, death and the church. Then obscure things, like holy bread. She liked the taste of holy bread on her tongue. There was a little church in her village with a large statue of Mother Mary that wept on holy days. Sometimes, as a child, she polished the wooden pews and felt Mary watching her. 'Please don't cry,' she begged the statue. 'Please don't watch me. I'll do it all wrong.' She never told her mother that the statue frightened her. Suddenly she didn't feel holy. She couldn't remember the last time she had gone to church. She clutched the crucifix around her neck. She wasn't sure if she had abandoned God, or whether God had abandoned her.

'Thank you,' whispered Sammy. She locked her fingers together and closed her eyes tight. She thought about moorland, purple heather, the hills and crags. She thought about country cottages with straw roofs and curly garden gates. She thought about blossom trees and petals blown in the wind. Finally, she murmured: 'And God bless England.'

CHAPTER SIXTY-ONE

Slowly Ehsan walked down the canal tow path to where the water became wide and deep. He checked there was no one around. Only the distant hum of a busy factory and a lone car travelling by. Solitude. He felt it now. He sat on the path, his legs crossed like a child in a school hall. He sat still and quiet. The photo was in his hand. He looked at the smiling face of Samina, her cheek pressed against the man called Rob. White veins ran through the picture, where it had been folded in his wallet. He didn't know why he had kept it. But he knew that now the man was dead, the photo had to go.

Thinking about that night in Beaumont Road made him ill. Even now his head was hot and he felt water trickle down his forehead. With the palm of his hand he brushed the sweat away. Nasir had enjoyed telling him about the white man and his wife. He wondered now whether it would have been better not to have known. To be ignorant was bliss. That was an English saying he had heard many times. It was difficult to believe that Samina had done this. And he didn't want to believe it.

When Nasir told him about Rob he had become really angry. Nasir said they should teach him a lesson, that his wife was a whore. Ehsan had sworn at him, bashed Nasir's head into the wall. 'Never say these things about my wife again.' Then Nasir had backed down and agreed it was all the man's fault. Nasir had seen the man in their street. That was it. They should follow him and kick him in. Even then Ehsan had doubted it all.

But that day he and Samina went for a walk he saw it himself. He saw the white man Rob, in his car, watching them. And he remembered Samina's worried face, the way she had stumbled over her words, and her steps. And also the man in the car had screeched away in a temper. Everything made sense.

Nasir had followed the man back to Beaumont Road, got the full address. 'I know the neighbour!' Ehsan had exclaimed. 'Old guy. I pick him up a few times and take him to the hospital. I don't believe this. The fucking bitch.' He had almost choked. He remembered the man telling him about Sammy. Sammy. Samina. Sammy. Samina.

'She's always thinking she better than everyone else,' Nasir said. 'Bringing disgrace on this family. I had to tell you. For the family. You understand?'

Ehsan had nodded at his brother but events had spiralled out of control. He looked at the picture now and ripped it into shreds. He threw it like confetti and the paper pieces floated away on the water.

It was difficult to think straight. He pictured the man Rob begging for his life. He pictured the old man finding him in a heap, his head bashed in, covered in blood. Just a few days after, he had taken the old man to hospital with pains in his chest. The man trusted him. Now he looked at the palms of his hands. They were raw and pink, patches of white where he had scrubbed them hard with a scouring pad and bleach. The blood-drenched clothes from that night were bundled in a bag with a brick and thrown in the canal. And the hammers and cricket bat too. The old man had wept in the taxi. The old man talked about this Rob as if he was a saint.

Ehsan shook on the canal bank. That English school was partly responsible. Since then Samina had changed. And this was why he had married a girl from Pakistan. Because Suriya said girls from Pakistan understood the Muslim ways. He didn't want a Burnley girl who wore English clothes. They were too much trouble. Unruly, corrupted, difficult to handle, Suriya said.

He thought of Samina. Why was life so difficult? Now all he could do was hope and pray the new house would bring them together and make them forget the past. But when he looked into Samina's eyes he was ashamed. He wondered what she saw when she looked at him. A stray dog brushed past him, its fur matted with dirt. He kicked the dog away. Again he saw Rob's contorted face, pleading for him to stop. Whenever he closed his eyes the man called Rob was there. He prayed for forgiveness. He told Nasir that the guilt was killing him.

Since that night Nasir had talked of defending the family name. He wondered how Nasir slept. But Nasir was indifferent. He slept like a baby. He said family was everything. 'Brother,' he said, 'you are thinking like the English. Think about your family. You cannot let this play on your mind. Block it out. You did it for the family.' Ehsan thought about this. 'Honour,' said Nasir. 'It means everything.' Ehsan had nodded in agreement.

Now he looked up at the shifting cotton clouds in the big, big sky. A woman with a pram walked past. Baby bedding, all washed and white and pure. The water winked in the sun and teased his thoughts. Karma, he thought. Something bad will happen to me. A tile will fall on my head and kill me. My taxi will crash. I will be diagnosed with a terrible, deadly disease. I will die in my sleep. When they cut me open my blood will turn black. My heart will be dead and black. Black as my thoughts.

CHAPTER SIXTY-TWO

Food from many different countries filled the paper bowls and the classroom smelt of cinnamon, curry and fruit. Balloons were tied to the chairs and fairy lights twinkled on the walls. The women came dressed in fancy outfits. Sequins, lace, scarves and sandals swamped in gold. Huddled in groups most of the women forgot to speak in English and nattered in Urdu, Bengali, German and Czech. 'Like a carnival,' said Lenka, admiring Sammy's turquoise dress. 'Everything is such beautiful colours.'

Someone had brought in Indian music and the women danced and laughed. A few were crying because they knew this was the last time they would see their friends. Together the crying women swapped food, phone numbers and smiles. Behind her veil, even Zehnab seemed tearful and sad. She helped sprinkle silver confetti on the tables and decorate the chairs with ribbons. 'Everything look nice,' she said to Su. 'I will miss the classes, even you ladies.' She paused for a moment. 'After this I goes back to my old life of cooking and cleaning. Ahh. What can you do? This is life.'

She patted Sammy on the back. 'Suriya like you,' she said. 'Show me your sewing. Very nice.' Sammy smiled back at her. 'You make me some beautiful clothes, yes? Now you are an expert, I will be asking you to make things.' She held the confetti up and sprinkled some in Sammy's hair. 'Very pretty.'

'You mad,' said Sammy, playfully, shaking the confetti away.

'Like wedding,' said Zehnab. 'I love weddings. I love parties.

Let me go and find you some cakes.'

When Zehnab had gone, Lenka sat down and tasted an Indian sweet. She pulled a face and wrapped the sweet in a napkin. 'Sammy. I worry. How will we see you?'

'I will see you,' Sammy reassured her, but her words hung in the air like thick mist between them.

Eventually Lenka said, 'You can come to my house at any time. Just don't bring me these Indian sweets, OK. They are heavy and so sweet. Make me fat.'

For a while Sammy forgot about the past and danced and posed for photos. They played the game Twister and did an English quiz. Su was pleased. 'I know all this stuff about the Queen. Bobby say I like history book.' She hesitated and wondered what would happen next. For her and Bobby life had almost ground to a halt. She thought more and more about returning to Thailand. Sammy offered her a sweet. But Su clutched her stomach. 'I have bad stomach today. No eating.'

When the party was over, the teacher gave awards for attendance and the students clapped and cheered. Women began to say goodbye in tearful voices, gave chocolates and flowers to the teacher. Sammy gazed out of the window, down at the canal. The water was still and murky. Three swans circled an abandoned pram, changed direction and glided under the bridge. When the rain came she watched the water bounce off the pram hood. The rain prodded the canal like millions of silver needles. She placed her hand outside the open window. She felt it. The rain was deliciously cold.

Su turned up the music. 'Stay a while,' she said. 'Early.'

They talked about English music and *Coronation Street*. Su had been to Manchester to see the actors. 'Talk northern on that programme,' said Su. 'Me no want to talk like a northerner.'

Sammy took an envelope from her bag. 'Lenka. Put this in my book. Put with other poem. I don't want Suriya to find.'

The envelope was open, the flap simply tucked inside. 'Can I read?'

'Yes,' said Sammy.

Sammy looked suddenly uncomfortable and awkward. 'I wrote this poem for you and Su.' But before she could continue there was a big commotion and voices were shouting. 'What happening?' said Su, looking worried. 'Something is happening'

Through the window Sammy saw the teachers and many of the women by the canal. They waved their arms. She could smell it now. Fire. There was a fire downstairs. 'We are coming,' shouted Sammy, but the manager Chris was in a panic. 'Don't come down. It's on the stairs. How many of you are up there?'

'Three,' Sammy shouted.

Su and Lenka looked through the glass door. The smoke was beginning to rise. But there was no alarm.

'Jesus,' said the manager. 'The alarm isn't working.' He threw his hands up in the air and returned to his mobile phone. 'The fire brigade are on their way,' he told the crowd.

Lenka, Su and Sammy stayed by the window. 'Open all the windows,' called the manager. One window was jammed with paint and Lenka sat on the computer desk and kicked it free. 'Oh my God.'

'It OK,' said Su. 'Fire car come.'

Outside, Zehnab began to scream. Panic spread through the crowd. 'You have to get them out, now!' She watched the flames licking the windows, smoke billowing out, balloons exploding one by one. 'Jump!' she shouted. Chris Chan, the manager, looked at his watch.

'OK, you will have to jump.'

'No!' Su called back.

'Into the water,' the manager said, his face now drained and pale.

Su fell back. 'No. No water.'

Lenka grabbed her hand. 'Listen to me. Either fire kill you, or I will. Now you must jump.'

'Water kill me,' sobbed Su. 'I cannot jump. You jump. I cannot jump.'

Su stood motionless listening to the crackle of fire, glass smashing, wood crashing. She watched the empty pram bobbing in the black water. She felt the blood rushing through her head and placed her hands over her ears.

Sammy pulled her hands away. 'Su. You have to listen. We all jump together.'

'Water kill Tai, my mom, many, many children. Water take them away.'

'No, Su. You are safe.' Sammy cuddled the little Thai woman. 'For me, Su. You have to jump.'

'No. No. No.'

Su sat on the windowsill, terrified. Below everyone was shouting, voices shrill and then the sound of warbling like a radio not tuned in. The word jump, jump, jump echoed in her ears. More and more people appeared by the canal. Someone had gone to find a ladder. Mobile phones were buzzing and ringing. She could hear the sound of fire hissing and spitting. Then wood snapping.

'We wait for ladder,' she said, but no ladder came.

All across Burnley people saw the plumes of black smoke. From the bridge they watched and pointed; frightened voices talked about the building collapsing. Lenka began to cry. Smoke crept under the door and through the glass she saw thick clouds of black. But it was the angry roar of the fire that worried her the most. She knew it was closer. Now she saw the carpet spark, near the door, a whoosh as a flame danced around the bookshelves. The fire gripped the books and lashed them with flames. She thought of Anna at school, of her mother and then David.

'Now Su!' she said. 'Hold my hand and we jump together.'

Down below they heard a voice. Bobby was standing beside the canal, tears in his eyes.

'Come on, Su. Jump now. Please just get down here now.'

Su looked deep into the water. After that she wasn't sure what had happened. She wondered if Sammy had pushed her. She hit the water with a fierce slap. Her face stung, then she was sinking down. The water was black. For a moment she stayed suspended in it but then she heard a voice. Tai was swimming towards her. 'Swim, Sumalee,' he told her. 'Swim.' He took her hands and pulled her up. She gulped for air. 'Tai,' she shouted. 'Tai!' But he had gone. Then she thought of Bobby. She began to swim. 'Bobby! Bobby!' She needed to find Bobby.

Bobby jumped in and dragged her through the water. On the canal bank he sat beside her, his lips blue with cold, his back bent stiff.

'I love you,' he whispered. 'Please don't leave me.'

Su could only mutter, 'I not leave you Bobby Haywood. OK. I love you too, old man.'

Lenka sat on the ledge, her eyes watering. Her body was folded tight like paper. 'OK, Sammy, let's go.' She coughed as the smoke filled her chest. Sammy peered through the open window and hesitated.

'In minute,' she said. 'I jump this window. More space.'

'I will count,' said Lenka. 'After three. Don't be afraid.'

She counted and watched Sammy's face. 'Sammy!'

Sammy shook her head and climbed down. 'No way!'

'Sammy, what are you doing?' Lenka turned and saw the fire advancing across the room. The books crashed and tumbled down, papers lifted in the air. A million sparks like fireflies.

She pulled at Sammy's dress. Already the smoke whirled and looped around their feet. 'We don't have time. I can hardly breathe.' Lenka gasped and breathed out hard.

'Go on. You go, Lenka. This is the end for me.'

'No! I am not leaving you.' Lenka began screaming. 'I am not leaving you.'

'Please Lenka.' Sammy pulled away. 'This is my way. This is my choice.'

'No!' shrieked Lenka.

'You go Lenka. You go for Anna. Have a happy life.'

'I can't leave you. Please don't do this.'

The fire raged through the room. 'Lenka you have to go.'

'I can't leave you. You are my friend. I love you.'

'If you love me let me go. Please let me go.' In the smoke Sammy disappeared. Her hand slipped away. Lenka shouted her name. For many seconds she shouted her name. She was still shouting her name when she hit the water. Dirty water filled her mouth.

'NO. NO. NO. Sammy!' The women dragged her onto the muddy bank.

* * *

'Where's Samina?'

Suriya's voice rang out from the crowd.

Lenka looked at the fat woman. There were no words but the woman knew. Suriya collapsed on the ground and cried.

Wedged between Bobby and Su, Lenka sat huddled on the bank, her head in her hands. The fire brigade had arrived and she stood up. Raindrops sprinkled on her face. Across the canal she saw the lonely figure of a man dressed in black. He paused and looked at her for a moment and then Kamil was gone.

Like a paper lantern the burning building glowed a fierce orange colour, lighting the street below. Flames licked and whipped the walls, raging through the warren of rooms until one by one the glass windows erupted and the fire breathed black smoke into the damp air, hurling hot papers in the sky. As the glass crashed and smashed, the sirens sounded loud and urgent. Lenka and Su sat in the ambulance. They sat in silence. Lenka was thinking about Kamil and the fire. She would tell the police. She squeezed the water from her trousers and felt something sharp jab her leg. The zip was jammed on the little pocket and she forced it hard. A loud ripping noise and she had her house keys. But there was something else. In the palm of her hand was a square of paper folded tight.

She remembered Sammy's poem. The paper was soggy and bent and the letters smudged. Gently she blew the paper dry. She coughed and choked and the ambulance worker told her not to speak. But Lenka raised her voice even higher. 'Listen, Su.'

> 'My Beautiful England'
> If ever I shall die,
> I will think of you,
> My Beautiful England.
>
> I will think of green fields,
> And happy times with you,
> My Beautiful England.
>
> Plant a flower for me,
> Like the English people do,
> Somewhere,
> My Beautiful England.
>
> Forever I will sing for you,
> My voice chiming like bells
> Through the pipes in the hills
> My Beautiful England.

Lenka smoothed the paper flat. 'I can hear her. I can hear her voice,' she said as the ambulance sped through the grey streets. 'Can you?'

CHAPTER SIXTY-THREE

He had a good eye for flowers. So people told him. He stood in the kitchen thinking about a garden he had seen in a magazine, or a book. It had topiary bushes, a pagoda with jasmine and dented stone flags. By the kitchen door were some boots and a trowel. A trowel with a green handle and a curled mouth coated with dry, flaky earth. The boots were brown and scuffed with deep grips that bulged with grass. Slowly, he pulled the boots on, but his ankles were swollen and lapped over the leather rim. He picked up the stripy laces with each hand until the strings touched. He waited. What next? He knew these strings connected, tied somehow and he wrapped one string round and round another, sure that the process of tying a knot would come to him at any moment. He tried again, feeling his breathing become heavier and heavier. How could he forget this? Frustrated, Frank Nuttall left the laces loose, attempted to wrap them around the hooks, angry that even this simple task had beaten him.

Outside a tangle of weeds strangled each other in a battle to survive and the grass was bent and flattened. This was his garden, an abandoned wilderness with a lonely chair and a table that rocked in the wind. He stared at the trowel in his hand and wondered where to begin. The wet grass needed cutting. It had been overtaken by daisies and he sat in the middle of the lawn and hurled the trowel down. One by one he picked the daisies. He slit their bodies with a finger nail. Then he threaded them together and made an enormous chain. He had a vague memory of doing this as a child. He thought about the man called Rob. Much of that night he had forgotten. He placed the daisy chain around his neck.

Getting up was a struggle so he took a deep breath and staggered to his feet. He glanced at the path, the weeds strewn across the cracks. There was something that bothered him about that night. The man running. He had caught sight of his face in the lamp light and somehow he seemed familiar.

Time was measured by news bulletins. He hardly ate. When he thought of that night his life was a patchwork of memories that had come unstitched. The fabric of his life was incomplete. The same programmes he watched over and over again. The police had no leads. And the girl Sammy had disappeared into thin air, leaving threads hanging.

On the table the slab of butter was sweating and warm. He took a piece of plain bread and tore a chunk away. The butter made him feel sick. He was sure he was nearing the end. When he coughed, green phlegm splattered his hand.

His daughter had left him some magazines, a newspaper and some fruit. He sat in the front room and delved into the carrier bag. Bananas and grapes, but he couldn't face those now. He unfolded the local newspaper. Today there were colour photos, a building engulfed in flames. He read the headline. GIRL DEAD IN FIRE.

He fumbled for his glasses. He read the name. 'Samina Ahmed, aged 18.' A photo of the girl showed her dressed in a red shalwar kameez and headscarf. He read the article again and again. The girl's husband was a taxi driver. He lifted the phone. That was it. That was it.

He had found Sammy. He was about to speak. But he placed the receiver down. He thought of the little Asian girl, who visited every Wednesday. He thought of Rob and closed his eyes. Together now, he whispered. Then he thought of his wife and shut out the world.

CHAPTER SIXTY-FOUR

Burnley – five years later

Language can change your life. That was the message they gave to the students at the language centre. Below a waving banner the women stood in a line, waiting to be seen. They came with their friends, aunties, mothers-in-law. Inside the language centre the teachers milled around with forms and lists of names.

On the classroom wall a picture of Samina Ahmed was hung in a shiny gold frame, surrounded by smaller frames with hand-written poems. The teacher removed the glasses from her nose and smiled. This was the moment she had been dreaming of. The classroom was arranged. Dictionaries were stacked in the corner and there were workbooks in front of every seat. She had carefully pinned the maps on the wall. Maps of the UK and maps of the world and a map of Burnley town. She was ready.

When the students arrived they rapped their pens on the desks with nerves. The teacher began to speak. 'My name is Lenka. I am your teacher. I come from Poland.'

Lenka glanced at the leather briefcase on the desk, a present from her husband. Shiny buckles gleamed in the light and there was enough room for her files and books. 'You are a professional woman now,' her husband had said that morning.' She wrote her name on the board in bold black letters. She wrote Lenka Haywood. The students copied everything down.

'On this course you will learn about life in England,' she said, her voice carrying around the room. 'This course will tell you everything you need to know about life in the UK.'

In the corner of the room one student was crying. 'Two weeks in the UK,' she told the others. 'Miss my family.' Lenka sat beside her. 'When I came here I felt the same as you. At first life is strange and difficult. But you will learn, England is such a beautiful place.'

The girl nodded and wiped her eyes. After break the girl's mother-in-law came and asked to sit in the class. 'I need to see what you are teaching her,' she cried. 'There are no men in this class, yes?'

Lenka took the woman aside. 'You not speak Urdu,' the woman complained. 'Tcha. How can you teach English language?'

'So, in my job I need to speak Japanese, Chinese, Czech, German, Urdu, Bengali and Thai. Do you think this is possible?'

The woman pulled a face. 'You cannot come in my class. I am sorry,' said Lenka.

'But you act like you have something to hide,' said the woman, lifting her veil.

'No,' said Lenka. 'I am teaching English Language and Citizenship. Priti must learn on her own, without you watching over her.' Lenka glanced at the smiling picture of Sammy. But the woman was not happy and began to pout and sulk. 'If you want you can find lessons somewhere else,' Lenka told her. 'But still you will not be able to watch the lessons.'

The woman glared. Lenka stood up. 'This is England,' she said. 'Women come to classes on their own. Women are independent.' Lenka looked at the picture of Sammy again and listened as the clear vowels rose like balloons. 'This is England. Here women are free.'

CHAPTER SIXTY-FIVE

Five years later – Thailand

The skinny boy kissed his mother's cheek and ran straight through an approaching wave. He jumped and the wave threw him back. He giggled loudly and called in Thai, '*Du chan! Du Chan!*' Watch me! Watch me! Then he waved his arms and dived under the sea, a flash of red, in the deep blue water. Su watched him disappear and emerge again, coughing, spluttering, choking water.

'Come here, Aran,' she scolded. She wiped his face dry. In a soft voice she told him, 'Remember Aran, you can try to beat the waves but you cannot compete with destiny.'

On the beach Bobby held a giant stripy ball in the air. The boy ran to his father. Bobby ruffled the mass of blonde hair and thought of David. He saw the same curly hair and wide mouth. The boy was excited and began to kick the sand with his feet. Mai sat on the picnic blanket, before her a white birthday cake with sugary petals and leaves. Su smiled at her sister and listened to the gentle whoosh of the sea. In the distance a boat bobbed on the waves and skipping children chased a kite. She heard the gentle chink, chink of seashells dropping in a bucket. She closed her eyes just for a moment. When she opened them the world had changed colour and suddenly everything seemed bright and new.

'Five today,' Su said, squeezing the boy's cheek.

Aran began to speak in Thai. 'Sorry Mama. Thai, or English?'

'You choose,' said Su. 'Do you want to speak in Thai, or English?'

The boy shrugged his shoulders. 'Both,' he giggled.

Su threw him up in the air. 'Aran Sammy Haywood, you are Thai in your heart. Always Thai. But a little bit English.' Su thought for a moment. 'Like your name. Aran is Thai for the forest and the tree and Sammy is for friendship and being free.' The little boy sat on his mother's knee, his eyes shiny and wide. Su paused and looked up at the bright blue sky, the dazzling ball of orange sun. 'One day I will tell you all about Sammy,' she said, stroking his head. 'But enjoy your day. Tomorrow we are going home. Back to my beautiful England.'

WHY I WROTE *MY BEAUTIFUL ENGLAND*

Some years ago I began teaching English to a group of women newly arrived in the UK. The women were from many different countries and cultural backgrounds, including China, Iraq, Morocco, Pakistan, Poland and Spain. None of them shared a common language and few of them could say more than 'hello' and 'thank you' in English. Yet, despite language barriers, the women were communicating with sounds, gestures, smiles, pulling out photos of their children and loved ones. 'Difference' was not an issue to these women in the classroom and they were united in their desire to interact with others.

During the class a teenage girl aged just nineteen broke down in tears. She had been in the UK for three weeks and had heard the news that some family members had been killed in bombings in northern Pakistan. Her young sisters and brothers had climbed over the bodies of the dead. In England she found herself trapped in a loveless marriage and felt alone, anxious and afraid. But this was not the story of just one woman. It was the story of many. So many times the voices echoed in the classroom, always the same response: 'In our culture, if you are a woman, you do not complain. You accept everything.' From this moment, I knew I wanted to write a novel that explored what it's really like to be a female immigrant in England; specifically northern England.

Traditionally novels about the experiences of the immigrant have centred on those in the city. *Brick Lane*, by Monica Ali, *The*

Road Home, by Rose Tremain and *Honour*, by Elif Shafak all explore the immigrant's experience of London. The experiences of immigrants in a small northern town are markedly different, characterised by the environment in which they live. The women coming to Burnley had envisaged an 'ideal' England, based on pictures of London, the queen and Big Ben. England meant freedom and hope. The reality was described as being very different. On arriving they saw it as a poor town, with segregated communities, endemic with racism and a place where 'difference' mattered. One woman told me 'I was so excited to come here. But then I realised England was not this dream place everyone talks about. No jobs. Houses were boarded up. The town is far away from everything. I don't go out, except to English classes. In the town centre people shout abuse at me if I wear my veil.'

Whilst the novel is a work of fiction, it is also inspired by the story of Shafilea Ahmed, who was murdered by her parents in 2003. The novel deals with issues that are often 'unspoken' such as self-harm and suicide. Shafilea Ahmed was unable to make herself heard using spoken language and communicated her feelings via poetry. In *My Beautiful England*, Samina also turns to poetry to express her fears for the future.

In *My Beautiful England* I wanted to explore friendships across cultures, friendships amongst women and also notions of Englishness. The novel seeks to lift the veil on what life is really like as an immigrant. Although they face many challenges in the novel, the three female characters are all united in their quest for love, peace and belonging. Fundamentally, it is a novel about human stories and human tragedy, inspired by real stories that are often hidden and unheard.

ACKNOWLEDGEMENTS

y Beautiful England was born from the stories of many female immigrants. Thank you so much for sharing your experiences with me and for your courage and honesty.

Thank you also to Martin Hay at Cutting Edge Press for your enthusiasm and the writer Paul Pickering for believing in this book from the start and encouraging me to finish.

To my wonderful friends Joanne Howard, Tracy Wells and Patricia Fisher, I know I can always depend on you and that means so much. And Kathryn Wilson, Juliet Brough and Anita Chapman who read this book in its early stages, thank you for your support. And to my family, Shaun, Tom, Rosie and Abigail, I love you all dearly.

Finally, I owe much to my mother Ann, who always filled our house with love, laughter and books. That's where my passion for stories began.

Resourses

The below list is a selection of national and international org
established to support victims of domestic violence and honour abuse
information is available on their websites.

United Kingdom
Refuge- domestic violence refuges and practical help for women and child.
www.refuge.org.uk   Tel: 0808 2000

Karma Nirvana- supporting all victims of honour abuse and forced marriage.
www.karmanirvana.org.uk   Tel: 0800 5999 247

Women's Aid- a national charity working to end domestic violence against
women and children
www.womensaid.org.uk   Tel: 0808 2000 247

Southall Black Sisters – aims to highlight and challenge all forms of gender
related violence against women.
www.southallblacksisters.org.uk   Tel: 0208 571 0800

International Organisations
National Coalition Against Domestic Violence- works against violence towards
women and children.
www.ncadv.org

VDay- global activist movement to end violence against women and girls.
www.vday.org

Amnesty International- promotes women's rights, including ending forced
marriages and domestic violence.
www.amnesty.org.uk

End Violence Against Women International- educates people on how to help
domestic abuse victims.
www.evawintl.org